Flaws and All

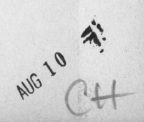

Flaws and All

Shana Burton

www.urbanchristianonline.net

Urban Books, LLC
78 East Industry Court
Deer Park, NY 11729

ISBN 13: 978-1-60162-852-7
ISBN 10: 1-60162-852-8

First Printing August 2010
Printed in the United States of America

10 9 8 7 6 5 4 3 2 1

Distributed by Kensington Corp.
Submit Wholesale Orders to:
Kensington Publishing Corp.
C/O Penguin Group (USA) Inc.
Attention: Order Processing
405 Murray Hill Parkway
East Rutherford, NJ 07073-2316
Phone: 1-800-526-0275
Fax: 1-800-227-9604

Dedication

This book is dedicated to my brother, Matthew Watkins. I'm so proud to have you as my brother. It's also dedicated to Deirdre Neeley, my "ride or die chick" who accepts me—flaws and all.

Acknowledgments

First and foremost, all praises go to God. Lord, you are my everything. I would've lost my mind a long time ago if I couldn't feel your presence. Through you, I'm blessed, I have peace, and I'm whole. Your love, grace, and mercy are always sufficient.

I would like to thank my family for keeping me covered with your prayers and your love. To Shelman: Through our marriage, I have learned that true love "bears all things" and how to love unconditionally. Having you in my life has made me a better person, and you will always be in my heart.

I thank my kids, Shannon and Trey, for adding so much joy and fulfillment in my life. You give me a reason to wake up every morning. I love you to pieces!

To my mother, Myrtice C. Johnson, who never stops fighting for me: I love you more than I could ever say. You're my bestest friend (smile).

To my father, James L. Johnson, Sr.: Thank you for challenging me in ways no one else dares to. Your intelligence and wisdom never cease to amaze me.

To my sister, Myrja Fuller: I admire you so much. Your strength and unwavering faith help me to be stronger. I know that you and Eric have never stopped praying for my family or for me, and I thank you.

To my little brothers, Jay and Matthew: Thank you for letting me be silly. You're both wonderful examples for your sons and nephews to follow.

Acknowledgments

I am so thankful that the Lord has surrounded me with so many wonderful people outside of family. The bonds between us transcend mere friendship.

To Demetrius Hollis: Since our GSU days at the Union Station, you have been my friend, brother, and the one person who will always tell me like it is with no sugar and no chasers. I consider you family.

To my two best friends, Deirdre Neeley and Theresa Tarver: You have taught me what it means to be a true friend. Thank you for always having my back.

To "Nottie Scottie": Thank you so much for all you do to support me and keep my books on the shelves in Louisiana.

To Andra Klyvert and Annie Stokes: I don't know what I did to ever deserve so much support and encouragement from the two of you, but I'm very grateful to have you in my life.

To Jimmy: thank you for being a real friend and a silver lining on those dark-cloud days.

To Millard: Who knew that a chance meeting in high school would lead to a whole book? Thanks for letting me take our story and run with it.

To my little sisters: Ashlei Cason, Brandy Whisby, Telea Thomas, Tashea Bryant and Cymphony Dawkins: You're not full-blown fabulous yet, but you're getting there! Keep pursuing your dreams and your writing. You make me so proud, and you inspire me as much as I've inspired you.

To my good friend Brian Harmon: Thank you for "getting" me and why I'm so passionate about my craft. I'm still impatiently waiting for *The Adventures of Blackman* to be introduced to the world.

To Aaliyah James: Thank you for making me laugh even when I don't want to. You're exactly what I need to stay sane when everything and everybody else is going crazy.

To my Urban Christian family: Thank you so much for all of the encouraging words, tips, and fellowship. I couldn't ask

Acknowledgments

to be in better company. Joy and Kendra, I know I gave you more than one headache revising this book, but I appreciate your patience and your honest criticism. I know whatever you tell me is only to make me a stronger writer.

To my publicist, Dee Stewart: Thank you for taking a chance on me and using your gifts and connections to bless me.

To Christa Rumph: Thank you for always coming through for me no matter how last minute I am. You have been a great business contact and an even better friend.

Thank you to my radio show co-host, Rod English, for making me feel comfortable enough to tell all my business on the air, and to Lady T for giving me the opportunity.

To Dwarka: There are so many words to describe what you mean to me, but I'll start with thanks for being a part of my life. Much love!

To my readers: I couldn't do this without you. I feel so honored to have your support. Publishing my work was enough for me, but having people respond so well to my books has been a blessing I never expected. Thank you to all of the reviewers and book clubs that have supported me since *Suddenly Single*. I know that it's loyal readers like you who enable me to do what I love and make a living from it. A special thanks goes to the following book clubs: Sisterhood, Mahogany Yells, Positive Minds, Ladies of Legacy, Words of Inspiration, Virtuous Woman, OOSA, Sista Talk, Readers With Attitude, and Women of Character. Much love to all of my Facebook friends as well (Hi, Chiquita, Donyella, and Tashia!)

To whoever reads this book: I pray that it makes you laugh, cry, and ministers to some part of your life. Feel free to contact me at jatice@hotmail.com, and let me know your thoughts. Be blessed and be a blessing to someone else. Enjoy!

Chapter 1

It's My Party . . .

Reginell Kerry sauntered into her sister's dining room and declared for all to hear, "Contrary to popular opinion, I'm not crazy and I'm not a slut!" The cocoa-skinned beauty inserted a cigarette between her lips with one hand and dug into her patent leather tote bag for a lighter with the other. The three other pairs of eyes in the room looked up at her. Clearly, Reginell had overheard them tossing out phrases like "must've lost her mind" and "belongs on a street corner" to describe the barely-there zebra-print mini-skirt and black halter top covering her svelte frame.

"I said the outfit was cute. It's just that the skirt is a little short for my liking," explained Reginell's soft-spoken cousin, Kina Battle. "Then again, what would I look like trying to stuff these size twenty hips and thighs into something like that?"

"Kina, you used to wear 'em just as short back in the day," recalled Reginell. "Anyway, you hags are just jealous because you're too old and religious to get away with wearing this."

"Is that so?" asked Reginell's older sister, Lawson. "All this time, I thought that it was because we were too classy and sophisticated to show our privates in public. Besides, the Bible says that women should 'adorn themselves in modest apparel,' and *modesty* is the last word that comes to mind when I see you prancing around in zebra stripes and—" She squinted her eyes. "Are those my open-toed Mary Janes strapped around your ashy feet?"

Reginell rolled her eyes. Having found a lighter, she stared into the leaping flame for a few seconds. "When you were little, walking around in your mother's pearls and high heels, did you think your life would turn out like this?" She lit her cigarette, took a pull, and blew out a cloud of smoke. "God knows I didn't."

"Let me see . . ." Spoiled housewife Sullivan Webb gazed at her butter-pecan reflection in her compact. "I'm richer than any of you will ever be, my husband is one of the most powerful preachers in Savannah, and on a good day, I can still squeeze into my high school majorette uniform. So, yes, my life is exactly how I imagined it would be!" She snapped the makeup case shut. "You, on the other hand, Reggie, chose to drop out of college, run to New York and after your imaginary music career, so you shouldn't be at all surprised that your life has turned into the mess we all know it as today."

Reginell puffed smoke in Sullivan's direction to show indifference. She pointed at Angel King's four-inch stilettos as Angel scuttled by carrying a thickly-frosted birthday cake. "Those things are going to kill you, you know."

Angel, the resident nurse and health nut, set Reginell's birthday cake down on the dining room table and fanned Reginell's smoke away from her face. "And *those* things are going to kill you!"

"Or us, for inhaling them," added Sullivan and snatched the cigarette out of Reginell's mouth.

"What are you doing?" cried Reginell.

Sullivan crushed the cigarette into an ashtray. "You may think that these cancer sticks make you look all grown and sexy, but don't suffocate the rest of us with your secondhand smoke."

"You mean I can smoke and suffocate you at the same

time?" Reginell gave Sullivan two thumbs up. "Finally, a plan we can all agree on."

"Ladies, there will be none of that today," sang Lawson as she punctured the cake with dainty white candlesticks. "And, Sully, cut the girl some slack; it's her birthday."

Reginell lit up another cigarette. "Thank you."

This time, Lawson swiped it. "Girl, are you crazy? You know I don't allow smoking in my house."

"I believe this is *Mama's* house," Reginell snidely informed her sister.

Lawson raised an eyebrow. "Well, she left it to me when she died, didn't she?"

"Yeah, 'cause you and Namon didn't have nowhere else to go when your rich baby's daddy kicked you to the curb," grumbled Reginell, setting her lighter on the table.

"*Reggie!*" scolded Kina in a harsh whisper.

Lawson flung her wrist, dismissing Reginell's remark. "It's all right, Kina. There ain't a soul in this room who doesn't know Mark was a one-night stand who left me barefoot and pregnant when I was sixteen, so I don't know who she thinks she's hurting by bringing it up now."

"Yes, but just because we all *know* about it doesn't mean we all want to be *reminded* of it," noted Sullivan as she swept her lips with a coat of lip gloss. Her eyes zoomed in on Kina's chubby fingers stealthily removing one of the candles from the cake. She licked the residual frosting and eased the candle back in place. "Kina, that is disgusting! Take that thing out!"

Kina seemed to crawl inside herself as all eyes shifted to her, caught in the act. Her olive skin turned beet red, and her hazel eyes fell downcast. "I was hungry," she whimpered. "I'm sorry, Reggie."

Sullivan exhaled. "Kina, if you're not going to stick to your diet, why keep going through the trouble of working with Angel? That's time she could be spending on patients who are actually serious about losing weight."

Angel smiled and gave Kina a tight squeeze. "Sullivan, chill out. It's just a little frosting. Pressuring and insulting her isn't going to make the weight come off any faster. And, Kina, while I know it's tempting to cheat, you've got to stick to that diet regimen I gave you. Kenny needs his mother healthy. We can't lose you over something as preventable as being overweight, got it? Nurse's orders!"

"The nurse needs to order her to get that germ-infested candle out of the cake," interjected Sullivan.

Reginell sat down in the designated birthday seat. "Dang, Sullivan, why do you have to be such a witch all the time? It's my party and my cake. Kina can lick every last candle for all I care."

"While it's no secret that you're not too particular about who or what goes in and out of your mouth," Sullivan spitefully retorted, in reference to Reginell's serial dating, "some of us tend to be a little more selective."

"What's that supposed to mean?" Reginell balked.

Sullivan gave her the once-over. "Do you honestly believe that there's anybody in this house—anybody in this state—who doesn't know you sleep around?"

Reginell narrowed her eyes. "And is there anybody in this city who doesn't know that you'll sell it to the highest bidder? We all know that's how you landed Charles and the church's hefty bank account."

Lawson clapped her hand over her sister's mouth. "Hey, watch out now. I can't have you two fighting in here. You know I just had these floors stripped."

Reginell slung Lawson's hand away. "I get so sick of her always coming in here trying to start something. You've got one more time to say something disrespecting me, Sully, and it's on!" threatened Reginell.

Sullivan spread a cloth napkin out over her lap. "You do an excellent job of disrespecting yourself without any help from me."

Reginell pounded her left fist into her right hand and backed away from the table. "That's it!"

"Whoa, whoa, whoa!" barked Angel, holding Reginell back. "I'm not about to be mopping up blood from the two of you on my one day off. Go back to your corners!"

"Sully, why do you have to say things like that?" whined Kina, cradling Reginell in her pudgy arms. "You know she's sensitive."

"Kina, Reggie is a big girl. In fact, that's what we're here to celebrate, right?" asked Lawson, lighting the candles. She smiled. "Wow, my baby sister is twenty-one years old today."

"Okay, who's going to sing?" asked Kina, hoping to be nominated.

"Let's just skip the song and go right to the birthday wish," said Reginell.

Lawson clasped her hands together. "All right, baby girl, make your wish!"

Reginell closed her eyes. She couldn't endure another year like the one she'd just gone through. Good things were bound to happen for her this year. She crossed her fingers underneath the table and blew out all twenty-one candles, praying that this time, this year, would be different. The ladies all applauded and cheered.

"So, what did you wish for?" probed Kina, already carving out a huge chunk of cake. She cut her eyes toward Angel, whose gaze was convicting enough to make Kina put half of it back.

"The same thing I've been wishing for since I was old enough to talk," Reginell replied. "I wanna sing."

"You can do that in the shower," said Sullivan. "Isn't it about time you started wishing for a real career?"

"I *wish* you'd get off my back. How about doing that?" uttered Reginell.

"And I wish you'd *stay* off yours!" returned Sullivan. "Try doing that."

"Lawson, can't you stop them for going on like this?" asked Angel in an exasperated plea.

Lawson helped herself to a slice of cake. "Girl, I can't control what's been almost two decades in the making. They've been like this ever since Sullivan stepped on Reggie's Easter basket when she was three and crushed all her eggs."

"I remember that," recalled Kina with a laugh. "Reggie cried all weekend."

Reginell drove a fork through her slice of birthday cake. "Crushing eggs, crushing dreams . . . it's all the same to you, isn't it, Sully?"

"Pipe dreams, like eggs, are made to be broken."

"It's not a pipe dream!" countered Reginell and sucked her teeth. "Why do I even bother talking to you?"

Sullivan concurred, "My sentiments exactly."

"Can you stop fussing long enough for us to open the presents?" asked Lawson.

"Oh, you better get used to all this bickering now that you're going to be dealing with it on a daily basis, Miss Teacher," piped in Angel.

"*Please!* It's either teach or go back to bagging pregnancy tests and toilet paper at Pick-n-Pay. Besides, I expect high school students to be emotional and high strung." Lawson pointed at Sullivan and Reginell. "Only God knows what *their* excuse is."

Reginell sulked. "See? Nobody ever criticizes Lawson for following her dream of being a teacher, so why do you all have to crap all over my dream of becoming a singer?"

Angel touched Reginell's hand. "There's nothing wrong with wanting a career in music, but the reality is that very few people actually become platinum-selling artists. Pursue something that's within reach. Dream big, but dream feasibly."

Kina nodded, cosigning on Angel's statement. "Look at me. The only dream I ever had was to be E'Bell's wife and

Kenny's mother. I knew that was something I could do, and I did it."

Sullivan was baffled. "Are you bragging or complaining?"

"Sully, Kina's a wonderful wife and mother, and that's enough for her," said Lawson.

"Well, even E'Bell's a step up from the felons that Reggie has dragged in over the past few years," replied Sullivan.

"Please, not again!" pleaded Angel. "Break out the prayer cloths . . . or the liquor!"

Lawson pulled out a bottle of Merlot from the buffet. "Here. Maybe if they're tipsy enough they'll stop arguing."

"At the very least, if *we're* tipsy enough, we won't care." Angel popped off the cap and filled her glass. "Drink up, Reggie. You can do it legally now."

Reginell passed her flute to Sullivan. "Sully, will you do me the honors? I want my first drink to be poured by someone who's no stranger to emptying a bottle of wine."

Lawson issued an ominous glare. "Reggie . . ."

Reginell smiled wickedly at Sullivan. "What? We all know that Sullivan has never met a drink she didn't like."

"The Bible says that a little wine is good for the belly," rationalized Sullivan. "There's nothing wrong with having a social drink every now and then."

"Yeah, it's when you drink every day like you do that it's classified as a problem," contended Reginell.

Angel groaned. "I can see where this is going. Was I the only one paying attention to Charles's sermon last week when he reminded everybody that the Lord instructed us to live peaceably with one another?"

"Amen," said Kina. "Try to get along for the next couple of hours, at least. This is supposed to be a party, remember?"

Lawson wiped her mouth. "And we can't celebrate this joyous occasion without giving thanks and praise where it's due."

"To God be the glory!" acclaimed Angel.

Lawson stood up. "Come here, li'l sister. Let us pray over you." The ladies all circled around Reginell and pointed their hands toward her with bowed heads. "Lord, we praise and uplift your name, and we come today thanking you for your many blessings and for everyone in this room.

"We come right now asking you to look down and bless my little sister, Reggie. Thank you for covering her with your blood for the last twenty-one years. I pray that you will continue to guide her and order her steps according to your will. Let her seek you first, so that all other things may be added onto her. Let her discern your voice from that of the enemy's. Keep her under your hedge of protection.

"Lord, I speak life, peace, and favor on Reggie and everyone gathered here today. We thank you for every good gift, and we have faith that we will receive whatever we ask in your son Jesus' name. Amen."

"Amen," seconded Angel as the ladies broke the circle and took their seats.

Lawson raised her glass. "We should make a toast to friendship and prosperity."

Sullivan hoisted up her glass. "I'll drink to that!"

"You'll drink to anything," mumbled Reginell.

Kina joined them. "To Reggie . . ."

Sullivan grunted.

"To my sister," said Lawson, putting her arm around Reginell. "And to all my other sisters standing around this table. I love you. To friendship . . ."

They clinked glasses with one another. "Here, here!"

"And to living out your dreams," stated Reginell, "no matter what it costs you."

Chapter 2

"I never tried to trap you; I loved you."
- Kina Battle

Kina closed her eyes and quietly recited, "You, Lord God, are my protector. Rescue me and keep me safe from all who chase me." Then she turned the doorknob, bracing for what was sure to come next.

"What took you so long?" barked her husband, E'Bell, the moment Kina stepped into their cramped apartment. He hurled the remote control across the living room, narrowly missing her head.

Kina closed the door behind her. "I'm sorry, baby. I just—"

"It's after eight o'clock!" roared E'Bell. "Didn't I tell your fat self to be here by seven-thirty? Didn't I tell you I had somewhere to be?"

Kina eased into the room, scrambling to find the right words to justify her actions and keep E'Bell's temper at bay. "I know you did. It's just that I got to talking with the girls and sort of lost track of time."

E'Bell put his six foot, nearly 350-pound frame against hers, pressing her into the wall. He shoved a finger in her face, filling her nostrils with his foul hot breath, which reeked of beer and smoke. "So, you just didn't care about what I had to do, huh? I guess nothing could be as important as you shooting the breeze with them same nosy broads you talk to every day as it is."

Kina bowed her head. "We were celebrating Reggie's birthday, and I forgot to keep up with the clock."

He grunted and cracked his knuckles. "Maybe you need something to help you remember that you got a husband at home while you're out partying with your friends. Maybe I should bust your head wide open to help you remember that next time."

Kina's mind flashed back to the last time E'Bell sought to "help her remember" something. It resulted in a detached retina and a swollen lip. That time, like the times prior that he'd gotten physical with her, she kept to herself and concealed it with makeup.

"Baby, I'm sorry. Please forgive me," begged Kina. "I'll make it up to you; I swear. Just tell me what I have to do."

"Do what I tell you without all the complaining and excuses. All I asked you to do is bring your tail home at a decent time, and you couldn't even do that right."

Tears leaked from her eyes. "E'Bell, I'm sorry. Please don't be mad at me."

"You're about an hour too late for that!"

"I swear it'll never happen again. You know how much I love you."

He dug his index finger into her temple. "You call this love, Kina? Look at how you just disrespected me by coming home late. I knew you were stupid, but I did give you more credit than that."

Kina wiped her eyes. "I didn't mean to upset you. I'm sorry I let you down. "

E'Bell turned away from her. "You see, this right here just proves I should've left you back in high school when I had the chance. Instead, I let you trap me into watching you get fatter every day and spoiling any chance I had of getting out of this dump."

"I never tried to trap you; I loved you. You're the only man I've ever loved."

E'Bell snatched up a pillow from the sofa, squeezing it between his large hands the way he used to hold a football. "I was the all-city football champ with a future just waiting for me to reach out and grab it. You took that away from me, Kina, and you don't ever take a man's dream away from him." He threw the pillow across in the room in frustration. "This ain't the life I wanted or the one you claimed we would have."

"I've always tried to make you happy and be a good wife to you," she wailed.

"You need to try harder." He grabbed his car keys. "I'm going out."

"Where are you going?" she asked timidly.

"You know better than to be questioning me like that. And you better not call me all night, either, whining about what time I'm coming home. I'll be here when I get here."

She looked down at the frayed carpet. "What about the baby? Is he asleep?"

"Kenny ain't no baby. He's eleven years old, but you'd never know it by the way you smother him all the time. He's too feminine as it is, all that crying he do. I told you I ain't raising no sissy."

"He's just a little sensitive, E'Bell."

"Yeah, and who's the one who got him like that? I swear you can't do nothing right." He pushed her aside and bolted out the door.

Alone in the room, Kina thanked God for sparing her from E'Bell's fists. His departure was almost a relief to her. The insults she could handle; in fact, his words hardly bothered her anymore. Years of experience had taught her when and how much to cry to make E'Bell feel like he'd gotten the best of her. The physical abuse was something else, though; something she could never get used to.

Kina took a moment to compose herself and tacked on a smile before going into her son's room. She didn't want him to know that she'd been crying again. She knocked on Kenny's bedroom door and opened it to find him sprawled on the floor playing video games. "Hey, sport, what are you playing?"

Kenny smiled up at his mother. "Mario Kart. I'm up to level eight."

Kina made her way inside. "Is that good?"

"Not as good as Cameron—he can get up to level ten—but it's close." He winced as his character succumbed to a mushroom, and then turned off the game system. "You were gone a long time. Where were you?"

"I went to see your cousins. It's Reggie's birthday, so we had a party for her."

"I wish you had taken me with you," he replied with a sigh.

She gathered him in her arms. "You missed your old mama, huh?"

Kenny smiled sheepishly. "I just like it better when you're home."

"Didn't you and your daddy have fun while I was gone?"

"Not really. I mostly stayed back here, and he stayed in the den."

Without having to ask, Kina knew that E'Bell had probably spent the afternoon drinking and staring at the television. Experience had taught her that too. "What did you guys have for dinner?"

He eased out of her lap and held up an empty bag of potato chips. "I had this."

Kina shook her head. She didn't expect E'Bell to be the nurturing caregiver that she was, but she did expect him to at least feed their son when she wasn't there. She went into the kitchen and returned with a glass of milk, carrot sticks, and a ham sandwich. "It's not a six-course meal, but it'll have to do for now."

"Thanks!" Kenny began devouring the sandwich.

"Wow, you were hungry, weren't you?" He nodded. "Did you remind Daddy that you hadn't eaten?"

Kenny swallowed a bite of his sandwich. "No. He said not to bother him and to stay back here. He did give me the bag of chips, though."

Kina masked her irritation. "Kenny, come sit with me for a minute. I want to talk to you." He hopped onto the bed and sat next to his mother. She tousled his head and kissed him on the cheek. "So, tell me what's going on in that brain of yours."

"What do you mean?"

"What are you thinking about? How do you feel?" He shook his head, but she could tell that he was holding back from her. "Kenny, come on now. You know that we don't keep secrets from each other."

Kenny looked down at his half-eaten sandwich and back up at her. "I heard you guys arguing," he revealed. "Daddy was yelling and calling you bad names."

Kina stiffened a little. It hurt and embarrassed her for Kenny to know how she was treated by his father. "Kenny, I know that you know better than to be eavesdropping on grown folks' conversations."

"I wasn't, Mama, honest. He was just talking so loud that I couldn't help it." Kenny paused a moment. "I don't like it when he talks to you like that."

"Honey, your daddy loves both of us. It's just that some-times he drinks too much, and it makes him act a little crazy and say a lot of stupid things that he doesn't mean."

"But he scares me when he does that. Can't you tell him to stop drinking?"

"I can't make him stop, Kenny. He's a man, and lots of men like to drink, especially when they have to work as hard as your daddy does. You're too young to understand this, but your father is under a lot of pressure between working, paying bills, and taking care of us. Drinking helps him to relax."

"Why can't he relax in other ways? Cameron's daddy works hard, too, but he doesn't drink to relax. He just plays golf."

Kina laughed. "Different strokes for different folks, baby. Mr. Nelson likes to play golf, and Daddy likes to drink. You and Cameron don't always like to do the same things, do you?" Kenny shook his head. "See?"

"I'm just scared he's going to hurt you one day."

Kina shook her head. "He won't do that."

"But what if he does?"

"He won't!" she stated with finality.

"He better not."

"Or what?" challenged Kina.

"I'd kill him!" vowed Kenny. "I'd kill anybody who hurt you."

"Kenny, you don't mean that, and it's a terrible thing to say, especially about your own father. You better not ever let me hear you talking about hurting or killing anybody ever again. You hear me?" He nodded. "I'm serious."

"I won't say it again, but I won't let anybody hurt you, Mama, not even Daddy." Kenny turned the game system back on. This time, he switched to a combat game. Kenny aimed at his targets and executed each shot with chilling precision. It unnerved Kina to see him shoot and kill his opponents so callously.

"This game looks violent to me, Kenny. I don't know if I want you playing this."

"Yeah—*take that!*" shrieked Kenny, striking his adversary. "Aw, come on, Mama. I'm just having fun."

As he continued to play, Kina saw the intensity in his eyes and recalled what he said about hurting E'Bell. She wondered if her baby had the capacity in him to kill, and the thought scared her to death.

Chapter 3

"Your parishioners don't have to like me;
they just have to respect me."
—*Sullivan Webb*

Charles walked past their Venetian-inspired bedroom, surprised to find Sullivan slipping into her nightgown. "I didn't hear you come in. Why didn't you tell me you were home?"

"Was I supposed to check in with you to prove that I didn't break curfew?"

Charles tottered into their bedroom and offered Sullivan a heartwarming smile. "Sweetie, you know I didn't mean it like that. I'm glad you're home. I missed you. This house is lonely without my better half. How was the party? Did Reggie like the gift?"

Sullivan sat down in front of her vanity mirror to brush her hair. "It was Coach—of course she liked it. The party was fine." She turned around to face him. "You know, if you're looking for something to fret about, you should worry about that hazardous car you've got me riding around in. I don't feel safe with it knocking that way."

"Baby, I told you to take it downtown and let Mike fix it."

"Mike who?"

"Michael Matthews from the church—older gentleman, married to Roslyn."

"Who's Roslyn?"

"She directs the praise team." Charles sighed. "Sweetheart, I wish you'd make more of an effort to get to know our members."

"Why should I? I know what those pseudo-sanctimonious heifers say about me behind *your* back."

"The congregation loves you, Sullivan. A few members just wish you would make more of an effort to be friendly, that's all."

"Your parishioners don't have to like me; they just have to respect me." She began examining her pores in the mirror. "Now, what about the car?"

"Just take it to the shop in the morning. You can trust Mike. He's been taking care of all of the church's vehicles for years."

"And you expect me to wait around at some greasy chop shop all day? Send one of your church peons to do it. Isn't that what you pay them for?"

"Those *church peons* are ordained ministers. They were hired to conduct the church's business, not to do my wife's bidding for her. Drop the car off, and I'll have someone pick you up and drive you where you need to go."

She huffed, "If that's the best you can do."

"I was about to go over my notes for Sunday's sermon, but I would love it if my gorgeous wife joined me for a glass of champagne out on the terrace instead."

Sullivan swiveled her body, stunned by the suggestion. "You mean the great and powerful Pastor Charles Webb is going to foul his body with Satan's elixir?" she posed mockingly.

"Only on special occasions, and tonight counts as one. You'll understand once I explain everything to you."

"Fine, whatever," grumbled Sullivan. Conversation on the terrace with Charles she could resist. Conversation on the terrace with drinks was another matter entirely.

Charles left to get the champagne as Sullivan threw open

the French doors leading from their bedroom to the balcony that overlooked their sparkling swimming pool. She leaned against the ornate railing, replaying Reginell's question in her head. Was her life really the way she'd thought it would be? Yes, she had the rich, successful husband. Yes, she had the 4,000 square foot Mediterranean house nestled on three acres. And, yes, she did look fabulous, but none of those things even came close to making her happy.

Charles had always been dapper and charming, especially when she met him right after graduating from college. Having the then-prominent forty-year-old pastor lavish her with attention and the social status of being First Lady of Mount Zion Ministries was enough to lure anyone. However, no one warned her about the monotony and boredom that came along with being a pastor's wife. She didn't know that she'd be expected to conduct herself as a doting, supportive spouse who smiled through hours of sermons and shouted "hallelujah" on cue. She detested the conservative suits with large, birdlike hats to match that Charles liked her to wear, nor did she delight in being confined to the ways and routines of the church. Everything about her rigid life with Charles contrasted with her wild, carefree spirit, and a part of her hated him for it.

Time hadn't been as kind to Charles as it had been to her either. He now had a portly belly from indulging in too many covered dishes from the deaconess board. His hair had started to gray and recede, and dark bags had gathered under his eyes from reading his Bible late into the night. He was a sharp contrast to the strapping young guest pastors Charles would invite to the church for Sullivan to drool over.

Nevertheless, Charles still looked at Sullivan with the same loving gaze as he did that twenty-two-year-old he fell in love with nine years ago.

"It's a beautiful night out tonight," observed Charles, walking onto the terrace.

"Feels like it's going to rain to me," countered Sullivan as a gush of August wind whipped through her hair.

Charles handed her a glass of champagne and reached for her face. "You look so beautiful standing there like that. I think I just fell in love with you all over again."

Sullivan rolled her eyes and guzzled down the drink. "I think I'm going to need a refill." She held out her glass to him.

He set her glass down on the railing. "Can I just hold you first?" Charles wrapped his arms around her from behind. Sullivan cringed at his touch. "There's a full moon out, and it's a beautiful night. I think that God is trying to tell us something. It looks like the perfect night to—"

"I have a headache," broke in Sullivan before Charles broached the topic of sex.

"That's the same thing you said last week and the week before that."

"Well, what do you want me to do, Charles? Lay there until I'm sick to my stomach and throw up on you?"

"No, I just want to make love to my wife. Is that so wrong?"

She rolled her eyes. "Later on, maybe. I'm not in the mood right now."

"Is there something I can do to get you in the mood?" he asked hopefully.

"You can stop pressuring me. It's pathetic."

He backed off, swallowing his pride. "I didn't mean to make you feel that way."

Sullivan exhaled. "Don't worry about it. Let's just talk about something else."

Charles took her by the hand. "You know I have that revival in Atlanta next Wednesday. I always preach better when I look out at the congregation and see my wife's beautiful face in the first pew. I would love it if you joined me."

She slid her hand out of his. "I have a life too, Charles.

You can't just make plans and expect me to drop everything to follow along with them. Besides, you know how much I detest going to those things, all that unnecessary whooping and hollering. Plus, I have a hair appointment that day. If I cancel this late, it'll be at least two weeks before Andre can see me."

Charles planted a kiss on her forehead. "All right, maybe next time. It was just a thought. Well, I guess now is as good a time as any to tell you this."

"Tell me what?"

"I've been praying about it, and I've made a decision about the county commissioner's seat." Charles refilled Sullivan's glass and passed it back to her. "I've decided to run. I hope I have your blessing."

She raised her glass and flatly stated, "Consider yourself blessed."

"It would mean a lot to me to have your support on this. It's not going to be an easy campaign. The incumbent is going to put up a tough fight."

Sullivan finished off her drink. "Fine, Charles. I know the routine. Do you want me to lick envelopes? Post signs? Kiss babies? Smile and look pretty for the camera?"

"A little enthusiasm would be nice."

"I'm thrilled, all right? So much so that I'm going downstairs to celebrate with another round."

Charles placed his hand over the rim of her flute. "Don't you think two glasses of champagne is enough?"

She peeled his hand off the glass. "If I thought that, I wouldn't be getting another drink, would I?"

Sullivan turned around and sashayed off the balcony and down the winding staircase to their kitchen. Once there, she reached her hand underneath the sink and pulled out a bottle of Tequila that she had stashed. She frowned when she saw that it was almost empty. Had she really drunk that much of it within a week's time?

She topped off a shot glass, noting that she would have to make a quick trip to the liquor store in the morning. She knew that Charles wouldn't let her wiggle out of sex, but there was no way that she could go through with it while sober. Nothing about him sexually stimulated her anymore. With a shudder, she resigned herself to the task at hand, already prepared to fantasize about the spring collection of Prada handbags while her husband made love to her.

Chapter 4

**"I love you, but I don't want to lose myself
in order to become your wife."**
—Lawson Kerry

Garrett Bryant poked his bald head through the kitchen
door and looked around as Lawson's 13-year-old son, Namon,
peeked over his shoulder. "Is the coast clear?"

The mere sight of the two men she loved most in the world
made Lawson's face light up. "They're all gone. You two can
come in now."

Namon whizzed by, stopping only long enough to give
his mother a peck on the cheek, and disappeared into the
bathroom.

"I think he had one too many sodas at the movies," explained Garrett. "All right, Namon got sugar, so where's mine?"

Lawson set down the dishes that she'd gathered and threw
her arms around Garrett's neck. "Right here." They reveled in
a long, passionate kiss.

"Is the birthday girl gone too?" he asked.

"Reggie had to work, so we might actually get the house to
ourselves tonight."

Garrett moved in behind Lawson, curling his arms around
her waist, towering over his five feet three–inch lady love.
"That's music to my ears."

"What do you have in mind? You wanna rent a movie or
watch TV?"

"Don't you want to see the surprise I have for you first?" he asked, taunting her.

"Oh, are you going to finish the dishes?"

Garrett chuckled. "Not tonight." He pulled a bandana from his pocket. "I'm going to have to blindfold you."

"Blindfold?" Lawson narrowed her eyes. "Just what kind of surprise is this?"

"Come on, be a good sport. I'm not going to hurt you. You trust me, don't you?"

She smiled and replied, "With my life," as he tied the scarf behind her head.

Garrett led her out the door and onto the back patio. "All right, take a look."

Lawson pulled off the bandana. She was amazed at every sight her eyes fell upon. Garrett had decorated the entire backyard with white Christmas lights, white scented tea candles, and long-stemmed white roses. The night sky was the perfect backdrop for the breathtaking scene. "It looks like something out of a movie back here," she said, awestruck. "When did you have time to do all this?"

He escorted her to a small glass table topped with different-sized covered trays. "I had my whole crew out here while you were having the party. You didn't even know it."

"This beats you doing the dishes any day!" Lawson took it all in, sniffing the roses and touching the lights. "It's all so beautiful, Garrett. This is the most romantic thing anybody has ever done for me."

"Baby, you're worth it. You deserve all the romance and happiness in the world, and I'm going to see to it that you have it and everything else that your heart desires." Garrett pulled out a chair for her. "I love you. Sometimes words aren't enough, though, so every once in a while, I like to show it too."

Lawson lifted the top of one of the covered dishes Garrett

had placed on the table. Underneath was a tub of lush strawberries and whipped cream. "Wow. As my grandmother used to say, who wouldn't serve a God like this?"

"That's what this is all about, baby: treating you like the queen God created you to be." He caressed her hand. "There's only one thing missing from this picture."

"What's that?"

He smiled nervously, his chocolate brown eyes shining. "Open the middle tray."

Lawson reached for the silver tray in the center of the table. "A calendar?"

"Go to January."

She flipped the calendar five months ahead. January fifteenth was circled in red ink. "What's this?"

"That's our wedding date."

"Wedding date?" echoed Lawson, surprised. "We're not even engaged yet."

Garrett kneeled down in front of her. "I'm hoping to change that right now. Open the tray on your right." With her hands trembling, Lawson lifted the top and discovered a black velvet box inside. She opened it and saw what she assumed was to be her engagement ring.

"We're Christians. When we got saved and realized that God didn't want us living in sin, we agreed to abstain from having sex and for me to get my own place until we got married. But that was two years ago. Since I know I'm not going to be able to keep my hands off this voluptuous body of yours much longer,"—he stroked his fingers along her frame—"I better go ahead and make you an honest woman."

"Aren't I an honest woman already?" she teased.

"Not in the eyes of the law. I know we don't need a ring or a piece of paper to define what we have, but I want us to stop playing around and do this for real. Here, let me do the honors. . . ." Garrett took the box out of her hand and cleared his throat. "Lawson, you already know how much I love you and Namon. I believe that God has a plan for us that can only be carried out by us as man and wife. I would be proud and humbled if you'd agree to see that plan through to fruition with me. Be my wife, Lawson. Say that you'll marry me." He presented the ring to her.

Lawson fidgeted nervously in her seat. "Baby, this is all so romantic, and I've known for a long time that you're the man I want to spend the rest of my life with. . . ."

Garrett grinned from ear to ear. "That sounds like a yes to me!" he declared and moved in to kiss her.

She staved him off. "Sweetie, I love you, and I know that I'll be ready to give you that answer you want to hear . . . someday."

Garrett was taken aback. "*Someday?*"

She gingerly put a hand on his shoulder. "Garrett, you're the one—I know that. And in the not too distant future, we're going to go before God and our family and friends to pledge to be together for the rest of our lives. But I can't make that leap until God places it on my heart."

"Which probably won't be on January fifteenth," inferred Garrett, rising.

Lawson sighed and lowered her head. "Maybe, maybe not. I can't answer that."

Disappointment settled on Garrett's face as he closed the ring box with the ring still inside.

"Baby, this doesn't mean no. It's just—"

"Whatever, Lawson," grumbled Garrett under his breath.

"Honey, we've talked about this. You've always known that I wanted to wait until I got my degree before we got married."

"I understood and respected that, but you have your degree now. We've been together almost ten years, Lawson. I'm thirty-six years old. I'm getting a little too old to still be calling you my girlfriend."

"It's only been two months since graduation," Lawson

pointed out. "Now that I'm starting this new job, I need to focus on that for a while. Once things settle down, I'll be ready to set a date. I want everything to be right before we make that commitment."

He sat down and leaned back in his chair. "How long have I been hearing that?"

"Please be patient a little longer." She reached for his hands. "I've been trying to get back on my feet since I was sixteen years old. Now that I've finally gotten to a place where Namon and I don't have to struggle so much, I want to take some time to savor it."

"I know." Garrett kissed her hands. "All I want is to be able to share it with you."

"You *are* sharing it with me. We're building a life together."

"I want to make it official, though. Being Uncle Garrett and Lawson's boyfriend isn't enough for me anymore. I want to be Namon's dad and Lawson's husband."

Lawson circled her arms around his neck. "It's going to happen for us, baby. I promise. I just need a little more time."

Garrett's tone shifted. "Yeah, I hope that's *all* you need."

She pulled away, a little offended. "What's that supposed to mean?"

"It means that if you don't know whether you want to marry me after almost ten years together, then maybe I'm not the one you really want to marry."

"Don't be ridiculous! I love you, but I don't want to lose myself in order to become your wife. I have to know that Namon and I will be okay with or without you."

"You're never going to have to worry about that. If I wasn't committed to you, do you think I would've stuck around this long?" Lawson shook her head. "All right, then, what more proof do you need?"

"Can't it be enough that we're in love? There's no rush. I'm not going anywhere," she assured him.

"That's the problem. We're not moving toward anything, just going in circles."

"I know it may feel that way sometimes, but we're making progress," Lawson told him then sat down in his lap. "We're going forward and planning our life together. I just need to do what feels right for me. You've been taking care of us while I went to school and worked dead-end jobs, and I love you for that. Now it's important to me that I actually have something to offer you other than my problems. There's a lot I still need to do financially and spiritually before I even *think* about setting a wedding date."

"You sure you're not holding out for something better?"

"What could be better than this, huh?" she asked and softly kissed him on the lips. "I love you, Garrett, and I will be your wife one day. I just need time to figure out who I am outside of being Mrs. Bryant. I won't be happy as your wife if I'm not happy as Lawson. You understand that, don't you?"

He sighed and rubbed the small of her back. "I guess I have to."

"This is temporary. You're gonna be stuck with me whether you like it or not."

Garrett smiled and opened the ring box again. "Well, hold out that beautiful hand of yours so I can slip this ring on it."

Lawson's eyes averted. She stood up, cramming her hands into the pockets of her jeans.

"You don't even want to wear my ring?" spat Garrett.

"If I wear the ring, it'll invite all kinds of pressure and questions from outsiders."

"Dang, you really know how to kick a man when he's down, don't you?"

Lawson tried to touch him, but he dodged her. "Garrett, don't be like that."

"I just got down on one knee and begged you to marry me, and you said no. How do you expect me to react?" He snapped the ring box shut.

"I didn't say no. I just said not now."

"Not now? It's been ten years, Lawson! If not now, when? From where I stand,"—he tossed the box on the table—"you might as well have said not ever." Garrett walked away and left her standing alone in the midst of their romantic oasis.

Chapter 5

> "The last thing I need for God to send me right now is another man to break my heart."
> —*Angel King*

Angel's dates usually ended with a polite kiss at the door and a promise to call the next day. It was a promise that neither party would fulfill for weeks at a time, if at all. This is why she didn't know why her girlfriends would expect anything different after her date with Don, a man she'd met at church and again for coffee after Reginell's party.

"What's wrong with him?" quizzed Lawson, forcing her size nine foot into a size eight ankle-strapped python pump while they were out shopping the next day. "He looked like a nice guy."

Reginell watched as Lawson waged a losing battle with the shoe. "You thinking that shoe *looked* like it might actually fit you is proof that looks can be deceiving."

"He's nice," conceded Angel. "He's also very, um, *husky*."

"Do you think he's too big?" asked Kina, feeling insecure due to her own weight.

"Don't act like y'all didn't notice," voiced Reginell. "He could barely fit through the aisle to go talk to her."

Sullivan eyed a pair of jeweled sandals. "A man should only be that big in two places. The bank account is one, and I'll leave the other to your imagination."

Angel grinned. "Something tells me that you're not talking about his heart."

"Hardly!" spat Sullivan. "Believe me when I tell you that Mr. Big Stuff is fat in all the wrong places. Dump him, girl. There are other fish in the sea. Notice I said fish, not whales!"

Lawson pried her foot out of the shoe. "Yeah, he's a little heavy set, but it's endearing on him, kind of like a chocolate teddy bear."

"Now, Lawson, there ain't nothing teddy about that bear, and you know it!" jibed Angel. Then she felt remorseful. "Am I being totally shallow?"

"Yes," retorted Sullivan. "Don't say that like it's a bad thing. Can you imagine all that weight rolling over you in bed, Angel? You're a scrawny little thing. You could easily get lost in one of his crevices and never be heard from again."

Lawson rubbed her feet. "Aren't we a little too old and too evolved to break up with or reject someone because of their weight?"

"No!" exclaimed Reginell.

Lawson sighed. "So, little things like kindness and spirituality don't matter, huh?"

Sullivan shook her head. "Not when the man they're attached to is weighing in at three hundred pounds."

"Angel, are you seriously going to listen to a woman who once dumped a man because he wore winter white in June?" raised Kina.

"A man who doesn't take care of his health is a turn-off," admitted Angel. "If he won't take care of himself, what makes you think he'll take care of me?"

"We're women of the millennium. We don't need a man to take care of us," boasted Lawson. "We can take care of ourselves."

Sullivan whipped out Charles's debit card. "Hmph! Speak for yourself."

Angel shook her head in pity as Sullivan walked to the counter to pay for her shoes. "To be honest, I just don't think

I'm ready for anything serious yet. Between work, you guys, and church, I don't have time to be obsessing over some man who's probably just going to lie and cheat his way through the relationship anyway. I'd do better to keep praying and waiting for God to send me my prince. Plus, Don has a son, and where there's a baby, there's a baby's mama."

"And where there's a baby's mama, there's bound to be drama," finished Reginell.

Angel nodded her head. "Precisely."

"What about that broker, Bryce what's-his-name? You almost seemed to be serious about him at one time," said Kina.

"Bryce was never officially my boyfriend. Yeah, he was good on paper, but we rarely ever saw each other. Whenever we did go on dates, if they could be called such, we were constantly being interrupted with phone calls and text messages. There was never a love connection there. I just happened to find the only other person who's as busy as I am, and who has as little use or time for a love life as I do."

Sullivan returned with the sandals she purchased. "If you ask me—"

"And for the record, I didn't," interjected Angel.

Sullivan rolled her eyes and continued. "If you ask me, the reason that you keep finding things wrong with every man you go out with is because you keep comparing them all to Duke. I don't think you've ever really gotten over him."

"Du'Corey?" Angel laughed to herself. "That was *so* eight years ago."

"I have to admit it, Angel. I agree with Sully on that one," weighed in Lawson. "You haven't really dealt with it, and you never had closure with that situation."

"Yes, I did," countered Angel. "It's called a divorce."

Kina placed her hand on Angel's shoulder. "That's not the same thing. You won't even talk about what happened."

"What's there to talk about, Kina? We got married, it didn't work out, and we got a divorce. End of story."

"To this day, I've never seen anything like the love between you and Duke," recounted Lawson. "Feelings that intense don't just go away because you want them to."

"You don't even celebrate Christmas anymore because of what went down," added Reginell.

"Can you blame me?" Angel's mind flashed back to that fateful Christmas Eve eight years prior. After nearly a year of trying to conceive, she had just found out that she was pregnant and had planned to give her husband the positive pregnancy test as a Christmas present. The surprise was all hers, however, when he came home and announced that his mistress, a woman named Reese, had just delivered their baby. He then professed his love for his baby's mother and told Angel that he was leaving to start a life with his new family. He packed his bags and never looked back.

"It's no wonder you had that miscarriage," replied Lawson.

"Don't forget about the mental meltdown," Sullivan replied absently. Everyone scolded her with burning looks. "*What?* It's not every day that one of us spends some time in a mental institution."

Lawson feigned disappointment. "Sorry. How could I forget to bring up the part about my best friend nearly losing her mind with depression and having to be hospitalized after she tried to kill herself?" she asked sarcastically. "Good grief, Sullivan! Is there at least one sympathetic bone in that anemic body of yours?"

"I have lots of sympathy for Angel!" argued Sullivan and glanced in a mirror. "And my body is flawless."

"I just thank God that you had so many people praying you through it," said Kina.

Reginell pushed Sullivan away from the mirror. "Duke was the love of your life, Angel. You don't just get over that."

"*He* certainly did!" scoffed Angel.

"Well, with him back in D.C. now and you in Savannah, at least you don't have to worry about bumping into him wherever you leave the house," said Lawson.

"I don't know, Angel. Sometimes the past has a way of catching up to us when we least expect it," warned Kina.

Angel shook her head. "Not in this case. Duke can rot in hell for all I care."

Sullivan pointed at Angel. "You all hear that? You can only wish that kind of suffering and pain on someone you love."

"Love is overrated. My marriage to Duke was proof of that. Whatever feelings I may have had for him died the same time our baby did, and nothing can bring either of the two back."

"Never say never," Sullivan cautioned her.

Kina shook her head. "God won't send you a husband until you deal with your issues with Duke."

Angel sighed. "God can send me some more patients or money to meet this month's payroll. He can even send me the seven hundred dollars to pay for these beautiful shoes." She looked longingly at the pricey short-cuff platform boots before placing them back on the pedestal. "But the *last* thing I need for God to send me right now is another man to break my heart."

Chapter 6

"I don't know what came over me."
—*Lawson Kerry*

On Monday morning, Lawson woke up feeling the same nervous tension that she always battled on the first day of school as a student; only now, she battled it as a teacher.

"You'll do fine," Garrett assured her when he called that morning to pray that Lawson had a productive day and a smooth school year. His words calmed her, but the panic which had temporarily subsided arose again, tightening the knot in Lawson's stomach by the time she reached the campus of North Central High School.

Lawson's first official day as an American history instructor was filled with pre-planning meetings, skimming over student and faculty handbooks, and adjusting scheduling conflicts. By noon, she was already overwhelmed and wondered if it was too late to get back her old job as a cashier at Pick-n-Pay.

"Be sure to have your lesson plans turned in before you leave on Fridays, and we have department meetings on Wednesdays at three," droned Lydia Paul, her middle-aged social studies department chair. Lawson nodded, trying to process all of it, while Lydia doled out rules and policies as she led Lawson on a campus tour. "Any questions?"

"I have a million questions," confessed Lawson. "I didn't realize there was so much to learn in such little time. I don't think college really prepared me for all this."

"One thing you'll learn very quickly is that teaching is on-the-job training. College classes can offer you theories about what goes on in the classroom, but nothing prepares you like actually being in the trenches."

"You make it sound like we're going to war."

"That's the way it feels most days. Don't you worry." Lydia patted Lawson on the back. "You'll have more help than you can stand, especially from your mentor. All new teachers have one specifically assigned to them. I believe you're one of Coach Vinson's mentees. He's the teacher support specialist for our department."

"Dang, how bad is it if I need an assigned specialist to keep me from jumping off the roof?"

Lydia laughed. "It's not that bad; I promise. We just want to make sure you have all the support you need. Coach Vinson's a peach. You probably saw him during the meeting. He's pretty hard to miss." She nudged Lawson. "He's a cutie-pie."

"My head is so full right now that I wouldn't have noticed if Jesus Himself walked into that meeting."

"Whenever you are too distracted to notice a good-looking man or the Second Coming, you know you're working too hard," teased Lydia.

"When will I have a chance to meet him?"

"His room is not too far from here. We can stop by there so I can give you two a proper introduction." Lawson nodded and added Coach Vinson to the growing list of people and places that she needed to remember.

Lydia stopped in front of a closed door. "Here we are. Let's see if Coach is in here." She knocked on the door and turned to Lawson. "Coach Vinson is the best. All of our new teachers credit him for getting them through that first year in one piece."

Lydia knocked again. This time, a bronze-hued man in sweats with deep-set eyes and a set of full lips answered. Lawson saw what Lydia meant by calling him a cutie-pie. "Hey, and welcome back, Lydia." His voice was a little hoarse, but friendly nevertheless. "What can I do for you lovely ladies today?"

Lydia gestured to Lawson. "*This* lovely young lady is the reason why I'm here, Coach. I wanted you to meet your new mentee, Lawson Kerry."

He gazed at Lawson with eyes as wide as his smile. "I saw your name on my list and had planned to drop in to say hello after lunch. Welcome aboard."

Lawson received his handshake and studied his face. There was something familiar about that smile. She apologized when she realized she was staring. "I'm not crazy," she clarified. "You just look so familiar to me. Are you from around here?"

The coach nodded. "Born and raised. I hope that's not your best pick-up line," he joked. "If so, I've got to warn you—it's been used."

He smiled again, and Lawson blinked and shook her head to readjust her vision. His smile, in fact, was very familiar because she'd seen that same dimpled grin for the past thirteen years, and as recently as that morning. For a split second, Coach Vinson looked as if he could be Mark, Namon's biological father.

This kind of thing had happened before. It wasn't unusual for Lawson to pass a man in the grocery store or on the street who looked like the fading image of Mark that she managed to hold on to in her mind. Perhaps this was just one of those times.

She realized that he had said something to her again. "I'm sorry, what did you say?" asked Lawson, still lost in her thoughts.

"I asked if you were from Savannah too," he repeated.

"Um, yeah . . ."

This man's last name was Vinson. Wasn't that Mark's last name? She couldn't remember; she could barely remember her own name at that moment. This guy couldn't be her son's father. It was impossible. Or was it?

He continued talking, and she only knew this because his lips were still moving, but she had no idea what he was saying. His words were crowded out by her inner thoughts. *He can't be Namon's dad*, she told herself. After all, what were the chances of the two of them being teachers and both working at the same school?

"Yeah, I went to private school myself . . ." she heard him say when she tuned in to the conversation again. She smiled and nodded to appear interested.

Mark went to private school too, she thought, and he had already admitted to being from Savannah and appeared to be around her age. Lawson could feel beads of sweat spouting on her forehead. She had trouble catching her breath. She needed to know his full name. Once she had that, she could relax again. She felt like she was losing her mind.

"I remember my first day as a teacher," he said. "I looked just as confused and distracted as you look right now." His saying that triggered another thought: If Coach Vinson was the same guy she slept with in high school, he would've remembered something about her, yet there wasn't a glimmer of recognition when he set eyes on her.

I know I'm not that forgettable, she said to herself. *Especially not after what we did.*

"Coach Vinson played professional football overseas before coming to North Central," reported Lydia.

Lawson thought back. If she remembered nothing else about Mark, she did know that he was a football player in high school. It was all he talked about. The name. She needed his full name to put the matter to rest once and for all.

"Forgive me, but what did you say your name was again?" Lawson asked and held her breath for his response.

"You can just call me Coach. Everyone does." He looked her in the eyes. "But my real name is Jamarcus Vinson."

This guy's name was Jamarcus. Crisis averted! Perhaps he was just one of those lookalikes that everyone is rumored to have. Then it dawned on her: Mark could just be short for Jamarcus.

She swallowed. "Do you have a nickname? Jay or Marcus, perhaps?"

He laughed. "The only person who calls me Jamarcus is my great-grandmother, and she's ninety-six, so I let her get away with it. Most people just call me Mark."

Most people just call me Mark. The words echoed a thousand times in her head, and Lawson felt her body go limp.

Mark caught Lawson just as she lost her bearing. "Are you all right?" he asked, propelling her back up.

Lydia was alarmed. "Do you need me to buzz the office?"

"No, I'm all right," Lawson insisted. "I just got really dizzy for a second."

"Here, sit down." Mark ushered Lawson into his classroom and seated her at his desk. "Is that better?" She nodded.

"I'll get you some water," offered Lydia and darted out of the room.

Mark crouched down beside Lawson. "The first day can be a little overwhelming. Just take a couple of deep breaths and relax."

Lawson closed her eyes and tried to control her breathing. "I don't know what came over me."

Mark placed his hand over her forehead. "Have you eaten anything today?"

"I was too nervous to eat." Lawson couldn't stop staring at him. Along with his dimpled smile. Mark had also given Namon his amber eyes and broad shoulders.

"Well, we can't have you passing out from starvation on your very first day. The first rule of teaching . . ." He opened his desk drawer and revealed an assortment of potato chips, snack cakes, cookies, and trail mix. "Never run out of snacks. Take whatever you want."

Lawson selected a small bag of crackers. "You've got quite a stash here."

"Any teacher worth his or her weight has one of these, but you can feel free to raid mine until you build up one of your own."

"Thank you." Lawson tried to open the wrapper, but she was trembling so badly that it slipped out of her hands.

"Here, let me." He tore open the bag and fed her one of the crackers.

"I'm not that fragile. I can feed myself," she said.

"Well, as your mentor, my job is to take care of you, and I plan to do just that." He smiled again, reminding her of what caused her to faint in the first place. "Do you have family around here?" he asked her. "Is there someone I can call to pick you up in case you're too sick to drive home?"

"Yes, my family is here . . . I have a sister," she sputtered, not knowing exactly what to say. "And a child . . ." A child—*his child!* A child he never knew existed.

"You look like you could keel over at any moment."

"I'll manage." Lawson tried to stand up, but swooned, still lightheaded.

Mark helped her back to the chair. "I'm sure you'll manage just fine eventually, but right now, you're going to let me take care of you. You sit right there. I'll be back with some aspirin." His eyes met hers, and he flashed another grin.

The smiled revealed it, and the name had confirmed it. There was no mistake about it: Lawson was staring into a pair of eyes that she hadn't seen in fourteen years. She was looking at the face of her son's father.

Chapter 7

"Is he flirting with me?
Do I want him to be?"
—*Sullivan Webb*

Sullivan double-checked the address Charles had given her. She cringed when she discovered she was in the right place. The automotive center that Charles had sent her to was not the boutique service station she was expecting, but a run-down garage right smack in the 'hood. The dank, dark carport, the oil-stained concrete slab of a parking lot, and the pile of junk cars rusting in the back were almost more than Sullivan could stomach. If her car hadn't cut off during the last three traffic lights, she would've risked driving home. The only thing worse than breaking down on the highway, however, would be breaking down in this neighborhood.

As Sullivan inched closer to the entrance, she felt something thick and sticky wadded to the bottom of her heels. With her pride reduced to ashes, she scraped the gum off her shoe and walked in. She spied two long legs encased in blue coveralls extending from underneath a black Caprice. She coughed to get the person's attention.

A young man rolled out from underneath the car. He looked up at her and rubbed his oil-doused hands on his uniform. He spit out a toothpick. "Can I help you?"

His face had *thug* written all over it. Sullivan didn't know whether to answer his question or to run for her life. She clutched her purse. "Are you Mike?"

He unraveled the ends of one of his cornrows. "Who wants to know?"

"I do. My car over there"—she pointed to her white BMW— "is acting weird. My husband told me to bring it here and let Mike check it out."

The man staggered to his feet. "Hand me the keys. I'll take a look at it."

Sullivan sized him up. "Are you Mike?" she asked again.

"I'm Vaughn. Mike's not here."

Sullivan crossed her arms in front of her. "I think I'll wait for Mike."

"Suit yourself, but it's gon' be a while." He disappeared underneath the car again.

Sullivan checked her watch. Patience was not one of her virtues. She thought she heard gunshots fired in the distance. A few minutes later, sirens blared, and she saw an ambulance zoom by. Car or no car, she had no intention of sticking around long enough to be in need of an ambulance herself. "Excuse me . . . Van."

"Vaughn," he repeated from beneath the car.

"Right. Do you know who I am?"

He rolled out and took another look at her. "Nope."

"I'm Sullivan Webb, wife of Pastor Charles Webb," she boasted. He showed no sign of being impressed or even having heard of either them. "Surely you're familiar with Mount Zion Ministries."

"Is that a church or something?"

"It's not *a* church; it's *the* largest church in Savannah, and one of the most prominent churches in Georgia." Vaughn's expression didn't change. Sullivan, not used to being in a place where Charles's name carried no clout, was flustered. "The point is that I'm a very important person."

He reached into his pocket and pulled out another toothpick. "And?"

"And . . ." Sullivan didn't know what else to say. Being treated like the common folks was a new experience for her, and she was compelled to drop the haughty attitude. "And I think I'll take you up on your offer now," she added quickly.

Vaughn stood up and held out his hand, waiting for the keys. She dropped the keys in his opened palm, but still clung to her clutch bag. He chuckled and said, "Lady, I don't want nothing you got."

Sullivan kept a close eye on him as he wheeled her BMW into the carport. Vaughn left the engine running while he popped the hood open and began his inspection. "When's the last time you had a tune-up?"

"I don't know. That's my husband's domain. I just drive it."

"It looks like you're due for one, but that's not the problem. It's the vacuum valve," he explained, bent under the hood of the car, tinkering with the knobs and wires that were as foreign to Sullivan as the car itself.

"Just tell me how long and how much it's going to take to fix it."

He slammed the hood down. "Ten minutes, tops. Just need to get the parts."

"Don't you people keep spare parts lying around? God knows you've got everything else here."

"Nah, not for this kind of car. We mostly deal with Chevys, Fords—cars like that. For what you need, you should go talk to Lance over at Auto World."

"Listen, Mister . . ."

"Vaughn," he finished, bearing a crooked smile. "Vaughn Lovett."

"Yes . . . Vaughn. Anyway, auto parts aren't really my forte." She reached into her purse and pulled out one of Charles's business cards. "Be a sweetheart and run down there and pick it up. Have the store bill us."

"That's not really my job, ma'am."

"Sure it is. You're the mechanic, aren't you?"

"I can put it on for you and all, but we expect the customers to get their own parts. It helps keep costs low. This way, you're only paying for labor. I'll write this up for Mike, though. He ought to be back by Thursday."

"*Thursday?* I can't wait that long."

He gnawed on the toothpick hanging out of his mouth and thought for a moment. "I suppose I could ride down there and get it, assuming you give me the money."

"I don't give money to strangers. That's why I asked to be billed."

Vaughn nodded. "I can respect that. Like I said, Mike'll be back on Thursday."

"Wait." Sullivan pressed her fingers against her temples. "How about I go with you to Lance at Auto Land, or wherever you were talking about. You can pick out the part, and I'll pay for it."

"That's cool. How do you propose we get down there, though?"

Sullivan frowned. "Don't you have a car?"

Vaughn pointed his finger. "You see that Buick over there?" Unfortunately, she did. "I guess it ain't the kind of car you're probably used to riding in."

Sullivan grudgingly followed him to the battered vehicle. He opened the passenger's side door for her. "Don't worry. Brown Sugar will get you there and back in one piece."

"I wouldn't count on it," muttered Sullivan. She dusted off the faded tan cushion before sitting down. Their eyes locked for a second before he slammed the door shut and climbed in on the driver's side.

Sullivan unbuttoned the top of her blouse. "Can I have a little air, please? It's burning up in here."

"Sorry. No air conditioning. The windows aren't automatic either. You have to roll 'em down and cool off the old-fashioned way." He cranked up the car and turned up the volume on the stereo, filling the air with Al Green's "Love and Happiness."

"Is that a tape deck?" she asked incredulously.

Vaughn put the car in drive and pulled out into the street. "Al just doesn't sound the same without one."

Sullivan scooted closer to the door with her hand scaling across the handle; she wanted to be prepared should the need arise for her to make a quick escape. She silently prayed that God would give her a quick hand and an even quicker foot. If not having air conditioning wasn't a sign of his having a chemical imbalance, still clinging to a tape deck certainly was.

Vaughn took notice of her. "I'm not going to hold you against your will."

"I'm not afraid of you," Sullivan stated and eased her hand away from the door.

"I don't want you to be. I'm not a scary guy." He grinned. "Women love me."

"I bet." Sullivan took a closer look at him. He wasn't half bad once she got past the cornrows and rogue image. There was something appealing about his piercing eyes, thick brows and lashes.

"Here we are," said Vaughn, pulling into the parking lot at Auto World. "It'll only take a minute." He jumped out of the car and jogged around to her side to open the door. He extended his hand to assist her.

"Thanks," she said, accepting his gesture. "Very cavalier of you."

"Well, you seem like the type who'll sit in the car all day until a man comes and opens the door for you."

"Is that supposed to be a compliment or an insult?"

He shrugged. "However you want to take it."

Sullivan stood idly as Vaughn and the sales associate talked shop. Her eyes drifted over his defined biceps bulging through his sleeves. His skin was a deep, rich chocolate that oozed sensuality. The blue uniform hid most of his body, but his sculpted physique was still visible through the fabric. Sullivan cocked her head to the side and narrowed her eyes while scrutinizing him. He was almost sexy.

"You ready?" asked Vaughn, snapping her back to life.

"Huh? Yeah, I'm ready. How much is it?"

Vaughn shook his head. "I paid for it. No big deal."

"Are you sure?"

"It's the least I could do for making you ride around with no air to cool that nice body of yours."

Is he flirting with me? thought Sullivan. *Do I want him to be?*

"I'll have you ready in no time," promised Vaughn once they got back to the garage. "Why don't you go over there and have a seat?" He pointed to a rusty folding chair a few feet away from the car.

She inspected the chair and looked down at her cream-colored pants. "I'll stand."

Vaughn laughed and raised the hood of the car. The more Sullivan watched him—bent over the hood, sweaty, and peppered with oil and grease—the more intrigued she became. Sinful fantasies about him floated in and out of her mind to the point where she had to scold herself into staying focused. She reminded herself that even looking at a man with lust was considered adultery. More importantly, she was the wife of a pastor, and a rich one at that. If she had to cheat, she was definitely going to cheat up.

"It's all ready for you," Vaughn said and tossed her the car keys.

"Thank you, Mister . . ." She had forgotten his first name again.

"Vaughn," he told her. "My memory's screwed up too. That's why I write everything down." He took her hand and rolled it over the tattoo of his name etched in old script on his forearm. His arm, a rock-hard mass of muscles covered in smooth skin, was a direct contrast to Charles's flabby arms wrapped in what felt like worn luggage.

"I have a feeling that I'll remember that now," she said, nearly breathless.

"I think you will too."

Sullivan looked up at him. "How old are you, Vaughn?"

"Twenty-three."

She blushed. "You're practically a baby, almost young enough to be my son."

Vaughn smiled. "Younger brother, maybe, but not son." He wiped his hands on a towel hanging from his pocket and grabbed a soda from the nearby cooler. He popped open the can. "You thirsty?"

Sullivan held out her hand. "Sure." He passed her the can, which she carefully wiped before taking a swig from it. She passed it back to him. Their fingers touched in the exchange. Then he tossed it back without thinking.

"You didn't wipe it off," she squawked. "Aren't you afraid of getting my germs?"

He extended the can to her. "Nope. Are you afraid of getting mine?"

Sullivan brought the can to her lips to prove that she wasn't. There was something sensuous about placing her lips where his had been.

Vaughn glanced over at her BMW. "That car suits you. I could tell you were all high class when you walked in." He took a sip from the can before giving it to her again.

"I'm a woman who likes nice things. What's wrong with that?"

"I didn't say anything was wrong with it. I like to see a black woman doin' it big. I just hate that you're so stuck up."

"Stuck up?" she balked. "You stare at the underbelly of a car all day. What would you know about being stuck up?"

To her surprise, he didn't seem offended. "You've got a slick mouth," he said with a slight laugh. "I like that."

Sullivan smiled a little and took another sip. It was nice to have her acid tongue appreciated for once. After her thirst was sated, she returned the can to him. Instead of drinking it as he'd done before, Vaughn stroked the side of her cheek with his thumb. "Had enough?" he asked.

She told him that she didn't know and closed her eyes, trying to remember the last time she wanted to be kissed so badly.

"I'm sure there's plenty to drink where you live. You know— champagne and whatnot." He passed her the can again.

"You don't always need all that if you're thirsty. Sometimes, a regular old soda can quench your thirst just as well . . . if not better." She fumbled the can.

Vaughn caught it. "Why are you so jumpy? Do I make you nervous?"

Sullivan stared him down. "You're too young to make me nervous."

"I'm not a kid, Mrs. Webb."

"Compared to me you are," she mused. "You'll find out what I mean when you get a little older."

"Are you going to be the one to teach me?" He moved closer to her and set the can on the hood of the car. She didn't know how to respond to him, but it didn't matter. She couldn't have formed a complete thought in her head even if she tried. His lips were mere inches away from her own, close enough to kiss him if she wanted to. He lightly brushed his cheek across hers. Her mouth dropped slightly. He whispered in her ear, "You're way too beautiful to be so wound so tight."

That said, he backed away from her and walked out of the garage. Sullivan was still standing there, her mouth gaping and her body fully awakened.

Chapter 8

"People can change, but they usually don't."
—Angel King

It was a typical day at the Guardian Angel Personal Care Center, which Angel owned and operated and where Kina worked as her administrative assistant. Angel had always known that health and healing was her ministry, and she devoted her life and work to offering home-based nursing care as an alternative to nursing homes and hospitals. As usual, it was barely noon, and Angel had already worked herself to the point of exhaustion and was nodding off at her desk.

"Why don't you get out of here?" urged Kina, clearing her own desk as she got ready to break for lunch. "You can't help the patients if you're dozing on them."

Angel yawned. "I know. Just five more minutes . . ."

"You've got to start getting some rest, Angel. You've been on duty for almost twenty-four hours straight. Aren't you the one always on me about taking care of myself?"

Angel stretched. "You're right; I'm beat. I just need to get through today."

"If you had a man at home, he'd make you get in that bed and rest," jeered Kina.

"Shoot, when I did have one at home, resting was the last thing he wanted me to do in bed. Duke used to always—" She bit her lip and started shuffling through her mail.

"Duke used to always what?" prodded Kina. Angel continued

busying herself with mundane tasks. "It's okay to talk about him, you know."

Angel shook her head. "It doesn't matter. The things he was saying to get me into bed were probably the exact same lines he was spitting to his mistress."

"It is possible that he's a changed man, Angel."

Angel rolled her eyes. "People can change, but they usually don't."

Kina looked down at her watch. "Let me get out of here and pick E'Bell up some lunch. Lord knows he'll have a fit if I'm late and he has to eat what's in the cafeteria."

Angel gave her a quick hug. "I'll see you at one."

Kina turned around before heading out of the door. "Oh, before I forget, a woman named Theresa McNair called you when you were on the phone earlier." She reached into her desk and pulled out a small slip of pink paper.

Angel skimmed over the message. "Do I know her?"

"I don't think so. She has cancer. The doctor's given her six months. She wants you to add her to your client roster and says she'll pay you up front, in cash."

"She must be loaded. I'll have Jess call her in the morning."

"No, she only wants to work with you. She was real adamant about that."

"I don't know why. Jess has the same qualifications that I have; I wouldn't have hired her if she didn't." Angel stuffed the number into her pocket. "I'll call her, but she'll have to wait until tomorrow. I have way too much on my plate right now."

"She really wants you to stop by today, if possible. It doesn't matter how late."

Angel rolled her eyes. "She sounds pushy. If I wanted to deal with an attitude or an ego, I'd call Sullivan."

"She sounded more desperate than pushy. I'll see you in an hour."

Angel bristled at having to add more weight to her overloaded plate, but she took it in stride. "God, you said that you wouldn't put more on us than we can bear, and I'm holding you to that!" she issued as she dialed the number.

A little girl answered the phone. Children always gave Angel's spirit a lift. "Hey, sweetie, is your mother home?"

"I'm right here," replied a woman who apparently picked up the phone shortly after her daughter did. "Hi, I'm Theresa. You must be Angel King."

Angel was surprised. "Yes. How did you know?"

"Credit the wonders of technology and the caller ID box," replied Theresa.

"How are you, Mrs. McNair?"

"I'm fine. What's a little cancer when there's a beautiful day outside like today?"

"I'm glad to hear you say that, especially under the circumstances. A lot of people in your condition would've lost faith by now."

"I won't, as long as there's life in this body—however long or short that may be."

"Well, my job is to extend that time as much as possible. I don't want you to miss a second more of that little girl's life than you have to. Do you have any questions about your illness or my role in your treatment?"

"After more than a year of doctor's appointments and chemo and needles, I think I know just about all there is to know about cancer, but I would like to know more about exactly what it is you do."

"Basically, we make sure you have the best medical care possible without ever having to leave your house," explained Angel. "I work with your doctor to make sure all of your medical needs are taken care of, while making sure your emotional and psychological needs are met as well. I do it all, from administering medicine to helping out with the laundry if I have to. I work on a contract basis of three times a week for three months at a time. Sometimes insurance covers this service; sometimes it doesn't. Just depends on the kind of coverage you have."

"I would like to contract you for the next six months, all cash, all up front."

"Are you sure?" asked Angel. "I haven't even quoted you my prices."

"The cost isn't an issue for me. I'm just ready for us to get started. I don't have time to waste."

"Okay, we can set up a time for a home visit and go from there. My secretary said that you wanted me to stop by today, but I'm booked for the remainder of the afternoon. Can we shoot for another day this week?"

"Sure," Theresa said and gave Angel directions to her house.

"By the way, how did you find out about us?" asked Angel before hanging up.

"Oh, I don't know. I think I came across your Web site or something." Theresa told her good-bye and quickly hung up the phone.

Theresa's rushed good-bye unnerved Angel, especially when she remembered that Guardian Angel's Web site wasn't up and running yet.

Theresa looked down at a family portrait, rubbing her hand over the picture of her husband. "God, this has to work," she prayed. Theresa thought Angel King seemed nice enough on the phone, but there was no telling how she'd react if she knew that the woman she'd just agreed to help had spent the last eight years living the life Angel was supposed to have.

Chapter 9

"The less he remembers about that night, the better."
—Lawson Kerry

"This so-called emergency better be good," warned Sullivan, barging into Lawson's living room. Reginell and Kina were seated next to Lawson on the sofa.

"Do you think she would've called you if it wasn't important?" snapped Reginell.

Sullivan smacked her lips. "What's your problem?"

"I'm just not in the mood for your mouth today."

"Did I miss anything?" asked Angel as she breathlessly entered the room. "I would've been here sooner, but I got tied up with work."

"You're fine. Have a seat," instructed Lawson.

Sullivan looked around the room. "All right, the gang's all here, so what's up?"

Lawson closed her eyes briefly to collect her thoughts. "Something happened today, and I want you all to tell me what you think I should do."

"Garrett dumped you, didn't he?" guessed Sullivan. "How many times have I told you that he wasn't going to let you lead him on forever, Lawson?"

Lawson shook her head. "We had a little tiff, but that's not what—"

"What did you guys fight about?" questioned Kina.

"I don't want to talk about it. Garrett isn't the reason I wanted to see you."

Reginell replied, "Well, it's out there now, so you might as well confess."

Lawson relented. "He asked me to marry him after Reggie's party, but that's not why I called you over—"

Angel's mouth dropped. "Garrett proposed, and you kept this from us for three whole days?"

"You didn't even tell me. I'm your sister!" complained Reginell.

Sullivan inspected Lawson's hand. "Where is the ring? Or is the diamond too small to be seen with the naked eye?"

"I can't believe you didn't say a word about it while we were out Saturday," said Kina.

"Ladies, *please!*" cut in Lawson. "I'll fill you in on all the details later. Right now, there's a more pressing matter at hand."

"What could be more pressing than you getting married?" asked Angel.

Lawson took a deep breath. "Seeing Namon's father today."

A hush fell over the room. Sullivan's eyes nearly bulged out of their sockets. "You saw Mark? Are you sure it wasn't just someone who looked like him?"

Lawson nodded. "It was him. I'm positive."

"Did he track you down?" quizzed Kina. "Did someone tell him about Namon?"

"No, I saw him at work. He teaches at North Central. Get this: not only does he teach at the school, but he's also been assigned as my mentor."

"Girl, stop!" shrieked Sullivan.

Angel winced. "Dang, small world, huh?"

"*Too* small!" seconded Lawson. "I almost passed out when I saw him. It was completely surreal, like one of those out-of-body experiences. What am I going to do?"

"You need to pray about this and ask God for direction," suggested Kina. "The Bible says He'll give you wisdom if you ask for it."

Reginell lowered her voice. "Does Garrett know?"

"No. I called and asked him to come over when he gets off work. I plan on telling him everything then."

"Lawson, exactly what happened between you and this Mark person?" inquired Angel. "I didn't meet you guys until Sully and I were roommates in college, and Mark was already out of the picture by then. I'm out of the loop here."

Sullivan bolted up. "I want to make it clear that it was not my fault! I just introduced them. They got into the baby-making business all on their own."

Lawson spoke up. "I was a virgin. Mark is the one who took it there, not me."

"You tagged along for the ride—literally and figuratively," quipped Sullivan.

"Okay, so what happened?" Angel asked again. "All I know is that Mark got you pregnant, moved to Virginia to play football, and that you never heard from him again. There's got to be more to the story."

Lawson sighed. "That really about sums it up."

"No, it doesn't," cut in Sullivan. "Don't you remember, Lawson? We were at Manny's graduation party. I was gorgeous as usual, and you were . . . you."

Angel huffed. "Can we skip the *Sullivan-is-fabulous* parts and get to the point?"

Sullivan cut her eyes at Angel. "Without that, there really isn't much of a story."

Lawson closed her eyes and leaned back. "I can still hear K-Ci from Jodeci wailing, 'So you're havin' my baby, and it means so much to me' during Mark's and my first dance at that basement party. That's really where Namon's conception began."

"You did it at the party?" asked Reginell.

Lawson chuckled. "No, we did it at his house. Sully and I had just turned sixteen, school had dismissed for the summer,

and we were ready to party. Sullivan always made it a practice
to keep two boyfriends—one at our neighborhood school, and
one from one of the swanky private schools across town."

Sullivan threw in, "Every teenage girl needs her *good* boy
and her *hood* boy."

Angel deadpanned, "I'll be sure to write that down."

Lawson continued. "Anyway, her private school boyfriend,
Manny, had just graduated and was throwing a party at his
house. Sullivan insisted on dragging me along with her, claiming that Manny had this cute friend that I just *had* to meet.
Then she introduced me to the finest boy I'd ever laid eyes
on."

"Sullivan has nothing if not good taste in men," admitted
Reginell.

"His name was Mark, and he'd just graduated too. We
settled into a corner of the room to talk. He told me about
his full athletic scholarship to Virginia Tech and his plans to
leave in two weeks for football camp, and I told him all about
me. When Jodeci came on, he asked me to dance."

"Bump and grind is more like it," amended Sullivan.

Lawson remembered how Mark cupped her body close to
his as they swayed to the music. By the time Jodeci reached
the bridge of "Forever My Lady," she was convinced that she
was in love. "A little later," narrated Lawson, "Sully busted in
on us in a frenzy because her other boyfriend, Anwar, was on
his way over. Mark didn't want me to leave, so he offered to
take me home so Sullivan could escape."

"See, if you had left with me, none of this would be
happening," Sullivan crowed.

"Will you stop butting in? I want to hear the story," said
Reginell. "Now, go on."

"Well, after a few more songs, Mark was ready to go. It was
still early and his parents were out for the night, so he invited
me over to talk and watch music videos."

Angel looked on in disbelief. "And you believed that was all he wanted to do?"

"I was sixteen and naïve," admitted Lawson.

Sullivan murmured, "Try stupid and gullible."

"Things started out innocently enough. At first, we really did just watch TV. Then he put his arm around me. An arm on the shoulder led to a hand on the thigh, which led to a kiss, which led to his other hand sliding underneath my shirt, which led to us conceiving Namon on the couch in his rec room.

"After that, Mark and I exchanged numbers, but neither of us called the other. The party was the first and last time we saw each other until today. I tried reaching out to him once I realized I was pregnant, but he'd already left for college by then. Manny cut Sullivan off after he found out about Anwar, and he was my only real connection to Mark."

Angel was enthralled by the story. "What did your mom say?"

"She wanted to know who the punk was that knocked up her sixteen-year-old daughter! I didn't tell her, though, until Namon was around six or seven. By then, I was well into my twenties and involved with Garrett. I resolved a long time ago to raise Namon the best I could without his father, and that's what I did."

"Do you regret not trying harder to find Mark?" asked Angel.

"I do now!" retorted Lawson. "I wouldn't change anything, though. Namon has been the joy of my life. Who knows what would have happened if Mark had known about him? His parents had money. They probably would've tried to take him away from me or made us bounce Namon back and forth between the two of us. I have to believe that things turned out the way they were meant to."

"Well, now that Mark is back on the scene, I think you

need to tell him," said Kina. "He has a right to know that he has a child out there."

"No, he doesn't!" disputed Sullivan. "Lawson doesn't know anything about this guy. He could be crazy or God knows what else. Why would she expose her son to him?"

Angel agreed. "Sully's got a point, and who's to say he won't go after custody?"

Lawson grimaced. "You think Mark would do that?"

"Would you blame him?" asked Reginell. "If it were me, I'd do everything in my power to get my kid back."

"Me too," admitted Kina.

Lawson panicked. "I hadn't considered that. If this thing winds up in court, any lawyer could argue that Mark is the victim here. What if I'm forced to hand over my son? I can't risk that. Losing Namon would kill me."

"Yeah, but think about what Namon is missing out on," countered Reginell. "All he knows about Mark is that he took off before Namon was born, and nobody has heard from Mark from that day to this one. Whether or not Namon admits it, you know he's curious about his real dad. Do you really want to deprive him of knowing the truth?"

Angel interposed. "You must think about Garrett in all of this, too, Lawson. He's been Namon's dad since Namon was three years old. Where does this leave him?"

"Bringing Mark into the picture would be a slap in the face to Garrett," said Sullivan. "After everything Garrett's done for both of you, he deserves better than that."

"He deserves better than what?" asked Garrett as he rushed into the living room. "It looks like you all are having a major estrogen session going on in here." To ease the tension, they all made a halfhearted attempt to laugh at his joke.

"Garrett, I think you need to sit down. We have to talk," said Lawson.

"Baby, if this is about Saturday night, it's cool. You were right.

We don't need to rush into anything. We love each other, and you, me, and Namon are a family. That's all that matters." The women exchanged ominous glances that Garrett picked up on immediately. "You're acting strange. What's going on here?"

Angel was the first to rise. "I think we better get out of here so they can talk."

Reginell followed suit. "Yeah. See you later, sis."

Sullivan leaned down and gave Lawson a quick hug. "Call me when you get everything figured out."

Kina squeezed Lawson's hand. "Think about what I said. He has a right to know." They all filed out quietly, leaving Lawson alone with Garrett.

Garrett took a seat next to Lawson. "Okay, what's wrong? This seems serious."

"It is," she confessed. "I ran into Mark today."

"Mark who?"

"Mark Vinson." She paused. "Namon's biological father."

"Are you serious?"

Lawson nodded.

Garrett slumped down into the sofa, blown away. "Was it just a coincidence, or has he been looking for you?"

"Coincidence. He works at North Central."

"Did he say anything to you?"

"We spoke for a minute, but I don't think he had any idea who I was."

"How do you feel about that?"

She sighed. "I'm relieved. The less he remembers about that night, the better."

"Why? I mean, you are gonna tell him about Namon, aren't you?"

"I wasn't planning on it, not unless it becomes absolutely necessary."

"Lawson, the man *is* Namon's father."

"So what? What contribution has Mark made to Namon's life that I couldn't have gotten from the local sperm bank?"

"That doesn't matter. He still has a right to know—they both do."

"Who cares about Mark's rights?"

"A judge might, for one."

"What about *my* rights? I've been raising Namon by myself since I was in high school. Don't I have the *right* to protect him and make sure he's well adjusted? Don't I have the right to decide who should and shouldn't be a part of his life? It's not only my right, Garrett; it's my duty as his mother."

"It's Mark's duty, too, as his father."

Lawson jumped up, her temper flaring. "Just whose side are you on?"

Garrett held her. "Yours. You don't even have to ask me that."

"Then act like it," she replied coldly. "You said that you wanted to adopt Namon. Do you honestly think that Mark would just sign him over to you if he knew the truth?"

"I don't know what he might do, but we both know there has to be a public notice put in the paper about the adoption petition. He's bound to find out sooner or later."

"Well, I'm praying for *later*."

"It's already been thirteen years. How much more time do you need?"

"As long as it takes to protect my child. Who knows how Mark will react once he finds out we have a teenage son together?"

"Keeping quiet would be fine if Mark was off somewhere never to be seen or heard from again, but he's here, Lawson. You don't have much of a choice."

Lawson paced the floor as she contemplated her next move. "There's another alternative to telling Mark about Namon, and it might be the only way out of this." She entwined her hands with his. "We can leave."

Garrett exhaled. "*Leave?* Lawson, you can't be serious."

"I am!" she affirmed. She squeezed his hands and stated

emphatically, "Baby, let's do it! Let's get married, take Namon, and get as far away from here as we can."

"And leave your home, this new job, your church, and your friends? You know you don't want to do that, and I know that you're not a quitter. You're not somebody who runs from your problems; you deal with them."

"This is how I intend to deal with this one."

Garrett cupped her face in his hands. "Lawson, I love you. There's nothing I want more than for you to be my wife, but I can't marry you like this, or let you duck out like a coward."

"But, Garrett—"

"I said no," he stated firmly. "Running might be a quick fix, but that's not going to stop Namon from wondering about his biological father. You can't just hide this from him. You've got to face this situation eventually."

Lawson snapped her fingers. "So, just like that, you want me to hand over my son to a virtual stranger?"

"I'm not suggesting anything that radical. I just don't want you to do something that's only going to make things worse. We need to seek God on the matter and follow His lead. Obedience is better than sacrifice. He's not going to allow this man to take your son away from you. Have faith."

Lawson dropped her head into her hands and gave in. "You're right. What was I thinking?"

He wrapped his arms around her. "You weren't thinking; you were panicking. We'll figure this thing out, though."

Lawson lifted her eyes to meet his. "We?"

"Yeah. We're a team, right?"

Lawson managed a faint smile. "Right."

Garrett sat down, and Lawson swathed herself in his embrace. "So, when are you going to break the news to him?" he asked her.

"Are you talking about Mark or Namon?"

"I guess both."

"I don't know. Once the truth gets out, there is no turning back. That's what scares me," she admitted.

"Don't be scared. I'm behind you all the way, no matter what you decide. Namon is your son, so do what you think is best. Just remember, baby, no secret stays one for very long. Everything done in the dark eventually comes to light."

Chapter 10

"What kind of man just wakes up one day and decides to turn his back on his family?"
—*Angel King*

"So, what do you think about this Lawson situation?" asked Angel as she and Kina shopped for groceries on Kina's "approved foods" list after leaving Lawson's house.

Kina sighed. "That's a tough one. I know Lawson is just trying to look out for her son, but I don't think keeping him from his father is the best way to do it. Parents try so hard to protect their children, but sometimes nothing you do is ever enough."

"Are we still talking about Lawson here?"

Kina stopped. "No, I'm worried about Kenny," she confided. "He's been saying things I don't think a kid his age ought to be thinking about, much less be putting into words."

"What did he say?"

"He said he would kill E'Bell if he ever did anything to me. It kind of scared me to hear him talk like that."

Angel's eyes widened. "Kill him, as in murder?"

"Yeah."

Angel blew out a breath. "That's serious, Kina. What did you tell him?"

"I talked to him and told him that he shouldn't say things like that, but I don't know . . . something in his eyes made me nervous."

"What has E'Bell done that would make Kenny think he needed to protect you?" Angel had long suspected that E'Bell was abusive, but could never get Kina to admit it.

"Kenny heard us arguing the other night, and you know how kids are. He read more into it than there was. I mean, I know that E'Bell's not perfect," acknowledged Kina, "but he's given up a lot for us. Who knows where football would've taken him if he hadn't let it go to be with Kenny and me?"

"You've made a lot of sacrifices, too, you know," Angel pointed out, discarding the carton of chocolate chip cookies Kina had sneaked into the cart. "You had plans of your own. Not many eighteen-year-olds would be willing to give up their dreams to become the wife and baby's mama of some washed-up football player."

"E'Bell's not washed up, Angel. He's just in a bad place right now. Think about it. He was the one everybody had pegged to go pro; now, he's a janitor at the same high school where he was the star athlete. I can't blame him for being bitter about it."

"You never asked him to give up his career, or to drop out of school, or to become a janitor. Even if you did, it was his choice to do so, and he has no right to take out his shortcomings on you and Kenny."

Kina stopped pushing the cart. "Look at me. Do you see the cute size three cheerleader I was in high school? In case you hadn't noticed, my twenty-four-inch hourglass waistline has been replaced by this forty-one-inch muffin." She looked down at her torso. "This is not the body E'Bell fell in love with fifteen years ago."

"He's not exactly the Give-'em-hell E'Bell the newspapers used to call him either. The only six pack he can brag about now is the one in the fridge, but you accept him anyway. Why can't he do the same for you?"

"It's just different for men, especially for a man like him."

"E'Bell has no right to make you feel bad about yourself. No one does. And for the record, Kina, you're still a very beautiful woman."

Kina laughed. "On what planet? I looked through my yearbook the other day and just cried. I don't know what happened to me, my body, or to all that long hair I had."

"Well, your hair wouldn't keep falling out if you stopped stressing so much," Angel theorized. "All that stuff changes with time anyway. Besides, I like your hair short, and who hasn't put on a few pounds? I want you to focus on just being healthy, mentally *and* physically. We're supposed to be setting a good example for our clients."

"Speaking of which, have you met with that cancer patient yet?"

"Theresa McNair? No. I'm meeting with her tomorrow." Angel picked up a grapefruit and inspected it. "I get a really strange vibe about her."

"How come?"

"For one, she claims she found us through our Web site, but the site's not up and running yet, so she has to be lying."

Kina looked up. "The woman is dying, Angel. Does it really matter how she found us as long as we're able to help her?"

Angel exhaled and let it go. "I guess you're right. She has a small child, so I'm sure she needs all the help she can get." Angel paused a moment. "You know, if my baby had lived, she would be celebrating her eighth birthday next month."

Kina looked on with sympathy. "It still bothers you, doesn't it?"

"I try not to think about it most of the time, but I was thrown back into it when Theresa's daughter answered the phone. Hearing that little girl's voice brought up a lot of hurt that I thought was buried."

"You still miss him, don't you?" Kina asked softly.

"Who, Duke?"

Kina nodded.

"Staying busy keeps my mind from going there too much, but every once in a while, I'll have a moment like I did today." Angel exhaled. "I loved him so much, Kina. What kind of man just wakes up one day and decides to turn his back on his family?"

"Despite what happened, I think he really did love you. He just got caught up."

Angel shook her head. "You don't do what he did to some-one you love. He had me fooled for a long time, though. I'll give him credit for that."

"You'll meet the right man one day, Angel. I'm praying for it. Then you'll fall in love all over again and can put all that heartache behind you once and for all."

"Even if I do remarry, I'll never give my heart to another man like that again. It's too hard to mend once it's been broken."

Chapter 11

"You can't keep treating me like this, E'Bell."
—Kina Battle

"Good morning," said Kina as she set a plate of scrambled egg whites and turkey bacon down on the table in front of E'Bell.

He grunted and picked up the bacon. "What's this?"

"Breakfast," she replied. "It's turkey bacon. I think it's time we started eating healthier." She passed a plate to Kenny.

"Since when did I start telling you to think?" fired E'Bell.

Kina sat down. "Angel says that my cholesterol is really high and that I'm at risk for all kinds of problems like heart disease and diabetes. I have to change my diet, and you know you're always telling me that I need to lose some weight."

E'Bell leaned back in his chair. "You wanna lose some weight, huh? First, you stay gone all times of the night, now all of a sudden you want to lose some weight. You think I'm stupid, Kina?"

She shook her head. "I don't know what you're talking about."

"Oh, you don't? You're just gonna sit there and play the innocent role, huh? I know why you're doing this. I bet there's some lame cat up at the job you trying to impress," alleged E'Bell.

"E'Bell, I haven't met any men, honest."

He flung back his chair and stood over her. "Then what's with the new hairdo, huh?" He flicked a lock of her hair.

"Why are you trying to lose weight? Who you trying to look good for? Where are you getting the money for all this? Is this fool giving you money too?"

At that moment, Kina's primary concern was getting her son out of the room before things turned ugly. "Kenny, baby, go to your room and finish getting ready. Your bus will be here in a second."

"Answer me, Kina!"

She waited for Kenny to exit before responding. "This isn't a new hairdo, E'Bell. All I did is wash it. There is no other man."

"You think I'm stupid, don't you?" he repeated. "You laying up with this dude? You done had him in my house? Huh?" He backhanded her across the face, leaving a red splotch on her fair skin. "Answer me!"

Kina pressed her hand against her bruised cheek in a futile attempt to ease the sting. "I would never do anything like that, E'Bell. I swear."

He grabbed her by the throat. "If I ever find out that you had a man in here or that you've been sneaking around behind my back, I'll kill you; you understand?"

She tried but couldn't speak. All she could do was gasp for air. E'Bell released his grip on her neck. "And don't be making me this mess for breakfast no more. You cook what I tell you to cook." He sat back down at the table.

Kina heaved, trying to fill her lungs with the air that she'd been denied. "You can't keep treating me like this, E'Bell," she whimpered.

"I don't do nothing to you that you ain't done to me. Look at how you disrespect me. Look at how you go out your way to try to hurt me."

Tears fell from her cheeks into her lap. "When did I hurt you?" she wailed. "When have I ever laid a hand on you?"

"You took my dreams away from me. Don't nothing hit harder than that."

Kina sniffed and wiped her eyes. "You act like you ain't even sorry. If I hurt you, at least you know it wasn't my intention."

"Whether you tried to or not, that's what happened. You expect me to feel sorry for you? You want me to make things easy for you? When did anybody ever feel sorry for me? Who ever cut me a break?"

Kina cried, "All I've ever tried to do is love you, E'Bell!"

"Is that why you're sneaking behind my back—to show how much you *love* me?"

"There is no other man, baby. Who would even want me?"

"Better not be. I swear, Kina, if I ever caught another man in this house—"

"You won't," she vowed to him. "I love you; I just want to be with you. All I want is for you to stop fighting me."

When E'Bell glimpsed at her battered face, he felt remorseful. "I don't like hurting you, but you push my buttons and that sets me off. Then I can't stop."

"But everything I do makes you mad. It seems like I can't do anything right in your eyes."

"That's because you don't try, Kina."

"I *am* trying, but I don't know what else I can do to make you happy."

E'Bell stared into the wall. "You just don't know what it's like for me. Didn't *nothing* turn out for me the way I planned." He looked like he was going to cry.

Kina got up and put her arm around his shoulder. "The two of us can come up with a new plan. Don't you remember how much fun we used to have? Even in high school, everyone could see how perfect we were for each other."

E'Bell nodded. "I remember. I had everything then—my girl, my team, fans, scholarship offers." He swatted her arm off of him. "I could've played for any school in the country. NFL agents were already looking at me. Then it was all taken away."

Kina knew that any sympathy she had garnered from him had vanished the moment he mentioned football. "What do you want from me, E'Bell? I can't apologize for having our son."

"What about for trapping me? Can you apologize for that? You knew I was gon' make it big one day, so you made sure that you had your little insurance policy on my money."

"That's not true!" she protested. "Kenny was never my meal ticket. I had plans to go to college, too, you know. I had to realize maybe that wasn't God's plan for me, just like football might not have been His plan for you."

"There you go, Kina, always putting God in it when you want to worm your way out of something. People in the streets said you got pregnant on purpose. Even my mama told me that. Well, you still want half of what I got, Kina? Fine. Do the math and figure out what's half of nothing, 'cause that's all I got now."

"You've got me," she replied meekly, "and you've got our son."

He looked at her and sucked his teeth. "Like I said, I ain't got nothing."

Chapter 12

"You know me, okay? Biblically!"
—Lawson Kerry

"Miss Kerry!" called Mark from the school's parking lot. She saw him in her peripheral vision but pretended not to hear. She picked up her pace.

"Lawson!" Mark's footsteps were rapidly approaching her, making it impossible to go on ignoring him.

Lawson turned around. "Hey, I didn't see you."

He took a second to catch his breath. "You wanna tell me what's going on?"

Lawson feigned innocence. "You know, first day of school and all . . ."

"This seems to be a little more than first day jitters."

"I don't know what you're talking about," she replied, walking away from him.

Mark grabbed her arm. "I think you're avoiding me, and I want to know why."

Lawson eased out of his grip. "What makes you think I'm avoiding you?"

"For starters, I know you got my e-mail about the new teachers' luncheon yesterday that you didn't bother to show up for, nor have you returned any of my phone calls. In fact, you haven't said two words to me since Monday when you nearly passed out in my classroom. Tell me what's up."

"Nothing. I've been busy. I haven't had time for social calls."

He narrowed his eyes. "I believe there's more to it than that. I hope you're not embarrassed by what happened."

"No. Why would I be?"

"Well, some people get a little embarrassed when someone else sees them in a vulnerable position. You shouldn't feel bad about it, though. Starting a new job can be overwhelming, and the pressure and stress took a toll on you."

She shook her head. "You don't know me as well as you seem to think you do, Mr. Vinson. Now, if you'll excuse me, I have a job to do."

Mark crossed his arms in front of him. "Miss Kerry, I'm not letting you set foot into that school until you tell me what's bothering you."

Lawson's voice filled with anxiety. "Just let it go, all right?"

"I'll let it go as soon as you decide to be honest with me."

"Are you calling me a liar?"

Mark held up his hands. "Hold on. Nobody's doing any name-calling or making accusations. I'm just trying to find out what's going on with one of my teachers."

Lawson rolled her eyes. "I'm not *your* teacher. I'm not *your* anything!"

Mark was taken aback. "The last time I checked, you were still my mentee."

She huffed and blurted out, "Therein lies the problem! I want a new mentor."

Mark looked surprised and a little hurt. "Why?"

"I don't feel comfortable around you."

"Really? If I've done anything to make you feel this way, you have my sincerest apology. If you'd talk to me, I'm sure we could get to the bottom of this."

"I don't need your apology. I just need another mentor," snapped Lawson.

"Lawson, I know that I can come on a little strong sometimes. I don't mean anything by it; it's just the way that I am. I can take it down a notch if you need me to."

"Your personality isn't the issue."

"Then tell me what is. I'm positive that it's all some big misunderstanding."

"There's no misunderstanding." She hesitated before going on. "Working with you would just be too weird for me."

"Why?"

She stepped in front of him. "Look closely. Don't I look the least bit familiar?"

Mark narrowed his eyes, examining her face. "No, not really."

"You know me, okay? Biblically!" Lawson leaned close to him and whispered, "We slept together."

He recoiled. "We did?"

"Yes, in high school, Manny's graduation party."

"Manny . . . Are you talking about Emanuel Young?"

Lawson nodded.

Mark thought back and smiled. "*La-La?*"

"Now you remember?"

"Wow," he said in awe. "You look so different; not that it's a bad thing, of course! You're just . . . wow." He shook his head, amused by the revelation. "Why didn't you say anything sooner?"

"It's embarrassing enough that you didn't remember."

"Shoot, that had to have been, what, fourteen years ago?" He chuckled. "*So you're having my baby*," he sang in his best Jodeci impression. "You remember that?"

"I couldn't forget it if I wanted to," Lawson thought aloud.

"Yeah, that night was crazy! Girl . . . well, come here." Mark pulled Lawson into a bear hug before releasing her. "I hate we didn't keep in touch."

"Not half as much as I do," she mumbled. "At least then you'd know that nobody's called me La-La in years."

"So, that's why you've been acting so strange," he concluded.

"It's not every day that I end up working alongside the guy I lost my virginity to."

"You know, they say that you never forget your first," he added smugly. They began walking again. "If it means anything, I'm sorry I didn't call like I should've. I was young and couldn't see past football and college. I should've handled things better."

"When you know better, you do better, as my mother used to say. We were teenagers. Who doesn't make mistakes at that age?"

"Thanks for being so cool about it," said Mark as they made their way through the throngs of teenagers swarming the hallway. "Now that we've cleared the air, I hope that you'll change your mind about our working together. In light of everything, I really want to get to know you again. Just because we've seen each other naked doesn't mean that things have to be weird between us."

"Actually, it wasn't really weird until you said that."

He laughed a little. "You know what I mean. We're both adults. I'm sure we can handle it; assuming, of course, you'll still let me be your mentor."

Lawson relented. "I suppose we can try and see how it goes."

"Fair enough. I meant what I said about getting to know each other. By the end of the semester, I want to know everything about you from your favorite food to what student you want to throw over a bridge."

Getting to know the intimate details of each other's life was the last thing Lawson was hoping for. "You'll soon find out that I'm a very private person, Mark."

"That's what you say right now. Give me a few weeks, though," he dared her. "I'll have you spilling your deepest, darkest secrets out. You'll see."

Nothing frightened Lawson more than the possibility of him succeeding in doing so.

Chapter 12

"I think it's indelibly marked on my brain now."
—*Sullivan Webb*

Sullivan half listened as Charles chatted with her on the phone that morning, reminding her to pray for one of the deacons at the church who was having surgery that afternoon. Deacon Wade and his heart problems were the furthest things from Sullivan's mind. She was too busy trying to stop her thoughts from wandering to the wonderfully and fearfully made Vaughn Lovett.

"And don't forget to schedule a rehearsal for the children's choir this week," added Charles. "Next Sunday is fifth Sunday, you know."

"I still don't know why *I* have to do it," whined Sullivan as she sipped on her Morning Sunrise, a potent combination she created, consisting of grapefruit juice blended with ice, yogurt, and vodka. "You know I don't mix well with children."

"And you know that it's customary for the First Lady to direct the children's choir on fifth Sundays. It's only a few Sundays out of the year. Surely that's not asking too much."

"Would it matter if it was?" she fired back. Another call came through before Charles could answer her. "That's my phone. I have to take this call." She hung up without another word to her husband and clicked over to the other line. "Hello?"

"May I speak to Sullivan Webb please?"

She was caught off guard by the velvety voice on the other end of the phone. "Yes. Who's this?"

"It's Vaughn from Supreme Auto on Sexton. I fixed your BMW the other day."

A grin snaked across Sullivan's lips. "How could I forget? Hello, Mr. Lovett."

"You remembered my name this time."

Sullivan smiled into the phone. "I think it's indelibly marked on my brain now. Now, to what do I owe the pleasure of this phone call?"

"Huh?"

She giggled. "Why are you calling me?"

"I just wanted to make sure the car's running okay. I'm the new guy, so Mike likes for me to do follow-up calls to make sure everything's all right after the first day or so. You haven't had any problems, have you?"

"Nope. You took very good care of me, if I do say so myself."

"Just doin' my job. Glad I could help." Silence passed between them as Sullivan scrambled for something to say to prolong their conversation. "Well, it was nice meeting you, Mrs. Webb. If you have any problems, just holler at me. You know the number."

The thought that this could be their last time speaking was sobering for Sullivan. Their brief connection may not have amounted to much, but his presence was a welcomed break from the monotony of her routine life. "So, this is it, huh?"

"I hope so," replied Vaughn. "It's not too good for business if your car is breaking down every week."

She scrawled his name with her finger. "Well, we'll always have Auto World."

"I'm sure we'll see each other around," he assured her. "Hey, a customer just walked in. I'll check you later."

The easiest and smartest thing to do at that moment would've been to hang up, but Sullivan wasn't always prone to doing things the easy or the smart way. "Vaughn, wait!"

"'Sup?" She heard Vaughn tell the customer he'd be right with him.

"Maybe we should get together for coffee some time."

"That's cool."

"Maybe, like, one day this week," she ventured.

He hesitated. It was only for a second, but it was long enough to make her want to rescind the offer.

"On second thought, maybe we shouldn't. Forget I said that."

Vaughn cleared his throat. "When?"

"Excuse me?"

"When do you want to hook up . . . for coffee?"

Sullivan sighed, relieved. "Are you free Thursday?" She crossed her fingers.

"Yeah."

"What time?"

"How's seven?"

She puckered her brow. "In the morning?"

"Yes. Some of us have to work, you know."

She acquiesced, giddy from the prospect of seeing him again. "Seven it is then."

"Cool. Can't wait."

"Is Starbucks okay?"

"I don't really get into all those lattes and mochas. I was thinking about just a regular old cup of joe at McDonald's or someplace like that. There's one a couple of blocks from here."

McDonald's? She didn't even know where the nearest one was, but she'd spend all night staking out every one of them if she had to. "Mickey D's is fine. I'll see you tomorrow, Vaughn." She hung up the phone and squealed with excitement.

As Sullivan made her way upstairs to find something to wear for her date with Vaughn, she caught sight of one of her wedding photographs, mounted up above the staircase, staring back at her. The guilt bolted down on Sullivan at once. What was she thinking? She was the pastor's wife, for

God's sake. How could she risk her reputation by cavorting with the family's mechanic? How could she do that to Charles, who had never been anything but good to her?

"I can just about hear those three stooges right now," grumbled Sullivan, thinking about Angel, Lawson, and Kina. She mocked them: "Remember what the Bible says, Sully. Have respect for marriage. Always be faithful to your partner because God will punish anyone who is immoral or unfaithful in marriage."

Try as she might, she couldn't argue with what the Word says regarding marriage and fidelity. Lawson, Kina, and Angel's wrath would be nothing compared to God's. Sullivan flipped through the call history on her phone to find the garage's number to call Vaughn and cancel their date.

As quickly as that repentant moment came, however, so did the memory of Vaughn's electric touch and seductive smile. Sullivan put the phone away and decided that God knew she would never do anything to intentionally hurt Charles. This was just coffee. After all, didn't the Bible also say that people should be kind to others because many people have entertained angels without even knowing it? Vaughn could be one of those angels for all she knew. It wouldn't be a far stretch, considering that he certainly had the body of a god.

The twinge of guilt tried to creep in again, but she wasn't perturbed. It was nothing that another shot of Morning Sunrise couldn't cure.

Chapter 13

"Sometimes the past is just better off staying there."
—*Angel King*

After a thirty-minute drive to the suburbs, Angel found herself on Theresa McNair's doorstep. She rang the doorbell and ran her hands over her smock to smooth it out. Standing in front of the large brick Tudor was intimidating. It didn't matter that the people inside needed Angel much more than she needed them.

A striking but frail woman appeared at the door with a little girl in tow. "Are you Angel King?" the woman asked.

"Yes, and you must be Theresa McNair." Angel extended her hand to her. "It's a pleasure to meet you."

She shook Angel's hand. "Same here. And this is my baby, Morgan."

"I'm not a baby," argued the little girl in afro-puffs. "I'm almost four years old!"

Theresa laughed. "She doesn't like it when I call her a baby. Please come in." She stepped aside to allow Angel to pass through. "And please, just call me Theresa."

"You have a beautiful home," observed Angel, admiring the elegant décor. She did notice that the living room was conspicuously absent of any family pictures.

"Thank you, but it's not the fixings that make this home special as much as it is the people in it." Theresa extended her hand toward the sofa. "Have a seat."

"Thanks." Angel sat down and pulled out her checklist. "Basically, what I want to do today is meet your family, get to know you a little better, and tell you what you can expect throughout this process."

Theresa sat down and invited Morgan to join her. "Well, there's not much mystery there. I'm going to die. I've accepted it, my husband's trying to accept it, and together, I'm hoping we can get the kids to accept it, too. Would you like some tea?"

"I would, thank you." Angel was struck by how calm Theresa seemed as she poured the tea and spoke of her own death with the same ease one might show when talking about the weather. "I didn't realize you had a whole clan here. I sort of got the impression that you were a single parent."

Theresa handed Angel her tea. "No, we're a family of four. My eight-year-old, Miley, is at ballet practice with her dad. We want to keep the kids' routine as normal as possible."

Angel sipped her tea. "Will I be meeting Miley and your husband today?"

Theresa tensed up. "No, I just wanted the two of us to talk for now and kind of get a feel for one another, you know?"

"I understand." Angel began pulling out papers from her bag. "I know that you probably want to know what my credentials are before turning your life over to me. I graduated with a degree in nursing seven years ago, got my masters—"

Theresa stopped her. "I'm more interested in getting to know you as a person, not as a nurse. After all, we're going to be spending a lot of time together, and you may very well be the person at my side when the Lord calls me home. If you're going to be around my husband and my kids, I want to know everything there is to know about Angel King."

Angel was caught off guard. "Exactly what do you want to know?"

"Anything. Are you married? Do you have kids?"

Angel shook her head. "No husband and no kids. I got married really young, but we divorced several years ago. While I don't have any kids of my own, I do have a godson, Kenny, who I'm really close to."

Theresa seemed surprised. "You've never thought about having kids?"

"Sure, I mean, what woman hasn't? I sort of gave up on it after—" Angel bit her lip, reluctant to reveal her most painful moments to a virtual stranger.

"After what?" pressed Theresa.

Angel swallowed the lump in her throat. "I was pregnant once, but I had a miscarriage soon after my ex-husband filed for divorce."

"Oh, no! I'm so sorry to hear that." The news appeared to hit Theresa particularly hard, which Angel found odd.

Angel set her cup back down on the table. "Don't worry. I'm fine now. Besides, I'm still young enough to have more kids if the time—and the man—is right."

"So, you want kids?"

"Someday, yeah. Until then, I have Kenny to fill that void. If anything ever happened to his mother, I wouldn't hesitate to raise him."

Theresa was quiet, thoughtful. Angel suspected that she might be worried about what would happen to her own children after her death. Angel touched her hand. "Are you all right?"

"I'm sorry. I was just thinking about you losing your baby right after losing your husband. My kids and my husband mean everything to me. I just can't imagine what that must've been like for you."

"Losing my marriage was tough, and losing my baby even tougher because I'd tried so hard to get pregnant."

"What happened? With your husband, I mean. I can't imagine any man leaving his pregnant wife."

"The same thing that always happens," replied Angel, thrown by Theresa's line of questioning. "Someone comes along who's prettier or more exciting, and the wife you have at home doesn't seem so special anymore."

"I'm sure it was more complicated than that. I don't think anyone, male or female, ever walks out on their family without agonizing over it first. People don't make that kind of decision lightly, especially when there are kids involved."

"Duke never knew about the baby," disclosed Angel. "I doubt if it would've made any difference, though, once that predator got her hooks into my husband."

"Why didn't—"

Angel interrupted her. "I'm sorry. I'm not really comfortable talking about this."

Theresa looked embarrassed. "Of course, I understand. Forgive me. I shouldn't have been so invasive."

"It's all right. Sometimes the past is just better off staying there, you know?"

Theresa nodded.

"Now, tell me about your treatment. You mentioned something about chemo earlier."

Theresa sighed. "For all the good it's doing. I feel so much worse afterward that I'm starting to wonder if it's even worth it."

"If it gives you one more hour with your family, I believe it is."

Theresa shook her head. "No matter how much time I've got, I don't think it'll be enough to right all the wrongs I've done."

"If I haven't learned anything else in this business, I've learned that you can't live your life looking back, especially not now."

"You must have a very forgiving nature," Theresa assumed.

"I try to." Then Angel thought of Duke and how much he had hurt her. "I'm not always successful, though."

"You forgave your husband and his lover. That says a lot about the kind of person you are."

"I never said that I forgave either of them," clarified Angel. "So, what does *that* say about the kind of person I am?"

"It says you're human, I suppose."

They were both quiet until Theresa looked down at her watch. "Well, my husband will be home soon. I didn't tell him you were coming today. I think if he sees you, it would freak him out too much. He doesn't like to think about me being sick. If he comes here and sees a nurse . . ."

"I understand," said Angel, rising. "Having me here is like having a casket in your living room."

"It's just too soon. He couldn't handle that right now." She walked Angel to the door. "When will I see you again?"

"It's up to you. I can come as often as you want," answered Angel.

"Let's shoot for Thursday, around noon."

Angel agreed to the date and scribbled it into her appointment book.

"It was nice meeting you," said Theresa as she walked Angel to the door. "I think this is going to be a life-changing experience for both of us."

As she drove into the street, Angel looked back at Theresa McNair still standing in the doorway. Something about the woman made Angel uneasy, and she had an eerie feeling that Theresa McNair would be one of the patients who would continue to haunt her long after death.

Chapter 14

"He's not in my life anymore. Not in either of our lives."
—*Lawson Kerry*

"Hey, let me help you," offered Mark when he spotted Lawson trying to balance her books and a stack of papers as she made her way down the hall before first period.

"Isn't it a little late for you to be trying to carry my books?" joked Lawson as she transferred the pile from her arms to his.

"Better late than never. You really shouldn't take so much work home," he cautioned her. "The key is to give one hundred percent from seven to three, but from three to seven the next morning is your time. Otherwise, you're gonna burn out before Christmas."

Lawson unlocked her classroom door; Mark followed her inside. "And just how often do you take your own advice, Coach Vinson?"

"Not often enough," he admitted. "But there are a few things I never let work interfere with, like God, family, and, of course, Mariah."

The mentioning of another female caught Lawson's attention. "Mariah—is that your girlfriend?"

He laughed and set her books down on the desk. "I don't think that's legal in most states. Mariah's my daughter. She lives in North Carolina with her mother."

The possibility of Namon having siblings had never occurred to Lawson before. Now, Namon was suddenly someone's brother. "How old is she?"

"She just turned six. She's very smart, beautiful, charming—basically, the female version of me," he boasted with a smile. "What about you? Didn't you tell me you had kids when we met?"

Lawson knew that the question was inevitable, but it still hit her like a bullet. "You mean other than the thousand or so we have here?" she asked, hoping to divert the conversation. She nodded. "I have a son."

"Cool. I've always wanted one myself. What's his name?"

"Namon."

"How old is he?"

She gulped. The last thing she needed was for Mark to start doing the math for Namon's birth and conception. "He's not much older than your daughter." She cleared her throat and opened her laptop. "You know, I've been meaning to ask you about last year's graduation test scores and if you have any ideas on raising the scores in social studies. I found a great Web site that I think the kids will love. It's got all kinds of sample test questions, quizzes, games, and it's set to rap music."

Mark sat on the edge of her desk. "You've got all year to worry about that. I want to hear more about you. We rarely get a minute to talk like this."

Lawson laughed nervously. "Me? I'm boring; just ask the students."

"Has teaching gotten in the way of you spending time with your son?"

Lawson sat down at her desk. "Not really. Thankfully, Namon's old enough to entertain himself most of the time. Plus, my fiancé helps out a lot."

"Oh, there's a fiancé?" he inquired. "I should have known you were way too beautiful to still be on the market."

Lawson was surprised to find herself blushing.

"So, when's the big day?"

"We haven't really set a date yet. Soon, though. What about you? Are there any wedding bells in your future?"

"Nope. I'm not as lucky in love as you are. I haven't found *the one* yet."

"What about Mariah's mother?"

He shrugged. "Tasha came close. I'm kind of traditional, I guess. I think if you get a girl pregnant, you ought to man up and give the baby a name and a family with a stable home. Unfortunately, Tasha's not so traditional. She was all for getting married when I was playing football overseas and still had a shot at the NFL. Once I got injured and was cut from the team, life as a teacher's wife didn't have as much appeal. Before I knew it, she was on to the next guy with a football contract."

"Did you love her?"

"Of course. She's the mother of my child. My daughter means more to me than anything, and Tasha is the reason I have her. Kids are a blessing."

Guilt crushed Lawson into silence.

"Marrying Tasha seemed like the right thing at the time, but I see now that we wanted different things out of life. We're still friends, though, for our daughter's sake. Mariah's my heart. I'd do anything for her, including befriend her gold-digging mama."

Lawson found her voice. "I can tell that you really love your little girl. She sounds like a lot for your future kids to compete with."

Mark shook his head. "No competition required. I won't love any other seed of mine any more or any less than I love her. A child who's carrying my DNA is privy to the same love and treatment that she is."

"Do you think you want any more kids?"

"Sure . . ." Lawson perked up. "But not right now. First, I want to settle down and get married. Tasha's cool, but I don't want any more baby mamas. I want a wife, and even that's at least three years on down the road."

She bit her lip. "I see."

"So, tell me about this man of yours. Does he have kids?"

"No, but he treats Namon like his own son."

"That's good. How does Namon's dad feel about that?"

Lawson turned away, under the pretense of looking for papers. "He's not in my life anymore. Not in either of our lives."

"That guy doesn't know what he's missing out on. I love being a dad."

She felt a pang of guilt again. "Well, my class will be in here soon, so . . ."

"So, you're kicking me out, huh?"

Lawson smiled. "Something like that."

Mark stood to leave. "Before I go, how are your classes? Everything okay?"

"Everything's great! I actually love my job. Can you believe it?"

"That's good to hear. I'm sure the kids love you too." He moved a little closer to her. "You seem like the type who's easy to love."

"You didn't always think that," teased Lawson.

"It's not like you were interested." He blushed in mock humility. "You didn't want me. I was just some ol' jock. You probably went for the preppy, pretty-boy type."

"Mark, you *were* the preppy, pretty-boy type!"

He laughed. "Guilty as charged. I bet your son's one too. The next time Mariah's in town, we should get the kids together," he suggested.

"Right. We'll have to do that." *Over my dead body*, she thought.

"Who knows?" said Mark as he made his way out the door. "They might end up being as close as two peas in a pod, like brother and sister."

Chapter 15

"I can't resist a man who comes equipped with presents."
—*Sullivan Webb*

Brown Sugar was the first thing Sullivan spotted when she pulled into the parking lot at McDonald's. It was strange how the same car that made her cringe the first time she saw it just days before now made her smile. She pulled up beside Vaughn's Buick, did a quick inspection of her hair and makeup, and met him inside.

"Have you been waiting long?" she asked him when she approached his table after ordering her coffee.

He put down his sausage biscuit and wiped his mouth. "Not really. Sit down."

Sullivan sat down across from him, still giddy. She hadn't been this excited since she discovered online shopping. "It looks like it's going to be a pretty day today," she said, making idle chatter.

He nodded. "You want something to eat?"

"No, this coffee's fine." She lifted the lid and inhaled it. "Hot and black, just like I like it."

"That's how I like my women, too," he said and winked at her.

She wanted to melt. "I bet a man like you has no trouble in that department."

He shrugged his shoulders. "I do all right, I guess."

"What—a stud like you doesn't have a steady girlfriend?"

Vaughn shook his head. "I'm not really the relationship type."

She smirked. "Oh, you just hit 'em and quit 'em, huh?"

"I wouldn't say all that. I just have a hard time finding females I can vibe with. Not many women my age like doing the kinds of things I want to do."

"What kind of girl doesn't enjoy fuel injections?" she asked, teasing him.

"I can do more than just work on cars, Miss Sullivan. I'm also an artist. You should stop by my place and see my work some time."

Sullivan was impressed. "You paint?"

"Does that surprise you?"

"It surprises me when I meet anyone who loves art. There was a time when I wanted nothing more than to be locked away in my studio with a canvas and a paintbrush." She sighed, thinking back on that creative and carefree period of her life. "That was a long time ago, though."

"What happened to make you stop?"

"I don't know. Life, I guess."

"Do you still have any of your old paintings?"

"A few."

"Maybe you'll let me see them one day." His eyes twinkled. "I'll show you mine if you show me yours."

Sullivan blushed, feeling twelve again. "I'm sure that can be arranged."

Vaughn sat back and took stock of her. "So, is this what you do all day—sip coffee and look beautiful?"

"Not *all* day," Sullivan corrected him.

"But you don't work, do you?"

"No, not in the traditional sense."

"Then why aren't you using this time to paint?"

She thought about it. "That's a good question. Why *aren't* I painting?"

Vaughn reached for her hand. "The next time we see each other, I want you to have painted something, all right?"

Sullivan batted her eyes. "Are you planning on there being a next time?"

"You never know. . . ."

They stared each other down a minute before saying anything else.

"Before I forget, I have something for you," Vaughn said and reached down into his duffel bag and pulled out a small white sack.

Sullivan rubbed her hands in anticipation. "I can't resist a man who comes equipped with presents."

"I thought about you and got it when I stopped for gas this morning." He reached into the bag and handed her an apple turnover. "It's still warm. The deli inside the gas station makes the best pastries."

She raised her hand to decline. "I don't eat sweets first thing in the morning. It's bad for the stomach, at least according to Doctor Big Mama. Besides, I skipped breakfast this morning. I should probably have some real sustenance first."

Vaughn moved in closer. "I promise you it's worth any stomach pangs you may have to endure later." His voice was incredibly seductive. "Look at that flaky crust and the icing drizzled across the top. Here, smell it."

She inhaled the aroma of warm cinnamon and baked apples.

"Taste it." He licked his lips. "You know you want to."

Her eyes were fixed on his lips. "Just because I want to doesn't mean I should."

"I'll make a deal with you. If you taste it, we'll keep it between us, and no one ever has to know that you broke the breakfast rule, not even Big Mama."

The temptation was more than she could withstand. He clutched the turnover as she sank her teeth into it. She licked a bit of residual icing off of her finger. "That's the best part," he told her.

Sullivan smiled up at him. "I think I'll have one more bite."

He fed her another piece. "Careful—don't bite off more than you can chew."

She didn't know if he meant that literally or figuratively. "You got any more surprises in that bag of yours?"

"I have several tricks in my bag, but we'll save those for another time." Vaughn slid his hand over her knee and glanced at the clock. "I should probably be heading out."

Sullivan pouted. "So soon?"

He rose. "I've only been working for Mike a couple of months. It's too soon to start coming in when I feel like it. I know that you've got it made, but some of us have to make a living the old-fashioned way."

Sullivan stood too. "Well, it was nice seeing you again, Vaughn." Saying good-bye was harder than she thought it would be. "So, what now? Do we shake hands, give a pound?" she pondered nervously.

He smiled. "How about a hug?"

Sullivan shrugged and slid into his opened arms. He had the firmest back she'd ever groped, and he smelled like fresh linen. She had to stop herself from wrapping both her arms and legs around him.

Vaughn pulled away. "Why don't you let me take you to lunch tomorrow?"

She wanted to, she desperately wanted to, but she knew she couldn't. Coffee was one thing, but there was no way she could take this kind of risk again. "I can't. Nothing personal. I have a husband, remember?"

"I remember. I was just wondering if you did. Anyway, it's just lunch, Sullivan. If you don't want to go, say that. Don't make excuses."

"My marriage isn't an excuse; it's a legally binding agreement," she disputed. "I'm sorry if I gave you the impression that

Charles and I weren't happy; it wasn't my intent. My marriage is solid."

"You don't have to convince me."

"Plus, Charles is running for public office. That makes anything I do up for scrutiny. The last thing his campaign needs is a scandal."

Vaughn shook his head. "I couldn't have people all up in my business like that."

"You get used to it. Plus, I don't get nearly the attention that Charles does. He's the one out in the public eye campaigning. I'm just the supportive wife."

"It sounds like he's a busy little boy." He brushed his hand against her cheek. "Busy little boys usually don't have enough time to keep their women happy."

"I suppose Charles and I are the exception," she boasted.

"If you're so happy, Miss Sullivan, then why are you here with me?"

For once, Sullivan didn't have a snappy comeback.

Chapter 16

"I'm a grown woman . . ."
—*Sullivan Webb*

"Flashlight . . . neon lights," sang a tipsy Sullivan over the music as she staggered to her friends during the annual Labor Day cookout in Lawson's backyard.

"If the church could see you now . . ." mumbled Reginell, taking note of Sullivan's inebriated state.

"I'd just tell them I got a hold of some of the communion wine yesterday at church," slurred Sullivan and threw up her hands. "Let's get this party started! Who wants to boogie?"

Lawson sniffed into the plastic cup Sullivan was holding. "That smells like something stronger than communion wine to me, and I know you didn't get that from here because I put nothing but sodas and bottled water in that cooler."

"Fortunately, E'Bell was kind enough to share his secret stash." Sullivan raised her cup toward E'Bell. "Kina, tell that husband of yours that he's all right with me." Sullivan tried to dance, but found that she couldn't keep her balance.

Kina helped Sullivan to a chair and glanced over at E'Bell, who looked to be three sheets to the wind himself. "It's bad enough that he drinks that stuff. I'm not giving him any encouragement from you."

"Sully, you're the First Lady of the church, and here you are carrying on like some frat boy," scolded Lawson. "You're supposed to be setting an example."

"I'm sick of being First Lady, and I'm tired of setting examples," cried Sullivan. "I can't do this, and I can't do that. Gotta go to revivals and anniversaries and funerals and christenings. Gotta direct the children's choir. Gotta feed the homeless. Gotta visit the sick. . . ." She took another gulp from her cup. "Screw it! I want to dance, and I want to paint. I want to be myself, not stuck in some amen corner for the rest of my life."

Angel shook her head. "Sullivan, you're drunk. Maybe you should go in the house and lie down."

"See, there you go again, telling me what to do. I don't need to lie down. I'm a grown woman, Angel—*grown*!" Her eyes fluttered. "And I do what I wants to do."

"I am so thankful that it's just us out here," said Lawson. "Charles is not only a pastor, but he's also campaigning. He doesn't need this kind of press."

"Charles, Charles, Charles," mocked Sullivan in her best Jan Brady impression. "Why is everybody always worried about Charles? Nobody ever worries about me."

"Oh, we're *definitely* worried about you too," replied Angel, watching as Sullivan fought to stay awake. "Look at you. You're a mess, Sully."

"Did I hear somebody call my name?" asked Charles, approaching them from his post on the grill.

"Those ribs are calling *my* name!" replied Kina. "When will the food be ready?"

"Feel free to help yourself to the vegetable tray, Kina," urged Angel.

"Charles, didn't nobody call your name," barked Sullivan, slumped over.

Charles rubbed her back. "Baby, are you feeling okay?"

"I think she's a little lightheaded," explained Lawson, not wanting to reveal that Sullivan was completely wasted.

Charles was alarmed. "Do you want me to take you home, honey?"

"Let me guess. My behavior is not befitting of the First Lady of Mount Zion Ministries," recited Sullivan. "Well, you know what, Charles? I really don't give a rat's behind about what is befitting of a First Lady right now. I'm here to have some fun."

Angel pointed to the grill. "Pastor, those flames look a little high."

Charles turned his gaze to the flames leaping from the grill. "It does look a bit out of hand, doesn't it? Can you all keep an eye on her while I tackle this fire?"

Kina shooed him away. "Sure. You just make sure the food's all right."

Charles massaged Sullivan's neck. "I'll be right back, sweetheart."

"Take your time," called Sullivan as he rushed off to tend to the grill.

"God has given that man the patience of Job," assessed Lawson. "Charles is too good a man for you to treat him this way, Sully."

Sullivan rolled her eyes. "Maybe I don't need a good man." She turned up her cup. "Maybe what I need is a smokin' hot bad boy."

"Ain't nothing wrong with that!" chimed in Reginell.

Kina pinched Sullivan. "Girl, hush! Charles is standing right over there!"

Angel dunked her celery sticks into the vegetable dip. "I'm sure Lawson can help you out with finding a bad boy. Her school must be crawling with 'em."

Lawson chuckled. "Don't even get me started!"

"Burnout already?" asked Kina.

"It's not full-blown teacher burnout yet. More like a smoldering fire. It does get crazy at times, though. I was hoping to start working toward my master's next semester, but it looks like that might have to wait until the summer when things settle down some."

Kina stared at the ground. "Lawson, I envy the way you

just get in there and go after what you want without letting anything stop you. Here you are talking about your master's, and I haven't even started on my first degree."

"What's stopping you?" asked Reginell.

"I have my hands full with work and Kenny." Kina looked over her shoulder at E'Bell. "Plus, I don't know how E'Bell would feel about me spending all my time at school instead of at home, where I belong."

"I'm sure he'd be proud of you for going back to school," said Lawson.

Kina shook her head. "Then you don't know E'Bell."

"If you're worried about being away from home, you can always take classes online," suggested Angel.

"E'Bell would go ballistic if I blew our money on a computer."

"You can use the one at the office until you can afford your own."

Kina laughed to herself. "Shucks, I haven't stepped foot in a classroom in about twelve years. I would be light years behind everyone else."

Sullivan smacked her teeth. "Will you stop making excuses and just do it? I'm sure you can list a hundred reasons for why you shouldn't go to school, but twice as many for why you should."

Lawson caught the football Namon tossed to her. "Savannah State offers several degree programs and online classes. That's where I'm going for my master's."

Kina was still leery. "Maybe I'll give them a call next week."

"Call tomorrow," insisted Lawson, throwing the ball back to her son. "You would've talked yourself out of it by next week."

"What about E'Bell?" asked Kina.

Angel made a face. "What about him? This is something you need to do for you. If he doesn't want to better himself, that's on him."

"*Who* is *that?*" exclaimed Reginell when she looked up and saw two men entering through the gate into the backyard.

Lawson squinted her eyes to block out the sun. "That looks like Mike from the church. I don't know who that sexual chocolate is with him."

Sullivan raised her head and saw the two men greeting Charles at the grill. "What is Vaughn doing here?" she wondered.

"Sully, you know him?" asked Reginell, surprised and intrigued.

"Yeah, he fixed my car." Dazed, Sullivan stood up and walked toward them.

"Hey, sweetheart." Charles kissed her on the cheek. "You know Mike from the church. This is his apprentice. . . . Vaughn, isn't it?" Vaughn nodded.

"Sister Webb, it's good to see you," replied Mike. He reached out to shake Sullivan's hand, but she was too distracted by Vaughn to notice.

"What are you all doing here?" asked Sullivan, more to Vaughn than to Mike.

"Well, Pastor was kind enough to invite us when he came in for an oil change earlier. Business was kind of slow with it being a holiday and all, so we decided to take him up on his offer," supplied Mike.

"Sister Roslyn couldn't make it?" asked Charles.

"Roslyn said that she wasn't getting out of the bed before it was time to go back to work tomorrow. She believes in getting into the true spirit of Labor Day."

"Well, I can't blame her there!" said Charles with a hearty laugh. "You brothers can grab a plate and something to drink from the cooler. Relax and enjoy the fellowship."

Mike gave a slight nod. "Thank you, Pastor."

Vaughn followed up with, "Yeah, 'preciate it."

"Make yourselves at home," added Sullivan and nearly tripped over her own feet.

Charles caught her. "Whoa, I got you! You'll have to excuse her," explained Charles. "She's not feeling well. Baby, why don't you go inside and take a time out?"

"Don't talk to me like a child, Charles," Sullivan snapped.

"I wasn't trying to. I just think you should rest until you're feeling better."

Angel and Lawson walked over to offer their assistance. "We'll get her in the house, Pastor. Don't worry," said Angel, letting Sullivan lean on her for a crutch.

Lawson aided Angel. "Come on, Sully, lean on both of us," directed Lawson, trying to shift and balance Sullivan's weight between the two of them.

Vaughn stepped in and grabbed Sullivan by the waist. "I'll take her in for you. You ladies can stay out here and enjoy the party."

"Thanks!" exclaimed Lawson, happily passing Sullivan off on Vaughn. "She's a lot heavier than she looks."

"You need some help, son?" asked Charles.

Vaughn draped Sullivan's arm around his neck for extra support. "No, I got her."

"Thank you, brother." Charles returned his attention to the grill while Vaughn hauled the barely coherent Sullivan into the house.

"Are you trying to steal me away from my husband?" asked Sullivan once they were inside.

"Not hardly," grunted Vaughn. He smelled her breath. "Dang, girl, what have you been drinking?" Vaughn found an empty bedroom and eased Sullivan onto the bed.

"It's been a long time since another man has gotten me into bed," she replied, giggling.

"Go on and sleep this off. You probably won't even remember it in the morning."

Sullivan propped herself up on her elbows. "Then you might as well take advantage of the situation and kiss me if I'm not gonna remember it anyway."

Vaughn laughed and sat down next to her. "You're crazy, you know that?"

Sullivan clamped her arms around his neck. "Now, about that kiss. . . ."

Vaughn peeled her off of him. "Sullivan, what are you doing?"

"What does it feel like I'm doing? Come on, kiss me. You know you want to."

He gave in and kissed her on her neck. Sullivan began to moan. Vaughn sighed and pulled away from her. "We can't do this. Not with your husband right outside."

"Your lips feel so good. I don't want you to stop."

He rose. "Maybe not now, but you'll thank me when you wake up."

"Come on, just one little bitty kiss," cooed Sullivan.

Vaughn smiled, leaned in, and kissed her forehead. "Satisfied?"

She closed her eyes and nestled her head between two pillows. "That's not the kiss I wanted."

"Sorry. That's as good as it's gonna get." He removed a lock of her hair that had fallen onto her face. "Don't worry, beautiful. This won't be our last time in bed together. Your husband seems like a good dude. You're a pistol, though. He probably can't handle a woman like you."

Sullivan snored, already asleep. Vaughn laughed and covered her with a blanket. "Pastor Charles might not be able to handle you,"—he let his hand drift over her body—"but I sure can."

Chapter 17

"There are some sins I'm just going to have to live with."
—Angel King

"I thought I had scared you off," admitted Theresa when she found Angel waiting outside her door as scheduled a week after their initial meeting.

"Please. I come face to face with death every day. It takes a lot more than a round of Twenty Questions to put some fear in me!"

Theresa laughed and led her into the living room. "Point taken. After battling cancer, nothing much scares me anymore either."

Angel sat down and pulled out her notebook. "Let's get down to business, shall we? What's going on with you today? How are you feeling?"

Theresa sighed. "I lost some more of my hair today. I know it sounds vain, but losing my hair never gets any easier. You'd think I'd be used to that by now, or would have the guts to just shave it all off."

"It's not vain, and it's completely understandable. You're a woman. Our hair is our crowning glory. I freak out when I see more than a few strands in the brush. I can only imagine what you must be going through. You don't have to put up a front for me."

She squeezed Angel's hand and offered a slight smile. "Thanks."

"Do you have anything else to report?"

"I've been a little tired. I can't run around with the girls like I used to, which really puts me in a funk."

"Lethargy and depression are to be expected," cautioned Angel.

"It feels like cancer is taking all of the parts of my life that used to matter." Theresa's youngest daughter darted into the room and careened into Angel's lap. "I take that back. One of my most important parts is right there."

"She certainly is a friendly little thing, isn't she?" noted Angel as Morgan crawled into her lap.

Theresa smiled. "She's only four, but she has a discerning spirit about people. She's sort of naturally drawn to good people."

"You're pretty," said Morgan, fiddling with Angel's earrings.

"So are you," returned Angel.

"Do you want to come in the backyard and play with us?"

"Maybe later. I have to check on your mom right now."

Morgan wrinkled her nose. "Mommy's sick, isn't she?"

Angel and Theresa exchanged glances. Theresa cleared her throat. "Sweetheart, don't you remember that I told you that Mommy has a disease? Miss Angel is going to try to help me feel better."

"Is she going to fix the disease?"

"No, baby, she can't."

"Then what can she do?"

"Well," began Angel, "I can give her medicine whenever she starts to hurt, and I can make sure that she has everything she needs to be healthy." She smiled at the little girl. "And I can play with you when she gets too tired."

Morgan jumped out of Angel's lap. "Okay."

"Go outside with your sister. I'm sure she's wondering what happened to you," said Theresa.

Angel smiled as she watched Morgan sprint out of sight. "You know, when I look at your daughter, I can't help but think about the child I lost. She would be around Miley's age if she had lived."

"I'm sorry if being around my kids makes you sad," said Theresa.

Angel shook her head. "Don't apologize. I love kids. It's not your fault my baby died."

Theresa looked away.

"Anyway, we're here to talk about you and how I can make your life easier, not me and all my drama from relationships past."

Theresa faced her. "Angel, I want to ask you something first."

"Go ahead."

"I've been thinking about our conversation the other day and about forgiveness and all, and it got me wondering." She looked Angel in the eyes. "Have you forgiven your husband and the woman who took him from you?"

"Well, first off, she didn't *take* anything," emphasized Angel. "The other woman wasn't committed to me; he was. My husband chose to leave home all by himself. I'll never forgive Duke for what he did to me. I hope he and that tramp both get exactly what's coming to them."

Theresa withdrew from the sofa and watched Morgan and Miley playing through the bay window. "I'm sure both of them regret hurting you the way they did, but you have to be forgiving. The Bible says so. Holding all that resentment inside can eat you alive."

"I know, but whenever I think about what Duke did to me—what they both did—I can't feel anything but anger and animosity," Angel admitted.

"You're just as guilty of sinning if you refuse to forgive them."

Angel joined her at the window and lifted her eyes toward heaven. "I guess there are some sins I'm just going to have to live with."

"Angel, what would you say to the other woman if you ever came face to face with her? How do you think you'd react?"

She considered the scenario. "I'd like to think I'd be mature about it, but we're talking about a woman who swooped down, seduced my husband, got pregnant by him, and then rode off into the sunset with my life. By no means do I think that Duke is blameless, but I have to believe that there's a special place in hell for women like that."

Theresa shook her head. "You don't know that woman's situation. I'm sure she's had her share of guilt and suffering over it."

Angel laughed a little. "She and Duke are probably off living their lives, carrying on as if nothing happened. The only one who's had to suffer in all this is me. I didn't do anything wrong, but I got stuck with all the hurt."

"God has a way of healing all wounds, including yours. Forgiving the people who hurt you could be the first step in that process."

Angel smiled and teased her. "I thought I was the Angel in the room. You have much more compassion than the average person, but if your husband did that to you, I don't think you'd be as understanding. Their affair almost cost me my life, and it did cost my baby hers. I think they deserve their fair share of pain too."

"*Vengeance is mine, says the Lord,*" quoted Theresa. "Nobody ever gets off easily when they destroy other people's lives. Besides,"—she looked down at her decaying body—"God always makes sure everyone gets what they deserve one way or another."

Chapter 18

"Working for Angel is okay, but I have other dreams too."
—*Kina Battle*

It was a scene that almost made Kina's heart stop, but there he was. Kenny was seated on the floor of her closet, wielding his father's loaded gun.

"Kenny, where did you get that?" she screamed.

"I found it in here when I was looking for some paper for school. Is it real?" He traced his fingers across the gun and positioned it as if he were going to shoot.

Kina took a deep breath, "Very slowly, I want you to hand me the gun, all right?"

Trepidation darkened Kenny's face. "Am I in trouble?"

"No, I just don't want you to accidentally fire it. Your dad keeps it loaded."

He surrendered the gun to her, and Kina let out a sigh of relief. "Kenny, I don't ever want to see you with this gun again. You hear me?"

"Yes, ma'am."

She secured the gun into the holster and set it on a shelf far above Kenny's reach. He watched as she lodged it in place.

"Why does Daddy need a gun?"

"It's for our protection."

"Is he going to shoot somebody?"

"I pray that he never has to, but either way, you are not to come anywhere near this closet without permission. Got it?"

He nodded.

"You nearly scared me to death holding that gun. You could've killed yourself, Kenny. Do you realize that?"

Kenny dropped his head. "I didn't mean to scare you, Mama. I just wanted to look at it."

"Do you know how many children have hurt themselves or other people just because they wanted to look at a gun?" Kina's stomach churned as she heard E'Bell unlocking the front door. "Go into you room and stay there until I come get you."

Kenny, eager to avoid E'Bell's wrath, left without protest.

"Kina, where you at?" bellowed E'Bell.

"I'm in the bedroom," she called back and then said a quick prayer for her son's safety.

E'Bell appeared in the bedroom doorway with a can of beer and a scowl across his face. "Dinner ready yet?"

She shook her head. "I was about to start when—"

"You ain't even started?"

"I couldn't."

"Why not?"

"There was a situation with Kenny. He . . . he found your gun."

"What?"

"He found it in our closet and was playing with it."

"Why are you letting him go through my stuff?" he fired. He snatched off his belt. "Tell that boy to come here!"

Kina reached for the belt. "Honey, don't whip him. He was just in here looking for some paper when he found it. It ain't his fault. We should've hidden it better."

E'Bell bolted into the closet and began rummaging through the boxes, clothes, and shoes placed in there. "Where did you put it?"

She pointed to the shelf. "I didn't want him to be able to reach it. E'Bell, I've never felt safe with that thing in the house, now more than ever. Can't you get rid of it?"

"And what are we supposed to do if some fool tries to break

in and take the little bit of stuff I've managed to get?" He found the gun and removed the clip to make sure all of his bullets were still there. "Who's gon' protect us then—you?"

"God is all the protection we need."

"Yeah, God and this forty-four." He reattached the clip.

"At least hide it so Kenny can't get to it. Nothing scares me more than the thought of coming home and finding my baby dead on the floor with a bullet in his head."

E'Bell sucked his teeth and wiped Kenny's fingerprints off the gun. "Shouldn't you be cooking dinner instead of standing here looking at me?"

Kina treaded into the kitchen and began butchering a chicken for dinner. She hadn't gotten halfway through rins-ing off the legs before E'Bell stormed into the kitchen.

"What's this, Kina?" he demanded, holding up a crumpled brochure in his fist.

Kina recognized it at once and dropped the knife. It was the brochure containing her application for Savannah State University. "I–I don't know," she fibbed.

E'Bell yanked her by the throat, immediately cutting off her air supply. "You gon' look me in the face and lie to me like that?" He shoved her. She lost her balance for a second, but at least she could breathe again. "I know what you're trying to do," he alleged. "See, you think you're slick, Kina! When are you going to get this through that thick head of yours that you can't outsmart me? You're about as dumb as you are fat."

"I wasn't trying to trick you, E'Bell."

"Then why didn't you say nothing about it? Why did I find your application in a shoe box in the back of the closet?"

"I just put it there for safe-keeping. I haven't even decided whether or not I want to go."

"Oh, *you* hadn't decided, huh? Here it is that I had to quit school before I even got there because of you, and now you're trying to sneak and go behind my back."

"We can both go to school, E'Bell. You still have time to

apply and register for classes. Think of how much closer that whole experience could bring us. It would be like being in high school again."

"I'm almost thirty-three years old. What college do you think is going to put me on their football team?"

"Don't make school about football this time. You can get a degree in anything you want."

"All I ever wanted to do was be a football player. I wasn't some nerdy A student like you. I barely got out of high school. Nobody would've accepted me in their college if I couldn't play ball. Football was my one shot at making it big, at being somebody."

"E'Bell, with or without a football, you're still somebody."

"What—a janitor? On that field, I was Give-'em-hell E'Bell. Now, I'm just another janitor to sweep up behind a bunch of simple-minded teenagers. Do you know how it makes me feel to have to clean up after those kids? To have to polish the trophies and plaques that my sweat earned for that school? 'Round there, they treat me like I'm nothing, Kina, like some ol' has-been with a mop and a broom."

"You can quit and do something else," suggested Kina.

"Don't you get it? There *is* nothing else. This right here— this pissy apartment, dead-end job, a fat wife, and a son who can't even hold a football—this is it for me, and I hate it!" He ripped the application into shreds.

"E'Bell, no!" she cried and lunged at him, trying to retrieve the application.

He pushed her. "You think I'm gon' let you go to college after you screwed up my chances of going?"

Tears began flooding from her eyes. "I just wanted to make something of myself. Working for Angel is okay, but I have other dreams too."

"Yeah, I bet Angel and the rest of them silly broads are the ones who put this crazy notion in your head, too." He sprinkled the remnants of the application down on her like confetti. "You can forget about this school business, Kina. It ain't happening. If I ain't gon' be nothing, you ain't gon' be nothing. Now, get over there and fix me something to eat."

E'Bell grabbed another beer before settling down in front of the television. Kina milled around the kitchen, doing as she was told. On the outside, she appeared broken, which satisfied E'Bell. Inside, she couldn't help but smile a little and thank God for the college application that she had already filled out and submitted online.

Chapter 19

"Urges aren't the problem. You get in trouble when you act on them."
—*Lawson Kerry*

"Is it just me or are you on information overload?" asked Lawson as the seminar on best teaching practices that she and Mark were attending broke for lunch.

"Hey, at least it's a day away from the classroom, right?"

"I actually miss the little troublemakers. I hate that we got here so late. It was kind of hard to see from the back of the auditorium."

"Well, we can stand here and contemplate the mysteries of C.P. time, or we can grab some lunch. Take your pick."

Lawson zipped her bag. "I'm not really hungry. You can go on without me."

"Do you mind if I tag along with you? I'd much rather hang out with a beautiful woman than hang out by myself for the next hour and a half."

Lawson chuckled. "You wouldn't be saying that if you knew where I was going."

"Unless it's to hell in a hand-basket, I'm game."

"Not quite. Since we are downtown, I wanted to look at some wedding dresses."

Mark playfully puffed out his chest and tugged on his pants. "I think I'm secure enough in my manhood to handle that. Plus, there are bound to be some single women in there looking for bridesmaids' dresses, right?"

"I didn't think of that. You'd have to be a complete loser not to be able to walk out with at least one phone number."

Mark held the door open for her. "Well, I guess we're about to find out whether or not I'm a loser."

"A good-looking guy like you?" teased Lawson. "Not a chance!"

"So, she thinks I'm good-looking," stated Mark, blushing.

"Well, I'm sure she's not the first person to say that," said Lawson, playing along.

"First one in a while," said Mark as they walked out. "Well, the first one whose opinion I actually care about."

Lawson looked down at her feet as they continued their stroll. "Why would my opinion matter to you?"

Mark seemed embarrassed. "I don't know. If I had to guess, I might think it was because I still had a crush on you."

"It was hardly a crush, Mark. More like a wham-bam-thank-you-ma'am."

"I prefer to think of it as an instant attraction that thrust us both into the throes of passion."

"That must be why you never called," Lawson added sarcastically.

"I wanted to call," confessed Mark, "but I was scared."

"Scared of little ol' me?" They stopped at a red crossing signal.

"Scared of the way I felt around you. I know we were young, but the chemistry between us was pretty intense."

Her pulse quickened when she thought back to that night. "The light's green," she observed, relieved for the distraction. "The bridal shop is just across the street."

Mark looked in both directions. "Well, let's make a run for it. I don't want to be the one having to explain to the boss why you were arrested for jaywalking." Without thinking, he reached for Lawson's hand as they dashed across the street. Once safely on the other side of the street, they looked down at their entwined fingers at the same time. Mark quickly released her hand. "See, I got you here in one piece."

"Thanks." Lawson approached the store's entrance. "Are you coming in?"

"I guess so. I don't see anybody I know. I won't have to deny being here later."

"Have you ever been in one of these before?" asked Lawson after they walked in.

"No, I never had a reason to go into a bridal store . . . until now."

Lawson was oblivious to Mark staring at her. "These dresses are all so beautiful!" she exclaimed, admiring the intricate beadwork on one of the wedding gowns. She pressed a form-fitting strapless gown against her torso. "You think an up-do will be okay for this gown?"

Mark frowned. "Do I look like an extra from *Queer Eye*? How should I know?"

"What happened to being secure in your manhood?" She rolled her eyes and placed the gown back on the rack. "Considering that you're the one who insisted on coming, the least you could do is offer a valid opinion."

"I don't see the point of buying a dress if you don't have a wedding date."

"That is not the opinion I wanted, and we're setting the date very soon. He wants to get married in January, but I'm keeping my fingers crossed for next fall."

"What makes you think I won't have swept you off your feet by then?" asked Mark good-naturedly. "You might decide you want that ol' thing back!"

"Very funny." Lawson held up a beaded gown. "Oh, this one is gorgeous!"

"Are you sure you should be wearing white?"

"I have just as much right to wear it as your baby's mama does." She draped the dress over her arm.

"If you're likening yourself to Tasha, you ought to be wearing red."

Lawson laughed. "I still can't believe that I'm out here picking out wedding dresses with the guy who took my virginity."

He sidled up next to her. "I don't recall having to *take* anything; it was given to me. You were a *very* willing participant, remember?"

Lawson sighed. "Ah, to be young and full of hormones and questionable judgment." She opened the dressing room door. "I want to try this dress on, and you are not to go anywhere, understand?" issued Lawson and shut the door behind her.

"The least you could do is let me in," he teased.

"You saw all you were going to see fourteen years ago."

"You sure you don't need any hooks fastened or zippers zipped?"

"Positive."

Minutes later, the door creaked opened, and Lawson emerged in a strapless gown with a fitted bodice and a full skirt. "How does it look?" Mark's mouth dropped, and she panicked. "What? What's wrong with it? It's too much, isn't it? You're thinking I don't have the height to pull this look off, aren't you?"

Mark blinked a couple of times. "Well, *I'm* thinking about pulling it off," he murmured. "You look great, like . . . wow."

She faced the full-length mirror and beamed. "You think Garrett'll like it?"

"If he has eyes, he will. That's the one," he asserted, gazing at her as if he were seeing Lawson for the first time

Lawson squinted her eyes and swayed in the mirror. The thick folds of her dress rustled whenever she moved. "You think so?"

An attendant approached them and spread the train of the dress onto the floor. "You're stunning in that," she enthused. "Here, try this." She pinned a tiara with a veil attached to it onto Lawson's head. "It's perfect!"

Mark's eyes were glued to Lawson. "You're breathtaking.

I don't think I've ever seen any woman look more beautiful than you do right now."

"It looks like somebody couldn't wait until the wedding day," noted the attendant to Mark. "She's going to make you a beautiful bride." Mark grinned but didn't correct her. The attendant smiled and moved to assist someone else.

Lawson whirled around and placed her hands on her hips. "Mark, why did you let that woman think I was marrying you?"

"You didn't set her straight either."

Lawson gazed at her profile. "The dress is lovely, isn't it? But I probably shouldn't get my hopes up. Garrett may never speak to me again once he sees the pricetag. He's too practical to spend this kind of money on anything, especially a dress that I'm just going to wear for a couple of hours. This indulgence is going to take a huge chunk out of our wedding budget."

"Then tell him you got it on sale. I doubt that he'll call up here to verify it."

She thought for a moment. "I suppose you're right." She looked at her reflection again. "I don't like lying to him, but I do want this dress."

"You should get it. It's you all the way."

"I better take it off before they have to pry me out of it." Lawson glanced back at Mark, who was still staring at her. "What?"

"Nothing . . . I just can't believe it's you, that's all."

"If this dress can have that kind of effect on a man, I better get over to that cash register quick!" She hiked up the dress to step down.

"Wait!" Mark stepped out in front of her and lifted the veil from her face. "I just wanted to see you one more time. Your fiancé is a lucky man."

"Rest assured; I remind him of that all the time," Lawson added smugly.

Mark thought for a second. "I bet you haven't even been practicing, have you?"

She frowned. "Practicing for what?"

"What do you mean, practicing for what?" Mark pretended to be shocked and reached for her hand. "Didn't you know that the bride's first lover is supposed to be the one who rehearses the first wedding dance with her?" He swept her into his arms.

"Isn't the bride's first lover supposed to be the actual groom?"

"In theory. Then again, the bride's first lover and groom may end up being one in the same." He pulled her closer. "I bet there's something else you didn't know."

"And what's that?" she asked, giggling as he goaded her into dancing with him.

"I bet you didn't know that this platform right here doubles as a time machine."

"Is that right?" They swayed along with the music that could only be heard by the two of them.

"Yep. You see, it may look like we're dancing in the middle of a bridal shop, but we've actually leapt back into the nineties—specifically, graduation night at Manny's basement party." Lawson laughed out loud as he began singing in her ear. "*So you're having my baby, and it means so much to me . . .*"

"You're silly," said Lawson, but pretended with him nevertheless.

"I must be. I don't know what I was thinking all those years ago," admitted Mark, holding the small of her back. "I can't believe I didn't see what a catch you were."

"Mark, we were just kids. Even if we'd gotten together, I'm sure we would have screwed it up way before now. Things happen for a reason and work out the way they're supposed to."

Mark stopped dancing and lifted Lawson's chin toward him. "If that's the case, then why do I have such a strong urge to kiss another man's fiancée?"

Her heart fluttered. She was not sure of what to make of her feelings or Mark's words. "Urges aren't the problem," she said. "You get in trouble when you try to act on them."

"Well, what would you do if I acted on it? On second thought,"—he leaned in to kiss her—"I'm sure you can show me better than you can tell me."

Lawson shied away from him before his lips made contact with hers. "I think your time would be better spent trying to find us a good seat in the auditorium."

"Are you sure?" gambled Mark, not quite ready to give up his pursuit.

She nodded. "We work together, Mark. I'm trying to keep it ethical. Even if I wasn't, I would never do anything to hurt or betray Garrett. He's been too good to my son and me."

"Gratitude is no reason to stay committed to someone, especially when there's a man standing in front of you who would do anything to have another shot with you."

"My feelings for Garrett run much deeper than just gratitude."

He seized her hand. "But are you one hundred percent sure you want to marry this guy?"

"Do you know how much money I'm about to drop on this dress? If I wasn't serious before, I am now," she answered, attempting to lighten the mood.

"So, you won't even consider giving me another chance?"

She let go of his hand. "Mark, I'm going to marry Garrett."

"Okay. You're engaged, not married. Nothing is official yet."

"I love him—that much *is* official."

Mark nodded and heaved a sigh. "I take it that there's no chance for us to turn back the hands of time, huh? I mean, we are in this time machine, after all."

She shook her head. "I'm in love, Mark."

They were both silent for a moment, thinking of what could have been, but focusing on what was. "Like I said before,

Garrett is a lucky man." He touched her cheek. "I guess I'll have to look you up next lifetime."

Lawson smiled. "It's a date."

Mark exhaled and looked around the room. "Well, imagine that . . . the time machine got us to and from the nineties in one piece. And by the looks of it,"—he glanced down at his watch—"we didn't lose any time while we were gone. There are still twenty minutes left in our lunch break."

Lawson smiled. "Thanks for the dance lesson . . . and the quantum leap."

Mark kissed her on the cheek. "Anytime."

After Lawson took off the dress and paid for it, she and Mark left the store. She had her wedding gown tucked under her arm and her commitment to Garrett still intact.

Mark made a final plea on his behalf. "You know, there's still one thing I can do for you that your fiancé can't," he hinted.

"And what's that?"

"Find you a good seat near the front of the auditorium. Come on. Let's go."

Chapter 20

"My husband knows I'm no Girl Scout."
—Sullivan Webb

Sullivan had just gulped down a Morning Sunrise when her cell phone vibrated, signaling that she had an incoming text message: I have the day off. I wanna see you. She read it and smiled. It was from Vaughn.

Charles entered just as she turned off the phone. "And how's my lovely wife this morning?" He planted a kiss on her jaw. Sullivan's smile drifted into a slight frown. Charles sat down across from her at the table. "Guess who I just got an e-mail from."

"I don't make guesses before noon," replied Sullivan.

Charles poured himself a cup of coffee. "It was from John. It looks like I'm going to be a great-uncle again. My niece Michelle is pregnant. John's very excited, but it made me kind of sad."

She nodded in agreement. "I couldn't imagine having a kid at Michelle's age. She's only twenty-four, and she and Daryl haven't even been married a year. Now they have to be responsible for this whole other person. Nothing kills the honeymoon like a load of dirty diapers."

"That's not what I meant," clarified Charles. "I'm happy for them, for the whole family. I'm kind of sad for me. I thought I'd be the one making grandchild announcements. Here I am at fifty, and I haven't even announced my first child."

Sullivan rolled her eyes. "You have a career. You don't need kids."

"Sullivan, no job or any amount of money could ever replace bringing a new life into the world, not even work in the ministry."

"I think children are highly overrated. They're needy, whiny, and expensive."

"You make them sound like wives," joked Charles then changed the subject. "It looked like you were on the phone when I walked in. Is everything all right?"

The thought of Vaughn reignited her smile. "Yes, everything is fine."

"The car hasn't been giving you any more trouble, has it?"

She shook her head.

"See, I told you Mike would take good care of you."

Sullivan bit into her blueberry scone. "Actually, his associate Vaughn did all of the work. Mike was out of town."

"Vaughn is the young guy, right, the one with his hair all braided up?" Sullivan nodded. Charles shook his head. "You know I don't judge a book by its cover, but that young man looks like some common street thug if you ask me. I told Mike that having a guy like that around could be bad for business. Even the Bible says to avoid the appearance of evil. If I'd known Mike was away, I would've sent you somewhere else."

"Vaughn isn't a thug. He's an artist."

"I hope you don't mean a con artist."

"No, he paints."

"What—graffiti?"

Sullivan rolled her eyes. "You're so closed-minded, Charles. Anyway, I've been thinking about picking up a paintbrush again myself."

He sipped his coffee. "I thought you gave that little hobby up years ago."

"It's not little, and it was more than just a hobby. I would probably be the toast of New York, hosting my own art shows if I hadn't settled for married life with you."

"It's because the Lord has blessed us that you don't have to live like some *starving* artist. We have more than enough money to commission any painter you want."

"You're missing the point."

"Am I, darling?" He wiped his mouth. "I tell you what: why don't you go out and buy you some paints and an easel, if that's what makes you happy."

"I will. Thank you."

"Can I convince you to come downtown for a breakfast meeting with me this morning? I'm linking up with some of the campaign workers, and I would love to have you sit in on it. I want your input as much as I want theirs."

Meeting with Charles and his aides paled in comparison to a romantic rendezvous with Vaughn. "No, you go on ahead. I'm really anxious to get started with my painting."

"All right, I'll see you around dinner. I love you."

"Yeah, love you too," she echoed, but Sullivan's mind was already on other things, namely when and where she would meet Vaughn.

"Welcome to my lair!" was the greeting Sullivan received when she reached Vaughn's modest studio apartment after she'd called and agreed to meet him there.

She ducked underneath the doorway. "So, is this where all the magic happens?"

"This is it. Come on in."

The small apartment had an open floor plan. It housed a tiny kitchenette, a crocheted afghan draped over a loveseat, a wooden table that leaned on a broken leg, and a hand-me-down bed that was missing a headboard. Sullivan walked in and was immediately struck by the intense and passionate paintings mounted on myriad canvases between the sparse furnishings. "Is this all your work?"

"Yep, every one." He picked up a few clothes that were scattered on the floor.

"Vaughn, these are not just good; they're breathtaking . . . brilliant, even."

He tossed a shirt into the hamper. "I just do me, you know? I put the brush to the canvas and see what happens."

Sullivan was captivated by a painting depicting an elderly man playing a bassoon. "This is amazing."

Vaughn slipped his arms through the sleeves of a black hoodie. "So, you ready?"

"Ready for what? I thought we were hanging out here."

"I wanna show you something first. I want to take you to my favorite place."

Sullivan smiled at him. "You mean it's not the bedroom?"

He laughed. "Well, my second favorite place." Vaughn reached out for her hand. "Come on. We can walk. It's just a couple of blocks from here."

"Where are you taking me?" she asked him for the third time as they walked down the street hand in hand. She felt light and sexy, a feeling that she hadn't gotten from Charles in years. Vaughn took pleasure in torturing her, not telling where they were going.

"We're here," he announced at long last. She looked up at the building's marquee. "It's a new and little known art gallery, mostly black artists." He pulled open the glass doors. "Come on. Let me show you around."

She slid her arm into his, and they began the tour of the gallery. Vaughn stopped in front of a whimsical painting of a man and a woman in what appeared to be the inner city. "You see this? This is one of William H. Johnson's works. He's an artist who emerged in New York after the Harlem Renaissance." The piece was entitled *Moon Over Harlem*. "Look at his use of color in this one," pointed out Vaughn, admiring another work by Johnson. "Notice all of the saturated reds and oranges and bold brush strokes. This technique is called *sfumato*. It works very well for this kind of painting. It's beautiful."

Sullivan was surprised and impressed by his observations. "I studied his painting called *Midnight Sun*," she told him. "He created it in Norway. He had to climb around two thousand feet every day for about a month to capture the view from the top of a mountain. The result is just spectacular."

This time, Vaughn was the one who was impressed. "How do you know that?"

"I'm not just another pretty face, Vaughn. There's a brain in there too."

He turned her head to look at her profile. "This is a face that was made to be photographed and painted. I would never call it something as common as pretty."

"Thank you," she replied, enchanted by everything about him. Her attention turned to another painting. "And look at this one. Doesn't it remind you of some of O'Keefe's work?"

"How do you know so much about art, Sullivan?"

"I took about a thousand art courses in undergrad. You know, art history, art appreciation, et cetera," she answered off-handedly. Sullivan paused, transfixed by an Elizabeth Catlett painting. "Wow. I've never seen this one before."

"Wait a minute!" said Vaughn, recovering from his shock. "First things first, you said something about taking art courses. Where? When?"

"I graduated with a degree in art from Howard. I was into everything art in college. It was my dream to be an artist, or at least a curator."

"So, why didn't you pursue art more?"

"I fell in love. Art didn't seem so important after that."

"And you really graduated from Howard University?"

"Yes. What, because I don't work, you assumed that meant that I was stupid or something? Vaughn, you'd be surprised to know how many housewives are smart and talented. We're not all gold-diggers. *You're* the one I'm shocked by. I can't believe you've even heard of all these artists."

"Really, Sullivan, who hasn't?" he said as if it were required knowledge among the mechanic set.

Sullivan stopped at Eldzier Cortor's elaborately painted depiction of a black woman in the nude. "This is beautiful."

"I'm sure you'd be just as beautiful if I painted you that way." With a mischievous twinkle in his eye, he added, "You game?"

She smiled. "Sounds like fun, but I do insist on keeping my clothes on."

"We'll see about that." Vaughn held the door open for her. "I'm starting to see that there's a lot more to you than that gorgeous face and killer body, isn't there?"

"I'm just a woman, Vaughn."

He caressed her face. "Sullivan, I'm sure that you're not *just* an anything."

They walked back to his apartment, making conversation out of leaves turning for fall and everything else they passed. At no point did her husband or their marriage enter Sullivan's mind, until Vaughn introduced the subject.

"I wonder what your husband would say if he knew you were over here," he posed, unlocking the door.

Sullivan followed him inside. "What makes you think he doesn't?"

He went into the kitchenette and put on a pot of water for tea. "Oh, you actually told him that you were coming to see me today?" He looked back over his shoulder, tossing a seductive grin in her direction.

Sullivan was definitely falling in love with that smile. "Not in those words," she disclosed. "Not in *any* words, actually. Charles knows I have friends and a short attention span."

"And he's fine with that?"

"His philosophy is that as long as I come home to him every night, it's all good. He's very understanding."

"I'm sure he is, but there's a line between being *understanding* and being stupid."

"You and I aren't doing anything wrong, just looking at art and having tea."

Vaughn poured the water into two mugs and dropped a tea bag in them. "Can't you do that with him?" He handed her a cup.

"Charles and I just don't click anymore. We don't really have anything in common. Our personalities are so different."

"You're still there, so it can't be all bad."

"No, it's not *bad*; it's just . . . drab." She sipped her tea. "But I made a commitment to him, and it's not easy to just walk away from that."

"Yet you're here with me."

"I never said I was perfect."

"I bet you don't even give him any," joked Vaughn. "You know how y'all married women do—put a brother on rations with the booty after you get the ring."

"I was rationing it out way before I met Charles! Our problems don't stop and start with the bedroom, though. I just don't feel fulfilled."

"I think I understand," he said, nodding. "And I wasn't judging you."

"Thank you." Sullivan finished her tea and stood up. "Well, it's getting late, and I don't want to overstay my welcome."

He reached for her and wrapped his arms around her hips. "You aren't."

Vaughn leaned in as if he was going to kiss her, prompting her to jump back. Sullivan ended up grazing her hand against the still hot stove cap.

"Ouch!"

"Are you all right?"

She looked down at her hand. "It hurts, but I'll live."

"Let me see it." Vaughn reached out and caressed the injured hand before planting a tender kiss on it. His lips were soft and warm. "It's my mom's remedy for everything that hurts." He grinned. "That and telling me to lay down and take a nap."

"Thank you." She broke his stare and reclaimed her hand. "It feels better now."

"No problem. I guess you better go on and get out of here."

She nodded. "'I had a really nice time, Vaughn."

"Me too. Hey, don't forget your purse." They both reached for her purse on the table at the same time. Their fingers touched, but neither of them made an effort to move. Sullivan closed her eyes as he gently stroked her hand.

She was short of breath. "What are we doing?" she asked softly.

"I don't know." Vaughn linked his fingers with hers. "I just know it feels good."

"Then I guess a better question would be *why* are we doing it?"

"Because we both know that there's more going on here than we want to admit."

"What do you mean?"

Vaughn propped himself up against the stove. "Come on, Sullivan. You know exactly what I mean. You're just afraid to let your mind, much less your body, go there." Vaughn moved in on her.

Sullivan locked eyes with him, but pushed him away, not trusting herself enough to be enticed by those tantalizing lips a minute longer. "I should get out of here."

"You nervous?"

"No, I'm *married*, and I still do have one or two scruples left."

"Scruples and morals are just excuses people make up for not going after what they want."

"Be that as it may," she maintained, "I should still leave." *While I can*, she thought.

"That's probably best," agreed Vaughn and walked her to the front door. He planted a kiss on her neck. "Until next time."

"What makes you so sure that there's going to be a next time?" she challenged, trying to recover from the thrill of having his lips on her again.

"Sweetheart, with me," he promised, "there's always a next time."

Chapter 21

"I'll think about heaven later."
—Sullivan Webb

Angel laughed and adjusted the speed on her treadmill.
"You have the goofiest look on your face right now. I wish you
could see it." Sullivan rolled her eyes and continued her jaunt
on the treadmill next to Angel's. "All right, what gives, Sully?
You've been acting weird all week."

Sullivan smirked impishly and shook her head. "It's nothing."

"Stop lying and start spilling. Confession is good for the
soul."

Sullivan laughed to herself and divulged, "I have a crush."

Angel came to a stop, "As in a *dear-diary-guess-who-I'm-stalking*
crush?"

Sullivan winked an eye. "Something like that."

"Okay, I'll bite. Who is he?"

Sullivan's smile grew even wider. "Vaughn Lovett."

"Vaughn . . . isn't he the guy who was at Lawson's cookout?"

"That's him. We met when he fixed my car a few weeks ago."

"When did you start crushing on the help? He's cute, I
guess; he didn't really seem like your type. And by 'your type'
I mean *rich* and anyone who isn't Charles."

Sullivan eyed the calorie count of her treadmill's monitor. "He
has a few edges that could be smoothed out," she acknowledged.
"And not being Charles is a plus."

"And how does Charles feel about you having a crush on a
man other than him?"

She flung her hand. "What my husband doesn't know won't hurt him."

"Yeah, but when he finds out, he might hurt *you*."

"This thing with Vaughn isn't serious. We're just, you know, hanging out."

Angel cranked the treadmill back up. "It always starts out that way."

"And that's how it'll end," Sullivan insisted.

"Sully, your husband is running for office. The one thing his campaign doesn't need is a scandal and the public finding out that the preacher's wife has been having more than just her tires rotated with the family's mechanic."

Sullivan sulked. "I'm entitled to have a little fun, aren't I?"

"And isn't Charles entitled to a wife who can keep it in her designer pants?" Angel saw Kina approaching them. "Kina, you and I both know that you did not put in half an hour on that StairMaster."

"I'm tired," whined Kina. "I've had enough exercise for today."

"Running back and forth to the juice bar isn't exercise," noted Sullivan.

Kina groaned. "Let's just come back tomorrow."

"We can't," replied Angel. "Sullivan may be burning in hell by then."

Reginell climbed off the Gazelle and joined them. "Did I hear something about Sullivan going to hell?"

Lawson toweled off her forehead and walked over to where her friends were. "Sully, what have you gone and gotten yourself into now?"

"Nothing," answered Sullivan. She turned to Angel and snapped, "Has anyone ever told you that you have a big mouth?"

"You were going to tell us eventually anyway," said Lawson. "All right, out with it, and we need details."

"Especially the juicy ones," added Reginell.

Sullivan exhaled. "I was just telling Angel about this guy I know."

Kina rolled her eyes. "*Hmph!*"

"Don't look at me like that, Kina. All we're doing is hanging out. He's a mechanic, for God's sake."

"You're talking about the guy from the cookout, aren't you?" asked Lawson.

Reginell was amused. "You slummin', Sully?"

"No, that's what you do. I'm merely opening myself up to a new friendship."

"And just what part of yourself have you been opening up?" ribbed Reginell.

Sullivan swatted at her with a towel. "Speak for yourself and for whichever man you crawled out from under this morning."

"Don't y'all get started in here," warned Lawson. "I've been waiting for the Ab Cruncher to be free for an hour, and I can't have you getting us kicked out before I'm sexy."

Sullivan pinched an inch of flab from her exposed midriff. "You might be a little too far gone for the Ab Cruncher. You need to ask for the ab snap, crackle, and pop."

"We're getting off subject," broke in Reginell. "Back to Sully burning in hell . . ."

"You're playing with fire. You do know that, don't you?" chided Lawson.

"I'm not playing with it, merely *fanning* it a bit. Nobody's gotten burned yet."

"The operative word is *yet*," Kina reminded her.

"And I seriously doubt that argument will hold up on judgment day," added Lawson.

"You just don't know what it's like being married to Charles," protested Sullivan. "My marriage is so stifling and predictable. There's no passion, no fireworks, and don't even get me started on our sex life!"

"Yes, please spare us those particulars," pleaded Lawson. "I need to be able to look at him in the pulpit without having that visual."

Angel shook her head. "Pastor Webb is a good, spirit-filled, God-fearing man who loves you, Sullivan. He practically worships the ground you walk on."

"He doesn't—I don't know—*stimulate* me. I hate being treated like his doll; I want to be treated like his woman."

"He treats you with respect," argued Kina. "He never puts you down or calls you fat or makes you feel like everything that goes wrong is all your fault."

Sullivan eyed Kina, concerned. "Does E'Bell do that to you?"

Kina plastered a smile on her face and shook the question off. "You know E'Bell—he says the first thing that comes to mind whether he means it or not."

"You're still his wife, Kina. He's supposed to treat you with the utmost respect," reproved Angel.

"*Love your wife as Christ loved the church*," cited Lawson.

"E'Bell does love me. He just doesn't always know how to show it."

"Maybe he needs to learn to," said Angel.

"Or you should find you a man who can," added Sullivan.

"I don't know if I should listen to someone on Satan's V.I.P. list," muttered Kina.

Sullivan huffed. "Don't be so dramatic, Kina."

Lawson settled into the vacated Ab Cruncher. "Is fooling around with Vaughn the quickest way to get into heaven?"

Sullivan admired her reflection in the mirror. "Who's worried about heaven? I'm having fun right now. I'll think about heaven later."

Chapter 22

"This could be the revenge I've been waiting the past eight years to serve up."
—*Angel King*

Theresa panicked the next afternoon when Angel returned to her house unexpectedly after leaving an hour earlier. "What are you doing back here?" she demanded to know.

"I think I left my Blackberry in your living room," Angel replied. "It's silver, has a Mary Mary ring tone. Have you seen it?"

Theresa stopped short of letting her in. "Wait here." Theresa disappeared into the house and returned with it. She thrust the device at Angel. "Is this it?"

"Yes, thank you." Angel was put off by Theresa's hostility. "Are you all right?"

"Yeah, I'm fine, just tired. Have a great weekend."

"You look flushed. I can hang around for a minute if you need me to."

"That's not necessary. I'll be all right once I take a nap." Theresa looked past Angel into the driveway. "I'll see you on Monday."

Angel paused. "Theresa, I'm worried about you. You don't seem like yourself."

"My husband will be home any second now. If I start feeling worse, I'll have him call you. Good-bye." Theresa quickly closed and locked the door.

Angel shook her head and walked down the driveway to her car. She couldn't shake the feeling that there was something amiss with Theresa. As she was about to turn back around to check on Theresa again, a burgundy SUV pulled up beside her.

The driver threw the car in park and jumped out. "*Angel?*"

She whirled around in shock, seeing but not believing. "*Duke?*"

Her ex-husband's expression was a mixture of angst and anxiety. "What are you doing here?"

"*Me?* What about you?"

Duke crossed his arms in front of his chest in a defiant stance. "This is my house. I have every right to be here. What's your excuse?"

"I'm here to look after my patient."

He looked baffled. "What patient? Are you here to see Reese?"

"No, I'm here for my patient, Theresa McNair."

"You mean Theresa McNair King, my wife."

"*Your wife?*" Angel's blood ran cold when it dawned on her that his wife, Reese, and her patient, Theresa, were the same woman. "What kind of sick joke is this?" she shrilled.

"That's what I want to know!" cried Duke.

Angel was furious. "I received a call from Theresa McNair pleading with me to take her on as a patient. I had no idea that she was in any way connected to you, but I guess that was the whole point when the two of you concocted this vicious scheme!"

He slammed the car door shut. "Why would I scheme to try to see you?"

"I don't know, Duke. It's clear that both of you are very sick, twisted people. Wasn't my pain and my sanity enough for you the first time around? Did you really need to see my humiliation up close? What kind of monsters would do something like this?"

"My wife would never knowingly reach out to you." Duke's eyes morphed into narrow slits. "Is this some kind of game to get revenge? She's already sick. It wouldn't be hard to stage it to look like an accident."

"*Excuse me?*"

His voice was a sinister calm. "You wouldn't be the first nurse to off a patient, now, would you?"

Angel hauled her hand back and slapped him with all the force she could muster. "How dare you! How dare you question my professionalism or my integrity when you are the one who broke every vow you made to me to jump in the bed with this tramp!"

"That 'tramp' is my wife, and you will respect her," roared Duke.

"You mean like the two of you respected me and our marriage?"

"So, this is about revenge, isn't it?" he inferred.

"Duke, I have a life, despite the fact that you and your whore did everything in your power to shatter what was sacred to me. Trying to get back at the two of you is the furthest thing from my mind. *She* called *me*, remember? Don't try to flip it because you've been caught." She placed her hands on her hips. "Tell me, Duke, what were you hoping to gain from all this? Exactly what are you trying to accomplish?"

"For the last time, I didn't call you. No matter how sick my wife is, you are the absolute *last* person I would ever ask for help."

"It was me, Angel," confessed Theresa, who appeared behind them, startling both Angel and Duke. "I arranged the whole thing. I looked you up, I called you, and I set it all up. Duke had nothing to do with it."

Duke was as stunned as Angel. "Honey, why would you do a thing like that?"

"I wanted to make amends," she explained to both of them.

"I'm the reason that your marriage fell apart, and I didn't want to die without making things right."

Angel wasn't moved. "Where was all of this compassion when you were sleeping with my husband?"

Theresa lowered her head. "All I can say is that I was a different person back then. I was lost. Once I realized that I had to get my life together, I started making changes. The first thing I did is get right with God, and I asked Him to forgive me for what I'd done to you. Then I forgave myself, but I still want to earn your forgiveness too."

Duke put his arm around Theresa. "Baby, why didn't you just tell me what you wanted to do? Why all the secrecy?"

"This was something that I needed to do for me. I was afraid that if you knew, you'd try to stop me."

"You had to have known that we'd find out eventually," he pointed out.

"I knew I couldn't go on deceiving the two of you forever, and I didn't want to. I wanted to tell both of you, but I wanted to do it in my own way and in my own time."

Angel shook her head. "Look, Theresa, Reese—whoever you are. This is sick, and I don't want to be a part of any get-right-with-Jesus plan that you've hatched up. You'll have to get your redemption without me."

"This isn't just about wanting your forgiveness," justified Theresa. "I need you; my family needs you. Do you think I would've hired you if I wasn't confident in your work and your credentials as a nurse? Yes, I wanted to make amends for what happened with Duke, but I'm also in for the fight of my life with this disease. This is just as much about receiving the help and medical treatment that I need as it is about anything else."

"Reese, there are other nurses," said Duke. "You know that I'll spare no expense to get you the best care money can buy. We don't need my ex-wife to take care of you."

"It has to be Angel" insisted Theresa. "I don't want anyone else."

"Even now, it's still all about what you want!" Angel butted in.

Duke ignored her. "Reese, I don't want to deny you of anything, but I do want you to think long and hard about this."

"I have," she assured him. "God led me to this decision and to her."

"God told you to do this?" mocked Angel with a cackle. "God told you to lie to me about who you were? God told you to convince me to let my guard down and trust you with my most intimate secrets? He told you to create this whole farce, to deceive the man you claim to love for your own selfish gains? God really told you to do all that?"

"It wasn't like that," Theresa answered softly. "I know I hurt you, not just with my relationship with Duke but also by not being completely honest about who I am. None of that changes the fact that I need you."

Duke faced his ex-wife and spoke with difficulty. "This is awkward for all of us, but the bottom line is that my wife is sick and needs your help. If you're in, it's fine with me. I'm willing to go along with whatever you two can live with."

Angel put her hands on her hips. "Ain't this something? The two of you are actually giving me *permission* to wait on you hand and foot, to be there for your every beck and call. I get to have a front row seat to watch Theresa living it up with my husband and to chase behind her children when your affair was the reason that my child died. How noble of you to want me to be a part of that!"

"What child?" exclaimed Duke. "What are you talking about?"

Theresa looked down. "Maybe this was bad idea. It's obvious that this is asking way too much of you, Angel, and I'm sorry for putting you in this position." She started coughing. "I hope that you can accept—" Theresa's cough turned to a hack that forced her to double over to try to catch her breath.

Duke grabbed her. "Baby, are you all right?" Theresa was coughing too hard to respond.

Angel's conscience got the best of her. "We need to get her in the house."

Duke swept up his wife and rushed her inside with Angel in tow. He laid her down on the living room sofa. Theresa was clutching her chest and wheezing.

"What's wrong with Mommy?" asked Morgan, her eyes wide with fright.

Duke turned to Angel. "I think her bronchitis is flaring up again."

"She's okay, sweetie," Angel reassured Morgan. "Take your sister upstairs. I'm going to give your mother some medicine to help her feel better." She turned to Duke. "Get her something to drink."

Duke left without a word, and Angel propped the pillows up behind Theresa's back. "How are you feeling, Theresa? Can you talk?"

Her coughing subsided a little. "I'm in pain," she groaned.

Angel reached into her bag and filled a syringe with medicine. "This will help; it's something for the pain. Lay back and try to relax." She injected Theresa, who started to calm down almost immediately.

Duke returned with a glass of water. "Here, drink this, baby." He held the straw to his wife's lips while she took small sips from the cup.

"Thank you for staying, Angel," said Theresa. "You didn't have to do that."

Angel stood up to leave. "I'm a professional. I'd never leave a patient in distress. She should be fine for now. Call her doctor and let him know what's going on. You should get another nurse in here as soon as possible."

"Baby, I'm going to walk her out, but I'll be right outside."

Duke kissed Theresa's brow and followed Angel out to her car.

"Angel, please, won't you at least try to reconsider? I'll pay you double what Theresa offered."

Angel unlocked her car door. "It's not about the money, Duke."

"You're right; it's not about the money. It's about my wife getting the best nurse we can afford. I was married to you; I know how good you are at what you do."

Angel huffed. "Do you really want your ex-wife dispensing medicine to the woman you dumped her for? Like you said, this could be the revenge I've been waiting the past eight years to serve up."

"I know you, Angel, and it's not in your nature. You have too good of a heart to intentionally hurt anyone. If Reese trusts you, so do I."

"Don't let the name fool you. I'm not the angel that you're making me out to be." Angel opened the door. "It wouldn't work. There's too much history between all of us. Besides, can you honestly say that you'd be comfortable with me hanging around your wife and kids all day? Do you really want to come home from a hard day's work and have to see me?"

"It isn't about me or my feelings. Honestly, Angel, you're probably the last person I would've sought out, and had I known what Reese was up to, I would've put a stop to it. Not because I don't trust you, but because I wouldn't want to force any of us to relive what happened. But you're here now, and my wife wants you to stay. That's all that matters to me."

Angel bit her lip. "You really love her, don't you?"

"She's my wife and the mother of my children. Of course I love her."

"That's what makes this so hard," she admitted. "I can look at you and tell how much you love her, and it hurts, Duke. I can't lie. Seeing you together with your kids would only remind me of everything I lost, and I don't know if I can handle being reminded of that every day."

"It's tough for me too. You and Theresa are the only women I've ever loved. Knowing that my love for her is what hurt you is something I've had to grapple with all this time. It would be much easier to let you drive off and never have to look at you again, but we both know that running away from the past isn't going to solve anything."

"I just don't think that this is the right thing for me to do right now. Maybe if things were different . . ." Her voice trailed off.

"I understand," replied Duke, nodding. "Hey, what were you talking about earlier? What baby died?"

Angel brushed him off. "It's nothing. Don't worry about it."

Duke let it go. "I hope you reconsider staying, but we'll accept your decision."

Angel climbed into her car and fastened her seatbelt. "I won't lie and say it's nothing personal, because we both we know it is. I'll pray about it, but I don't think I'm going to change my mind."

Duke stood in front of her door. "No matter what happens, it was good seeing you again, Angel." He gently touched her face. "I'm glad life has treated you well."

His caress was hauntingly familiar and gave her a jolt that made her feel uneasy. Angel waved before closing the door and pulling out. As she drove on, she wondered if his touch made her uncomfortable because she no longer had feelings for him, or because she did.

Chapter 22

"Revenge is best served cold."
—*Sullivan Webb*

Lawson checked her watch for the fifth time since she, Kina, and Sullivan sat down to eat at Huey's on the River. "I'm worried," admitted Lawson. "It's not like Angel to run this late and not call anyone."

Sullivan shook her head and closed her phone. "Still no answer. Her phone's going straight to voice mail. Maybe we should ask a waiter if she's called."

"She probably hasn't found her phone yet," Kina told them. "She thought she left it at a client's house and was supposed to swing by and pick it up on her way over here."

"That was two hours ago. We should've heard from her by now," said Lawson.

Sullivan cleared her throat. "Not that I'm complaining, but we do seem to be missing another person. Where's that incorrigible sister of yours, Lawson?"

Lawson skimmed her phone for any missed text messages from Angel. "Reggie's at home asleep. I'm so proud of her. She's only been working at that insurance company a few weeks, and she's already putting in overtime. Poor thing was too worn out last night to make it to her bed, and passed out on the sofa. She's sticking with it, though. I never thought I'd see the day Reggie was working at a nine-to-five job and liking it." Lawson looked down at her watch again. "Even you have to give her credit for trying, Sully. A steady income and a solid future is what Mama always wanted for her."

"At least she's working, which is more than I can say for some people," mumbled Kina, directing her eyes at Sullivan. "You people *have* to work. I don't." Sullivan looked up and exclaimed, "Well, it's about time!" when she saw Angel approaching their table. "Where have you been?"

"We were starting to panic," said Kina. "I thought that you had been in an accident or something. Why didn't you answer your phone?"

"Is everything all right?" asked Lawson. Angel shook her head. "What's wrong?"

Angel sat down, eyes glazed over. "Remember the new client I told you about?"

Kina thought back. "Theresa McNair, right?"

"That's the one, except her name isn't Theresa McNair anymore. It's Theresa King. More to the point, she's Mrs. Du'Corey Jamal King."

Kina stopped chewing her food. "As in Duke's wife?"

"Exactly," replied Angel. "Can you believe it?"

"I can't and I don't! This is no coincidence, Angel," charged Sullivan. "It's obvious they've been setting you up the whole time."

"That's sick!" declared Lawson. "Why would they do something like that? Does the woman even really have cancer?"

"That much of it is true," confirmed Angel. "And *they* didn't plan it. *She* did. Duke didn't know anything about it."

Lawson raised her eyebrow. "Says who?"

"She admitted that it was all her doing. Duke was just as shocked as I was."

"Is she trying to prove something, or is she just demented like that? The nerve of her!" scoffed Sullivan. "I hope you told her where to go with that foolishness."

"She claims that she just wants to make things right between us before she dies. She wants my forgiveness," said Angel.

"That's fine. Tell her you've hidden it and that she has to go to hell to find it."

Angel managed to smile. "You know I can't tell a dying woman that. I did tell her that I wouldn't be working with her anymore."

"Good for you," cheered Lawson.

Kina frowned. "Why not?"

Everyone dropped their forks at the same time.

"Kina, this woman slept with Angel's husband and got pregnant by him," said Sullivan. "Why would she want to have anything to do with either one of them?"

Kina flung her hand. "That's all water under the bridge now. We're supposed to be operating in forgiveness. I know I do."

"You have to be forgiving; you're married to an idiot," reasoned Sullivan.

"I'm going to operate in forgiveness right now and ignore that," replied Kina. *"And be ye kind one to another, tenderhearted, forgiving one another, even as God for Christ's sake hath forgiven you.* Helping her is the right thing to do."

Lawson differed. "It would be a big mistake. There's too much bad blood there."

Sullivan spoke up. "Wait a minute. Kina might be on to something,"

"See, even Sully agrees with me," said Kina, vindicated.

Sullivan nodded. "Who says that this can't work out for the best? You know, Angel could add a couple of extra milligrams to her medicine here, a few extra pills there, and if Theresa *accidentally* overdoses . . ."

"That is *so* not what I meant!" insisted Kina. "Now who's demented?"

"I don't want to kill her," affirmed Angel. "I just don't want to treat her. I don't know why I even told Duke that I'd pray about it."

"Don't even waste God's time or your energy with that one," suggested Sullivan. "Tell both of them to kick rocks and keep it pushin'."

"Don't listen to Sully," advised Lawson. "What is God leading you to do? Listen to your heart." Lawson put her arm around Angel. "That's the part that He speaks to."

Angel sighed. "My heart is saying that I need to help her. Health and healing is the ministry that God gifted me to do. I just wonder if I'm strong enough to carry it out."

"That's why you've got our shoulders to lean on when it gets rough," said Kina.

"Kina, you can't expect her to be all clowns and smiles with the very people who nearly drove her to kill herself," insisted Sullivan. "Angel, you still have your therapist's number, don't you? You're going to need her if you keep listening to Kina."

Kina held Angel's hand. "God wouldn't have placed this on you if He wasn't going to give you the strength to carry it out."

"You've got all the answers, don't you, Kina?" Sullivan asked snidely. "But what about the answer to the most important question, the one everybody's scared to bring up?"

"And what question is that?" asked Lawson.

Sullivan faced Angel. "When it's all said and done, how do we keep the nurse from falling back in love with the patient's husband?"

It was the one question that no one could answer.

Chapter 23

"We're just kissing, right? It's no big deal, no crime committed."
—Sullivan Webb

"I've got a surprise for you," said Vaughn, after letting Sullivan into his apartment. "Close your eyes."

She beamed. "What is it?"

"Didn't I tell you to close those pretty eyes first?"

She did, and then Vaughn placed something hard and heavy in her hands. Sullivan opened her eyes. "Oh my God, Vaughn, you bought me a canvas! That is so sweet. This is one of the nicest things anyone has ever done for me. Thanks . . . I'm touched."

Vaughn downplayed the gesture. "It ain't nothin'. I'm sure your husband could buy you a whole gallery if you wanted him to. I'm sure he'd do almost anything to keep you happy. I just want you to start back painting again."

"That means a lot, Vaughn. More than you know."

Vaughn cupped her face and moved to kiss her. Before he could, his phone rang. Sullivan was both relieved and disappointed by the disruption. "I'll let it go to voice mail. Now, where were we?"

Sullivan reached for one of his paint brushes. "We were talking about art. No time like the present to start painting, right?"

Vaughn filled a palette and sat down to paint next to her. "What you got going on over there?"

"Why? Are you trying to steal my ideas?"

"No, just trying to get inspired."

She blushed. "And just what is it that I inspire you to do?"

"This . . ." Vaughn took the brush from her. Sullivan knew what was coming next. If she were honest with herself, she'd have to admit that she longed for it. He set his lips on top of hers, and his kisses were everything that she imagined that they would be—intense, lingering, passionate. Every place on her body that was ignited by his touch seemed to scorch with desire. Whenever he looked at her, she could feel herself dissolve.

"You're trembling," he whispered.

"I'm f-fine," she stuttered. "You broke my concentration, that's all."

"Dang, girl, you just can't admit it, huh?" They were close enough that she could hear his heart beating, or perhaps it was her own, which started to race whenever he was near her the way he was at that moment.

"Admit what?"

He leaned into her, his lips inches from hers, "That you want me."

"I don't know how you fit such a massive ego in this tiny apartment."

"Look me in the eyes and tell me that you don't want me, that it's not taking every ounce of willpower you have not to kiss me right now." He stroked her face. "I know you felt it from that first day we met."

"What makes you think that?" she asked breathlessly.

"Because I felt it too."

Sullivan could feel heat radiating from his body. "I told you . . . I have Charles."

"You also said that he's busy. Yeah, I see him all over the TV, making speeches and organizing rallies. Meanwhile, his woman is all alone, waiting for someone like me to scoop her up and show her what she's missing." He pulled her closer to him. "Relax. Kiss me."

Sullivan did, and with every lip-lock, her resolve and vows to Charles grew dimmer. "We're just kissing, right? It's no big deal, no crime committed."

"It can be whatever you want it to be." Vaughn slid his hand underneath her shirt and traced the outline of her body with his fingertips. His mouth soon followed. There wasn't an inch of her body that didn't crave to be kissed by those forbidden lips.

He pulled her into a long, passionate kiss and into a place where her husband, her vows, her morals, and her God no longer existed.

She pulled back from him, realizing that he had leaned against her canvas. "I'm getting paint all over your clothes."

"Then I guess you better take them off."

Sullivan peeled off his shirt and physically consummated that which had transpired in her mind a long time ago. It no longer mattered that Vaughn was someone she knew she should have nothing to do with. He was the type of man who'd leave a girl sprung and a quivering mess of her former self, while he moved on to the next lovelorn victim. She wanted more of him, and she didn't care that she belonged to someone. Sullivan's mind and her body already belonged to Vaughn.

Chapter 24

"A true lady never kisses and tells."
—*Sullivan Webb*

"Wow, Sullivan, you're glowing!" noted Lawson over lunch the next day, poolside at Sullivan's estate. "I guess ol' Chuck hasn't lost his touch."

Angel lowered her shades. "She does have that morning after look, doesn't she?"

Sullivan grinned and stretched out on the lounge chair next to Kina. "A true lady never kisses and tells."

"But a freak details it blow by blow!" jeered Reginell, laughing and slapping hands with Angel. "Go on and tell us what happened."

"Yeah, Sullivan, tell us which of the commandments you broke this time," pushed Lawson, biting into a ring of pineapple.

Sullivan pinned her hands behind her head. "I can't. It's personal."

"*Personal* gets checked at the door. You know that. Now, start talking."

Sullivan cleared her throat and sat upright in her chair. "Well . . . I cheated on Charles," she revealed.

Lawson nearly choked on her pineapple. "You did what?"

Reginell leaned back and crossed her legs. "Umph. I always knew there was a straight-up ho underneath all them designer clothes and foreign weaves."

"It takes one to know one," fired Sullivan.

"Sully, I can't believe you would do that to Charles," said Kina.

"Oh, I can believe it," said Angel. "I just want to know with who."

Sullivan smirked. "Vaughn."

Lawson's jaw fell. "The same Vaughn you said was rough around the edges?"

"He's not so bad." Sullivan giggled. "Actually, he was quite good!"

"It looks like Skankville just got a new resident," muttered Angel.

"Hold up, now," cut in Reginell, raising her hand. "I've got to side with Sully on this one. Sometimes you need to switch it up some. Variety is the spice of life."

"Good. She can put that on a T-shirt. It'll give her something constructive to do while she's roasting in hell," said Angel.

"God knows my heart," rationalized Sullivan.

"You have one of those?" asked Reginell.

"Look at you. You don't even feel guilty, do you? No repentance, no remorse," charged Lawson.

Sullivan shook her head. "I can't explain it. I do feel guilty, but it's only because I feel bad about not feeling guilty at all. I feel . . . *liberated*, if you can believe that."

"Sullivan, even if Charles never finds out, God knows, and He was watching you in the very act," scolded Kina.

Sullivan poured a glass of juice. "Kina, that thought is disturbing on so many levels. Vaughn is so amazing, and I'm not just talking about the sex. He's an artist, and he's so intuitive and creative. He makes me feel more alive than I ever felt in my whole life. In the past three weeks that we've been spending time together, I haven't had a single drink. I get love-drunk instead."

"Enjoy it now. It may be hard to feel alive once Charles finds out, because he's going to kill both of you," replied Lawson.

Sullivan kicked back her heels. "I don't even care if he finds out. I might even tell him myself. Maybe then he'll finally divorce me."

"All right, be careful what you wish for," prophesized Angel. "The Bible says that you shall have whatever you say. Life and death are in the power of the tongue."

Sullivan sighed. "Don't even get me started on the power of *Vaughn's* tongue."

"Sully, you're nasty," said Kina with a frown.

"That's not all she is," reproved Lawson. "Sullivan, you're an adulterer! I've seen you do some questionable things in your life, but this is outright wrong. Do you know what God says happens to people who are unfaithful in marriage? Don't you know how seriously He takes the marriage covenant?"

"Isn't Charles just as wrong for putting me out there?" shot back Sullivan.

Lawson rolled her eyes. "He hasn't put you out yet. Just wait. As soon as he finds out about Vaughn, you can say good-bye to this house, this pool, and everything else his name is attached to."

Sullivan stood firm. "Charles knows what kind of woman I am—at least he should after ten years. I need passion; I need excitement. He chose to stop providing that a long time ago."

"Regardless of what Charles does or doesn't do, you still have vows and a covenant to keep," admonished Kina. "Now, I'll be the first to admit that things are not always perfect between E'Bell and me, but I would never cheat on him. God takes a special offense to sins against your own body."

"That includes gluttony too," retorted Sullivan. Kina pushed her plate away.

"If nothing else, Sullivan, you saw what infidelity did to my marriage to Duke. Why would you want to put Charles or yourself through that?" asked Angel.

Sullivan sat up and griped, "I thought this was supposed

to be my sister circle! I tell you something in confidence, and you blast me for it. What kind of friends do that?"

"We're still your friends, but as your friends, we have to tell you when you've screwed up," said Lawson.

"And you *have* screwed up," stressed Angel. "You have to end it with Vaughn now! You need to stay as far away from him as possible before anyone gets hurt."

"Sully, what you did was foul even by my standards," weighed in Reginell.

"You said you understood," objected Sullivan. "You said variety is the spice of life."

"Yeah, but that was before I thought about how wrong it was to do that to Charles. He's a decent man, and you didn't even have the good sense to cheat up."

"Don't you recognize the tricks of the enemy when you see them, Sully? The devil knows the best way to the church is to attack the leaders and their families. You need to get on your knees and start repenting right now!" beseeched Kina.

"Might as well," agreed Reginell. "She's been on her knees for everything else."

"Obviously, I won't be going to Sullivan for marital advice," said Lawson.

"Oh, did you and Garrett finally set a date?" asked Kina.

"We're working on it. At least I have something to wear for the occasion."

"You got the dress?" exclaimed Angel.

Lawson nodded. "I bought it a couple of weeks back."

"You should've called me," whined Sullivan. "I would've gone with you."

"You were probably sinning that day. I didn't have to shop alone, though. Mark went with me."

"And you're talking about me?" mused Sullivan.

"Who takes their baby's daddy wedding dress shopping?" raised Angel. "Is this a part of the 'something old, something new' tradition that I don't know about?"

"It's not like that," said Lawson. "Mark and I are friends . . . sort of."

"Uh-oh, I smell trouble," said Reginell.

"There's no trouble brewing,"—Lawson avoided eye contact—"aside from him trying to kiss me."

"Did he *try*, or did he succeed?" asked Kina.

"He *tried*," Lawson stressed. "I told him I'm one hundred percent committed to Garrett."

"And are you?" pressed Reginell.

"Yes! Who do I look like—Sully?"

Sullivan refreshed her glass. "Not even on your best day."

Kina scooped up a handful of pralines. "Now that the two of you are friends, have you thought anymore about telling him the truth about Namon?"

Lawson shook her head. "I'm invoking the 'don't ask, don't tell' policy."

Angel's phone rang. She glanced at the phone number registering on the screen and decided to ignore the call. "I'm not in the mood to deal with those two today!"

"I take it that's Duke's wife calling," inferred Lawson.

"I haven't been able to force myself to talk to them yet."

"Angel, every day that you go on ignoring them, Theresa gets worse. Do you really want that on your conscience?" asked Kina.

"You at least owe them a response," said Lawson. "If you're not going back, let them know."

Reginell yawned.

"Are we boring you, little sister?"

"No more than usual. I'm just sleepy."

"I keep telling you that you're working too hard," cautioned Kina.

"Reggie, sleep deprivation is a real thing. It causes memory lapses, slows down your reflexes and your thought process," forewarned Angel. "You need to take better care of yourself."

"I'll be able to get all the sleep I need now that I'm getting my own place," Reginell announced.

Lawson looked up. "Reggie, are you moving out?"

"It's time, don't you think? I mean, you and Garrett will be getting married soon, and you're going to want the place to yourselves. And I know that Namon is tired of fighting me for the bathroom. I'm twenty-one now. I'm old enough to strike out on my own."

"Can you afford to do that?" asked Kina.

"Are you kidding?" spat Lawson. "She's making so much money that we find bundles of cash stashed around her room all the time."

"Have you been going through my stuff?" Reginell rolled her eyes. "Now I *know* it's time to move out."

"No, but if you don't want me going in your room, stop leaving all the dishes in there; then I won't have to go in there searching for them."

Kina stopped chewing. "Have you found an apartment somewhere?"

Reginell nodded. "I'm signing a lease at The Links."

"The Links? *I* can't even afford to stay there!" exclaimed Sullivan,

Lawson spoke softly. "Honey, isn't that a little out of your price range?"

"I'm making good money now, Lawson."

"You must be making *great* money," added Kina.

Sullivan scratched her head and asked, "Exactly what do you do at this insurance company? My cousin James works out there, too, and he's never even heard of you."

"I'm in customer service," boasted Reginell.

"So is he, but he's still living with his mama. What are you doing that he isn't?"

"Working my butt off, that's what!"

"Well, give him some tips. According to him, y'all barely make minimum wage."

"I will. I need to start making some new friends while I'm at it," hinted Reginell.

"What's that supposed to mean?" Lawson wanted to know.

"It means that I need to start hanging out with people who think like me and won't try to be all up in my business every five minutes. All you people do is sit around and gossip. Get a life!" snapped Reginell then flashed a wad of cash. "I believe this ought to be enough to prove that you all can stop worrying about what I can and can't afford."

"Who does she think she's talking to?" asked Sullivan in a raised voice.

Reginell pointed her finger and replied, "I'm talking to you and every other meddling person at this table. Lawson, I'll be out by the end of the week."

"Dang, Reggie, my period's on too, but you don't see me biting everybody's head off!" cried Angel.

"Whatever. I've wasted enough time with you females as it is. Later." Reginell snatched up her purse and jacket and stomped out.

Kina watched as Reginell rudely brushed up against Sullivan on the way out. "What's her problem?"

"It's gon' be me if she doesn't watch it!" called Sullivan loud enough for Reginell to hear.

"I don't know what's going on with her," said Lawson. "But I know my sister, and when she starts acting like this, it means one of two things. Either she's hiding something, or she's in trouble. Knowing Reginell, it's both."

Chapter 25

"Your death will only mean there's one less whore in the world."
—*Angel King*

The following Monday was Angel's first scheduled visit with Theresa since finding out her real identity. She dreaded seeing either Theresa or Duke again, but she had agreed to return and was determined to uphold her word.

"You came back!" exclaimed Theresa when she opened the door to Angel.

"I told you I would when I called yesterday," Angel replied coldly and walked in without being invited to do so.

Theresa didn't seem to mind. "Duke and I are so happy you changed your mind."

Angel pursed her lips together. "I suppose I should ask how you're feeling."

"The past couple of days were a little rough without you, but we managed. Please sit down. Would you like something to drink?"

Angel noticed that Theresa had prepared tea. "A glass of water would be nice," she requested to be contrary. Angel could tell that Theresa was tired, but she hobbled into the kitchen just the same to fetch Angel some water. "Do you have anything to eat?" Angel asked when Theresa returned. "I haven't had a bite all day."

"What would you like?"

"Do you have any fruit?"

Theresa smiled. "Coming right up." She came back with an apple.

"Thank you." Angel bit into the apple. "Do you mind getting me a napkin?"

Theresa, in no way perturbed, left to get Angel a napkin. "Anything else?" she asked after fulfilling Angel's request.

"I'm good for now," replied Angel. "On second thought, I would like a little more ice for my water if it's no trouble. It's not quite as cold as I like it to be."

Theresa picked up Angel's glass. "It's no trouble at all."

Angel's flesh reveled in watching Theresa march back and forth to her demands. *Serves her right*, thought Angel.

"Here you go," Theresa said and handed Angel the glass. Theresa lowered her body onto the couch, holding her back. "I've got to take a minute and rest these old bones. That walk to the kitchen isn't as short as it used to be."

"Are you in pain?" inquired Angel.

"A little. Mostly tired, though."

Angel filled a syringe. "I have something I think might help. Give me your arm."

Theresa pushed up the sleeves on her housecoat. "Be gentle. I hate needles."

"I'll try." Angel jabbed the needle into Theresa's arm. She yelped in pain. "I'm sorry. Did I hurt you?"

Theresa shook her arm to relieve some of the pain. "No more than you intended to."

"Excuse me?"

Theresa chuckled. "Come on, Angel. Do you really think I'm that stupid?" Theresa smiled. "Don't you know I was expecting this?"

"Expecting what?"

"I knew you wouldn't be able to resist sticking it to me— literally, it seems. I can't even say I blame you. I just hope you'll go easy on me under the circumstances."

"I'm a professional," stated Angel. "I would never use a personal vendetta to endanger any of my patients, including the ones with no moral compass."

"Relax, all right? I'm not going to turn you in to the Medical Review Board. I just want you to know that I understand. I know why you're angry with me, why you would love nothing more than to see me suffer right now."

Angel's defenses immediately flared. "If you think this is about you and Duke—"

"Of course it's about me and Duke! In your mind, I'm the slut who stole your husband and the reason your baby died. Why wouldn't you enjoy a little comeuppance?"

"Don't try to analyze me," snarled Angel. "You don't even know me well enough to make an attempt. You don't know anything about me aside from whatever lies Duke may have told you to get you into bed."

"I know that you loved him and that you wanted his baby more than anything in the world. I know that he hurt you. We both did."

"Were you worried about hurting me when you started sleeping with my husband?" inquired Angel condescendingly.

Theresa shook her head. "I won't lie; I wasn't. I knew he was married, but I wanted him and didn't care. After a while, neither did he."

Angel could feel her anger rising. "You're a disgrace to women everywhere. You're nothing but a common whore."

"Back then, I probably was," conceded Theresa. "I was wild. I partied all the time, lived for pleasure. I hurt a lot of people with all of my selfish choices, and your name is at the top of that list, which is why I wanted your forgiveness."

"*Forgive you?*" cried Angel. Her emotions took over. "It's all I can do to stand here and look at you! Do you have any idea what you and that son-of-a-gun did to me? I nearly lost my mind! I actually tried to kill myself and had to be put in a mental facility. If Kina hadn't found me when she did, I'd be dead right now. I haven't even had a serious relationship since my marriage to Duke ended nine years ago. Now you want to come here all contrite and telling me you understand? You know just where you can go with that, Theresa!"

Theresa folded her hands together and calmly asked, "Are you finished?"

"No!" shrieked Angel. "Let me tell you this: we were happy. We were committed to one another. Duke and I were best friends, soul mates! We fell in love the first second we laid eyes on each other, and you slithered in like the demonic serpent you are and destroyed all that. You knew he was married. You knew he had a wife at home, but you didn't care. You seduced my husband and got pregnant—no doubt on purpose. You sank your claws in him and held on until you got him in your house and in your bed."

"And Duke isn't to blame for any of this?"

"Of course I blame him! I blame him much more than I blame you because he was the one married to me. He was the one who made vows to me and came home and made love to me every night after hitting the sheets with you. Just the thought of his touching you the same way he touched me makes me sick to my stomach. At least he had the decency to walk away and leave me alone. You, on the other hand, deliberately set out to find me and to use me to clear your own filthy conscience."

"That's not what I'm trying to do, Angel."

"Really?" asked Angel with a crude laugh. "You're trash, Theresa, just a home-wrecking slut. As this cancer eats away at you, destroying your life, I hope that it is a constant reminder to you of how you destroyed my life. I hope it eats away at you like it eats away at me knowing that my child died because yours was born." Angel began to cry. "Duke is the only man I've ever given my heart or my body to. I know that he left home on his own accord, but it never would've happened if he'd never crossed paths with you. I'm *glad* you have cancer! I'm *thrilled* that you're dying! Your death will only mean there's one less whore in the world. I hate you, and if I thought I could get away with it, I'd probably kill you myself. Instead, I'll let nature do it for me. You're getting exactly what you deserve. If you sow pain and destruction, that's exactly what you reap!" Angel sank to her knees sobbing, angry, hurt, confused, and relieved all at the same time.

Theresa ran to her and held her. "It's okay," she whispered. "Let it out!"

"Don't touch me!" ranted Angel, trying to escape Theresa's grasp. "Get your hands off of me. Your hands have my child's blood on them, and you know it!"

Theresa clung to her even tighter. "We're going to get through this, Angel," she vowed. "I hurt you, and I'm sorry. I broke up your marriage, and I sinned against God and you as my sister in Christ. God told us to show love to one another, but I didn't do that. I was selfish, calculating, and cruel. I didn't care how my actions would affect you; I just wanted what I wanted. Now I'm asking you to forgive me. I have truly repented, and God has forgiven me. I pray that you will, too, not for my sake, but for yours. I pray that you can forgive Duke too. He never wanted to hurt you."

"You don't prove your love to your wife by sleeping with another woman!"

"Duke will explain everything to you in time. His version really doesn't matter, though. The important thing is that you release this anger and these negative emotions. You can't do what God wants you to do by bottling up all this hatred. You're blocking your blessings. All that hatred and resentment is going to destroy you just like this disease is destroying me. My physical cancer is just as real as your spiritual cancer. We both need to be healed."

Angel finally broke free from her. "I will never forgive either of you for what you did to me!"

Theresa sighed. "Then you'll always be in bondage. The last thing I want to do right now is say anything to hurt you even more, but the truth is that Duke and I have had a great life together. We have two beautiful daughters, we have good friends, and we're not wanting for anything. We've acknowledged our sins, and we've moved on. But you, you're still stuck in this sad, empty place because you won't soften your heart enough to forgive. What are you gaining by holding on to all of this pain? You've created this little prison for yourself, but you can choose to be the prisoner with the life sentence, or the warden who sets her free. Forgiving is the hardest and easiest thing in the world, but it's totally up to you."

"Shut up! You will never understand what it's like to be hurt this deeply. Like you said, you have your husband, your family, your life. You can't possibly know what this has been like for me."

Theresa stood in front of her. "Look at me. Along with everything else I have, did you forget that I have cancer too? My family is being taken away from me just like yours was, only slower, but you don't see me sitting around here bitter, blaming God because I got sick. I had just turned only thirty-one years old when the doctor gave me six months to live. I could be very angry about that, but what would that accomplish other than sending me to the grave that much faster? The devil may be winning this victory over my body, but he won't take my joy and my peace. Neither will unforgiveness."

"I've been carrying this around for nine long years," said Angel. "Getting beyond it is not as simple as you want to make it seem."

"Sure it is; you just do it." She took Angel by the hand. "Pray with me, Angel."

"I can't," she sobbed and shook her head. "Not with you. Anybody but you."

"You don't have to do anything but close your eyes and give it to Jesus." Theresa kneeled beside her and prayed, "Lord, we come humbly and boldly before your throne. We acknowledge you as Lord over our lives and as the one true God. We rejoice and serve you with gladness. We thank you for today and for your continued grace and mercy upon us. While we are all guilty of sin, we also know that you are good, are ready to forgive, and are plenteous in mercy to all who call upon you.

"Lord, I come to you on behalf of my sister Angel. My husband and I have wronged her, Lord, in the most deceitful and hurtful way. Even though we have turned from our wicked ways and have sought and been granted your forgiveness, we have yet to be given hers. God, help her to remember that your word says that if we don't forgive those who hurt us, you won't forgive our transgressions. Soften her heart right now, Lord. Deliver her from the stronghold that a hardened heart has put on her life. Help her to recognize that the devil's sole purpose is to keep her bound and in a perpetual state of hurt and depression. Forgive her for her sins so that she may be led to forgive others.

"In the name of Jesus, I release her right now from hurt and negative emotions. From this day forward, she shall walk in the spirit of love and forgiveness. We believe that all we ask in your son's name is done, and we claim the victory right now. Amen."

Theresa opened her eyes and found Angel shaking her head and quietly thanking God in agreement. Theresa wrapped her arm around her. "It is done, my sister."

Angel wept for a long time. The memories started flooding back to her at once: meeting Duke, her wedding day, the joy of finding out that she was pregnant, and the agony of losing her child; the devastating blow of hearing Duke tell her that he was in love with another woman and was walking out on their marriage, the indescribable heartbreak of being served divorce papers, and the feeling of being so hurt and so defeated that she sought solace in overdosing on painkillers that the doctor had prescribed her following the miscarriage. Despite it all, though, the Lord had brought her through it. She was still here, still alive. She was surrounded by friends who loved her, and she was in a position to do good in the world and help ease other people's pain. She was blessed, and it took the woman she despised most to remind her.

Angel looked up at Theresa through watery eyes and whispered, "Thank you . . . I forgive you. I forgive both of you."

Theresa hugged her and replied, "Thank you. God bless you." She squeezed Angel's hand. "Your life is going to be so much richer from this point on. You're free."

"For the first time in nine years, I *feel* free," she admitted. Angel wiped her tears and laughed. "Who would've thought, right?"

Theresa smiled. "Who would've thought . . ."

"Theresa, I want you to know that I really do believe you've changed. You couldn't have done what you just did for me if God wasn't in your life and in your heart."

"The God we serve can do all kinds of miracles, even save a wretch like me," replied Theresa. "I don't have any unrealistic expectations about us being best friends or anything like that, but I'm willing to try to be something other than enemies if you are."

Angel looked down. "Theresa, I'm willing to try, but I'm not going to pretend that the hurt is gone. It's a little less, but the sting is still there."

"I know. In time, though, I pray that each layer of forgiveness will be pulled back, and that you'll no longer be haunted by this. I know that you'll have to forgive me all over again whenever you think of the child you lost or see me with Duke, or any time there's a trigger that causes you to remember. But you took an important step today toward making peace with everything that's happened."

"And I promise to be a consummate professional from now on. I'm sorry for being a pain earlier. I know I was hurt, but that's no excuse. The welfare of my patients should always come first."

"It's okay. Even your halo leans to the side sometimes, Angel," kidded Theresa.

"Nevertheless, I want to do right by you as your nurse."

"So, does this mean you're sticking around?" Angel nodded and Theresa smiled.

"Duke will be so happy to hear this. If you'll excuse me for a minute, I want to call and tell him the good news." Theresa made a quick exit.

Duke. Now that she was no longer hiding behind her anger, Angel realized that there was another emotion lying dormant in her as it related to her ex-husband. Beneath the layers of hurt, betrayal, and resentment was buried the one emotion she'd fought to deny for nine years: love.

Chapter 25

"Don't try to tangle with me."
—*Lawson Kerry*

Mark entered Lawson's classroom that Monday afternoon just as she was packing up to leave. His presence brought the usual anxiety along with it.

"Do you have any extra dry erase markers?" he asked.

"I thought the new teacher was supposed to be borrowing from the mentor, not the other way around." She pointed to her file cabinet. "Look in there. Grab what you need."

"Thanks." He opened the drawer, pulled out a box of markers, and held up a wallet-sized picture of Namon in his football uniform. "Is this your son?"

The anxiety mounted. She'd forgotten about stashing the picture in there to keep Mark from seeing it on her desk. Clearly, the plan had backfired. "Yes, that's Namon."

Mark was mesmerized by the photo, "Cute kid. Kind of looks like me at that age."

The comparison left Lawson feeling sick. "He is the spitting image of Patrick Kerry, my father," she lied to throw him off.

"What's his name again?"

"Namon." She hoisted the picture from his grasp.

"He plays football, huh? How old is he?"

"He's in middle school," she replied, being vague to prevent Mark from asking too many questions.

"Oh, you must've had him pretty young?"

"Yeah, I was still in high school."

"Really? I don't remember you saying you had a kid when we met."

"I had him later." She crammed the picture into her wallet.

"Was his daddy a jock too?"

"Mark, why the sudden interest in my son?"

"I'm just curious about what you've been doing for the last fourteen years. Sue me."

"I've been working, going to school, and taking care of my child. Case closed."

"Do you get a lot of help from his dad?"

Lawson was visibly irritated. "Namon's father abandoned him before he was even born."

"That's messed up. I can't imagine ever doing that to a child of mine."

"Oh, really," she replied, ripe with sarcasm.

"I know you're wondering how I can say that when my daughter's in a whole other state; but I send money every week, I get her during the summer, and I'm up in Charlotte visiting her every other weekend. I refuse to be a deadbeat dad."

"I suppose that makes Mariah a very lucky girl." Lawson slung her purse strap over her shoulder and started walking out of the classroom. "Mark, I really do have to go. Namon has a doctor's appointment, and we can't be late. I'll see you tomorrow."

Mark walked out behind her. "He's not sick, is he?"

"Not really. He has thyroid problems."

"I do too. It's hereditary, you know."

She shrugged her shoulders. "I guess."

He stopped walking and thought for a moment. "That's weird, isn't it?"

"What?"

"That your son and I both have the same condition."

Lawson pushed open the exterior doors of the school and walked to the parking lot. "It's not that strange, Mark. Millions of people suffer the same ailment." She could tell by his expression that her answer didn't placate him as much as she wished it had.

Mark was hot on her heels. "How old did you say he was again?"

In her haste to get away from Mark, Lawson blurted out, "He's almost fourteen," without thinking.

"Fourteen? You made it seem like he was a lot younger." She began to sprint, but was no match for the former running back. "Dang, slow down, Lawson!"

She stopped. "Mark, I already told you that I have to go. We'll talk later."

"Lawson, wait . . . if he's fourteen, then that means he must've been conceived around the time we met, right?"

Lawson exhaled. "What's your point?"

"When is Namon's birthday?"

"How about I just bring you his birth certificate, okay? Then you can figure out how old he is, who his dad is, and every other question you have that's keeping me from getting my son to the doctor."

He acquiesced. "Go on. I don't want you to miss your appointment."

She sighed, relieved. "Thank you. I'll see you later."

As Lawson moved to leave, Mark stopped her as a new thought came to him. "Lawson, wait . . . that night . . . we didn't use protection, did we?"

"I'm sure we did," she lied. "I wouldn't be that careless with a guy I just met."

Mark thought about it some more. "I'm almost positive we didn't because I wasn't planning on having anybody over that night. It just sort of happened."

"If you say so," she replied in a huff. "Now I really have to leave."

"Why are you so agitated? Why don't you want to talk about it?"

"What's with the Grand Inquisition, Mark? We've already had this discussion. Why do you want to rehash it now?"

"I don't know. I guess I'm looking for the truth. Something's not right about this. I feel it in my gut." He parted his lips to say something then pursed them together. He shook his head and spoke again. "Do you mind if I take another look at that picture?"

"I *do* mind. I really don't have time for this."

"Then just answer one question for me. Who is Namon's father?"

Lawson swallowed and looked away. "A guy I dated in high school. Why?"

"What's his name?"

"You don't know him."

"Then why won't you tell me his name?"

She unlocked her car door. "Why are you doing this? Just let it go!"

"I have to know the truth, Lawson. What's his name?"

Lawson rattled "Johnny" off of the top of her head before getting into the car.

"Johnny who?"

She was flustered. "Johnny Jones or something. I don't really remember. Like I said, we don't talk anymore. We haven't communicated in years."

She tried to close the door, but Mark blocked the door with his body. "Lawson, you don't know a dude named Johnny Jones any more than you do Adam's house cat."

"Okay, evidently you have all the answers, Mark, so why are you bothering me?"

"I think . . ." He shook his head. "I can't believe I'm about to ask you this."

"Then don't."

"I have to." He gulped. "Lawson, is Namon my son?"

She pushed him aside. "Don't you think you'd know if you had a child here, especially if he was living in the same city as you do?"

"No, not if his mother didn't tell me. Lawson, look at me, all right?" He held the door so she couldn't close it. "Is Namon my child? Just tell me, Lawson. I have to know. Is he my kid?"

Tears started to burn in her eyes. "Please, just drop it, okay? I'm not asking you for anything. My son and I are fine. We don't need anything from you."

"I'm not leaving until I know the truth. You owe me that much."

"I don't owe you anything!" she raged.

"If he's not my son, just say it."

Lawson shook her head.

"From the moment we met again, you've been acting strange. I thought it was because we'd slept together, but when I saw that picture, I knew. Tell me, Lawson. Is Namon my son?"

"I'm begging you, Mark. Don't do this."

Mark crossed his arms in front of him. "Fine, then, I'll have him tested. Is that what you want? You wanna drag your son through that?"

"No," she sobbed.

He stooped down beside the car. "Please just tell me the truth," pleaded Mark. "I need to hear you say the words."

Lawson looked down at Mark. The weight of carrying this secret was finally too much to bear, and she knew that there was only one way to unload it, to free Mark and to free herself. She wiped her eyes. "You were right, okay?" She held her head down as she spoke. "We didn't use protection that night." He dropped his head too. "It was stupid, and we should've known better."

Mark looked up. "And Namon?"

She took a deep breath and went on. "We didn't use protection, and we ended up making a baby that night."

His body was trembling. "So, it's true then? Namon is . . ."

"It's true." She looked him squarely in the face. "Mark, Namon is your son."

Mark was seething. He didn't say anything with his mouth, but his eyes spoke volumes. His face was rigid, jaws tightened.

Lawson was actually terrified of him. "Aren't you going to say anything?"

"Why?"

"Because we need to talk about this. I need to know what you intend to do."

"No, *why?* Why would you keep my son from me all these years? How could you not tell me?"

"Mark, I didn't know how to contact you. I didn't know where you were—"

"That's bull, Lawson! You had my number. You knew where I lived."

"By the time I realized I was pregnant, you'd already gone to Virginia to play football. How was I supposed to track you down way over there?"

"We knew the same people. If you wanted to reach me, you would have."

"I left messages with your parents for you to call me."

"You never told them you were pregnant."

"How could I? I didn't know them. I barely knew you."

"All of this time, I've had a son out there who needed me, and you kept him from me. Where does he think I've been all this time?"

"I told him the truth: that you dumped me and never looked back."

Mark shook her head. "How could you do that to him? What kind of mother lets her child think that his father doesn't give a —" He lowered his voice as two teachers strolled by them on the way to their cars. "How could you let him think I didn't care?"

"You didn't! You dropped me quicker than a bad habit."

"Is that what this is about? You kept him from me because I didn't call after we had sex?"

"Don't flatter yourself, Mark. The fact of the matter is that you knew we didn't use a condom and that there was a good chance that I could get pregnant, but you were too caught up in being the big football star to ever look back."

"Things would've been different if I had known."

"Would they really? Admit it, Mark. You didn't want to know what happened. You didn't want to know whether or not I was pregnant, because if I was, then you would have to take on a responsibility that you had no intention of seeing through."

"I wouldn't have hesitated to step up. We Vinsons take care of our own. I would've done whatever I had to do to make sure that my son had whatever he needed, including a father. Do you realize that he has grandparents that he's never even met and a sister who he doesn't know exists? What gave you the audacity to think that you could keep him away from us?"

"I was sixteen, Mark. Do you have any idea what it's like to be sixteen and pregnant? Do you know how it made me feel having to see the disappointment in my mother's eyes when she found out that I was pregnant? Or the pain of having your body ripped apart during labor? I had my whole childhood taken away from me while you were somewhere carefree. And you have the nerve to stand here and judge? How dare you?"

"You had choices, Lawson, and that's what you chose to do."

"What kind of choices did I have? An abortion? Adoption? Leaving him in a trash can on the street?"

"You could've told me. My family has money. My parents would've given their last to make sure that Namon was taken care of. Heck, they probably would've raised him while we finished school."

Lawson pointed at him. "That's exactly what I was afraid of. I never wanted to give up my son, Mark. I wasn't looking for a handout or someone to drop Namon off on."

Mark looked at her. His gaze was cold and unyielding. "I want to see him."

Lawson took a deep breath and calmed down. "Okay, when the time is right, we can arrange some sort of meeting or a phone conversation."

Mark chuckled. "A *phone conversation?* He's my son, Lawson! You have dictated my relationship with him long enough." His tone became as sinister as his stare. "Sorry, sweetheart, but you're no longer calling all the shots where Namon is concerned."

"I'm his mother. Say what you want, but I'm the only parent he's ever known. Now, I'm willing to work with you, but if you try to threaten or intimidate me, I'll be the only parent he *ever* knows."

"Do you really think you're in a position to take this kind of stance? You don't want this thing to get ugly, Lawson. I'll assemble a team of lawyers who won't have any problem with taking you on with every resource, loophole, and outlet they've got."

"Don't try to tangle with me, Mark," she warned him.

"Then don't get in my way. I will have a relationship with him, and it won't be on your terms. Those days are over."

"I never said you couldn't have a relationship with him, but I'm not about to let you come out of left field, disrupting his life. Namon is a stable, well-adjusted young man, and I intend to keep him that way. Your relationship with him will have to be a process. Even then, it'll only be if that's what he wants."

"So, let me get this straight. You get to decide when, where, and how I meet my son, and Namon gets to decide whether or not he even wants to see me. At what point in this equation do I get any say?"

Lawson stood firm and looked him up and down. "You don't."

"Oh yeah? My son will know me, Lawson. I'm prepared to go after custody if you force the issue."

"Your threats don't scare me. No judge in his right mind is going to take a child from his mother to live with a stranger who happens to have the same DNA. Get real."

"It's real, all right. You may be his mother, but I've got the law on my side. You can't keep a child away from his father without just cause. I'm not afraid to have this thing go to court."

"And I will fight you every step of the way," added Lawson, moving in closer.

"Then get ready for the fight of your life," he advised before storming off.

Chapter 26

"I just need to be patient and wait on you to move in my situation."
—*Kina Battle*

Kina was still quivering. An argument with E'Bell over the past due light bill left her stripped of her pride and almost of her life after he ripped into her about not paying it on time. E'Bell then choked Kina to silence her when she reminded him that he was supposed to pay it, not her.

As usual, E'Bell stormed out of the apartment following the argument, presumably to get drunk or smoke marijuana with his friends. His activities outside of their house no longer concerned Kina. It was his actions within their four walls that she had just about had enough of. Kina loved E'Bell—there was no doubt in her mind about that—but she also knew that staying with him could very well end up costing her sanity and her life. Real love, she believed, shouldn't require her to sacrifice her body, her self-esteem, and her self-worth in exchange for affection. E'Bell never spoke life into her or put her needs ahead of his own. Living with him was becoming unbearable, and the last thing she wanted to do was leave a legacy of abuse for her son to repeat. She had to make a choice.

"God, I don't think I can take this anymore!" Kina cried out in prayer. "You said that we can cast all of our burdens on you. I need you to help me. You are my fortress and my protector. I need a way out for my son and me. I know that it is not your will for us to suffer like this. Give me your spirit of peace and the courage to do what I have to do. I need your guidance so I won't act out of emotion. I need to feel your presence, Lord, because right now, I'm so lost. I just need you to help me. Please don't abandon me. Not now, Lord!"

While cowering in a corner crying, Kina's first thought was to numb the pain with the box of doughnuts she had waiting for her on the counter. When she lifted her head to make sure they were still there, she spotted the telephone directory on top of the television. The Lord dropped it into her spirit to open the book. She turned to the yellow pages and discovered strength and resolve that she didn't have before. She began frantically skimming through law firms, searching for a divorce attorney.

Kina settled on family attorney Bette Walsh, whose full-page ad in the yellow pages guaranteed a free consultation. Kina picked up the telephone, took a deep breath, and dialed Bette Walsh's number, praying that she was doing the right thing.

"Good afternoon, this is the law office of Bette Walsh. Can I help you?" asked the receptionist on the other end of the phone.

Kina cleared her throat. "I, um, I need to speak to Ms. Walsh please."

"She's with a client at the moment, but I'd be happy to give her a message."

"Um, tell her Kina Battle called." Kina gripped the couch, urging herself to utter the words that she'd never had the courage to say aloud before. "Tell her I need a lawyer because"—she took a deep breath—"I want a divorce."

Kina left her phone number with the receptionist and hung up. She swelled with pride for taking that all-important first step. She lifted her eyes to the Lord and clasped her hands together and whispered, "Thank you for giving me strength and giving me a way out." Then Kina lifted both arms in praise and shouted, "Praises be to God!"

Kina fell back on the sofa laughing, intoxicated with joy. With one phone call, she had begun the process of setting herself free. Never again would she have to fear for her or her son's safety. She could go to school if she wanted, she could cook what she wanted. "Shoot," she said aloud, "I can even fall in love if I want to!" She started giggling to the point of hysteria, feeling something that she'd hadn't in a long time: hope.

Kina was brought back to reality after catching a glimpse of E'Bell's tarnished MVP trophy on their display shelf. Leaving him would not be easy, and she needed a plan. Kina knew that E'Bell would lose his mind if she flat-out told him that she was filing for a divorce, and there was no telling what he'd do to her once he got home if she had divorce papers served to him at work. She needed to find a safe haven for herself and her son. In order to do that, she would have to ask for help, which would mean admitting that she was trapped in an abusive marriage.

Kina's thoughts were interrupted by a knock at the door. She opened it and found her elderly next door neighbor. "Hi, Miss Janie, can I help you with something?"

"I'm just looking for my grandbaby," croaked Janie Carswell. "I need him to run down the corner to the store for me."

"Sheldon's not here," replied Kina. The woman nodded and dropped her head. "If you need something we have in here, I'd be happy to give it to you."

She squeezed Kina's arm. "That's mighty sweet of you, baby. You got some baking soda and some sugar?"

"I'm sure I do. Come on in." Kina invited the woman into her living room.

"You all right, baby? You look like you've been crying," Janie observed.

"Oh, it's nothing," said Kina, pasting on a smile. "These are tears of joy."

"I thought I heard some yelling over here earlier. I ain't nosey, but you know these walls are made out of paper." She rapped on the paneling. "You can just about hear each other breathing."

"My husband and I had a little disagreement." Kina went into her cupboard and pulled out a bag of sugar and a small box of baking soda.

"It's like that sometimes," conceded Mrs. Carswell, retrieving the items from Kina. "But y'all are young. You got plenty of good years ahead of you."

"I don't know about that," admitted Kina.

"Of course you do! You two are in love and you got that baby to raise together. Don't let some little argument make you throw in the towel."

Kina sat down on the sofa shook her head. "It's more than that. The marriage isn't working for us. I just don't think we need to be together."

"Hush all that!" ordered Mrs. Caswell. "That's just the devil talking! You know he comes to kill, steal, and destroy. He hates marriage, but the Lord says, 'I hate divorce.' The Bible says that divorce is treacherous, so don't even let that word come out your mouth! You just need to go somewhere and pray and trust God to make it all right."

"I have faith that He will make everything all right, but I don't believe God expects me to live in misery while I'm here on earth."

"Baby, the devil will tell you anything he can in order to move you out of God's will for your life. This ain't just about what you want. You got to think about that baby and remember that God told married folks to stay together. Don't give your family over to Satan. Don't let him have that victory."

"Miss Janie, you don't know the whole story or what I've been through."

Janie leaned against the arm of the sofa for support. "We all go through struggles, baby. My problems might not be same as yours, but when it comes down to it, problems are problems. There really ain't too much difference."

"I think Satan has a stronghold on my husband. I'll continue to pray for E'Bell's deliverance, but the best thing for me and my son to do is to get out while we still can."

"If you believe that Satan has a hold on your husband, that's even more reason for you to stay here and pray him through it. Your prayer could be the one thing that saves him. You can't make this whole thing about you. You've got to do what's best for your family and to do what God's word tells us to do. He ordered us to live at peace with one another, not strife. Don't let the devil use you or the people closest to you to further his plan to destroy your marriage. Do what God says."

With a heavy heart, Kina stammered, "I–I thought I was doing what God wanted me to do."

"That's why you've got to spend time with the Lord so you can discern his voice from the enemy's. All that talk about divorce and leaving your husband has got the devil written all over it. You need to get on your knees and repent for even thinking about it. Don't you know that divorce grieves God's heart?"

"I would never want to do that, not even unintentionally."

Janie hobbled to the door. "See, that's why the Lord sent me over here, to keep you from doing something foolish. Now, I thank you for my sugar and baking soda, and if you see that rascal of mine, send his behind home, you hear me?"

Kina struggled to hold back the tears as she opened the door to let Janie out. "Yes, ma'am."

Janie lifted Kina's chin. "Aw, don't look so sad, child. Be joyful. The Lord will forgive you if you ask Him to, and everything is gon' turn out just fine. You'll see."

Kina nodded and closed the door. She had been certain that the Lord was speaking to her, but now wondered if it was only the devil trying to lead her into sin. Perhaps she'd acted in haste. After all, God wanted her to be willing to bear all things and to be true to the covenant she made with Him and the vows she made to E'Bell.

"God, I know that you'll be faithful if I continue to pray and be obedient," prayed Kina. "You won't put more on me than I can bear. You said having trouble tests our faith and builds character. I just need to be patient and wait on you to move in my situation."

Her cell phone rang, and Kina picked it up without thinking. "Hello?"

"Hi, this is Attorney Bette Walsh calling for Kina Battle. Is she available?"

It was the call that just fifteen minutes earlier Kina had been waiting for. She thought of Janie Carswell's words and concluded that the call was just another attempt from the devil to move her away from God's will for her marriage. Kina sighed and replied, "Sorry, you've got the wrong number," and hung up the phone.

Chapter 27

"I've always known that this day would come.
I should've been prepared."
—*Lawson Kerry*

"Give me the name and the number of a good lawyer," demanded Lawson.

"Well, hello to you too," Sullivan said and invited Lawson inside her home.

Lawson took off her coat and flung it on the couch. "Mark knows."

"I thought you were going to hold off on telling him."

"That was the plan, but he figured it out. Now he's talking all kind of foolishness about custody and his rights and going to court."

"Nobody's taking your son away from you, Lawson. God will see to that, and if He doesn't, I will!"

"He acts like I'm just supposed to hand my son over to him, like the last fourteen years never happened," she ranted. "He's so angry with me right now. I have no idea what he's gonna do."

"Well, I know what I'm going to do. I'm calling in the whole cavalry, including Garrett. If Mark wants a fight, we'll give him one!"

"Sully, what if he really goes after custody?"

Sullivan folded Lawson into her arms. "He can try, but nothing is going to come of it. Lawson, you're Namon's mother, and you've been an excellent one at that, even though you started taking care of him since you were a kid yourself. You've spent your whole life sacrificing all you had so that Namon could have a good life. You don't have to prove that you've done your job as a mother; it's Mark who has to prove that he's a worthy father."

"How can we stop him?"

"I don't know . . . We'll seek God. We'll get a lawyer. We'll do whatever it takes to protect you and Namon."

Within minutes, after being summoned by Sullivan, the troops descended on Sullivan's lawn. First, Angel and Kina arrived, followed by Reginell and Garrett, all offering their prayers, pledging their support, and committing to move heaven and earth to keep Lawson and Namon together.

Lawson wiped the tears from her face with the back of her hand. "You know, I've always known that this day would come. I should've been prepared."

Garrett held her. "Baby, there's no point to playing the 'shoulda, woulda, coulda game.' We need to focus on our next move."

Reginell joined the two of them. "It doesn't matter what he does. Mark can't hurt us. You, Namon, Garrett, and me are a family, and nothing's breaking that up."

"Thank you, sis. It means the world to me that you even came."

"Lawson, we might fight sometimes, but I'm your ride or die chick for life," vowed Reginell.

Kina spoke next. "Cuz, everything is going to be fine. Somebody reminded me just today how much the enemy wants to destroy families. While I believe that Mark has a right to have a relationship with his son, he doesn't have the right to take Namon away from the only sense of family and stability that he's ever known. We won't let him."

"Thank you, Ki." The tears kept flowing. Lawson was moved by the outpouring of love from her family.

"I told you we had your back," assured Sullivan.

Garrett handed Lawson a tissue. "I think it's time to tell Namon the truth."

Lawson blew her nose. "I don't think we need to do that yet."

"Lawson, you said yourself that this man is unpredictable," said Angel. "What's to stop him from tracking Namon down and telling him himself? You don't want your son to find out like that. Then not only will he be confused, but he'll feel like he can't trust you. Don't leave it to chance."

"He thinks of Garrett as his father," claimed Lawson.

Garrett exhaled. "But I'm not, and he knows that. You don't want Mark putting his spin on things before you've had a chance to explain this to Namon."

"How do I even begin to do that? It was one thing when we didn't know where Mark was, but I've known where he is for weeks now."

"You can't worry about that now, but you do have to tell him. If you want, I'll speak to Namon myself, and I'll be right by your side when you break the news to him. Either way, Lawson, he needs to know that his dad is looking for him, and it's best if he hears that from you," said Garrett.

"Lawson, what are you so afraid of?" asked Reginell. "What's the worst that could happen? Yes, I'm sure it'll be a shock to Namon, but it'll also be a tremendous relief. They could actually end up having a great relationship. You don't want to stand in the way of that, do you?"

Lawson plunked down on the sofa and began sobbing again. "What if . . . what if Namon decides he wants to live with Mark?" she cried. "Or worse—what if Mark snatches him up and takes off? I thought about doing it, and probably would've gone through with it if you hadn't stopped me. What's to keep Mark from thinking the same thing?"

Kina sat down beside her. "He won't. From what you've told me about Mark, he seems to be a stand-up guy. I don't think he'd intentionally hurt you or his son."

Lawson shook her head. "You didn't see him today. You didn't see the look in his eyes. He was so angry that it scared me. People like that can't be trusted."

"Well, we know who *can* be trusted," proclaimed Angel, "and we need to put this into His hands. God told us to cast our burdens onto Him, and He will take of care of it."

"What will Namon think of me?" wondered Lawson. "I preach to him all the time about being responsible and thinking things through. How am I going to rationalize sleeping with a guy I barely knew? What kind of woman will he think I am?"

"He knows the kind of woman you are," assured Sullivan. "You're strong and you're kind and you love him more than anything in this world. Nothing you tell him about Mark is going to change the way he feels about you."

"I'm scared, y'all. I'm so afraid of losing my son and losing his respect. I have absolutely no control over the situation or what's going to happen next."

"You don't have to be in control, because God is," said Angel. "Trust Him, Lawson. Hasn't He always taken care of you and Namon? Put it in God's hands."

"We've all got your back," avowed Garrett. "Mark against us and God is like him fighting against an army with a handgun."

"That may be true," said Lawson, "but if Mark takes my son from me, all the support in the world won't matter. Nothing will."

"Jesus will work it out. Just pray," urged Kina.

"I am, but there's one thing we have to consider. What if God's on Mark's side with this? If He is, army or not, there ain't a thing in this world I can do about it."

Chapter 28

"To this day, I still don't know what went wrong."
—*Angel King*

As Theresa slept, Angel checked her vitals one last time before she got ready to leave. Satisfied with the results, she turned off the lights and tiptoed out of the bedroom. She bumped into Duke in the hallway.

"How is she?" he asked with concern.

"She's sleeping, but she's okay."

"Are you leaving?"

"Well, it's after five, so I should be heading out. Besides, you're here now. I'm sure she prefers your bedside manner to mine." Angel looked everywhere except at him. "I'll see you around, Duke."

"Angel, wait. If you have a minute, it would mean a lot to me if we could talk. Please . . . it'll only take a minute."

"Sure. Let's just make it quick." Angel followed him downstairs, tormented by her conflicting emotions. She had gone out of her way to avoid him; now, interacting with him was inescapable.

"Reese told me about what happened between the two of you," he began. "I want you to know how much it means that you found it in your heart to forgive both of us."

"I'm afraid your wife deserves more credit than I do. If it wasn't for her making me face the Lord and my own sins, I probably wouldn't be able to do this."

"Despite what you may think of her, Reese really is a remarkable woman. She's changed a lot since we met. You probably won't meet a woman more devoted to the Lord or to her family than she is."

It stung to hear Duke talk about his wife in such heartfelt terms. "I can see why you love Theresa. She makes it almost impossible to hate her."

"That's what makes her having this disease so unfair. Even in the midst of it all, she never gives up hope."

"Well, if that's all you wanted to talk about, I should get going." Angel headed toward the door.

Duke followed her. "There's one more thing. . . ."

Angel turned around. "What's that?"

"I never apologized to you. You didn't deserve to be treated that way. You were a wonderful wife, Angel. I was the one who messed up, not you. I hoped that you never blamed yourself for our marriage falling apart."

"Duke, if all of this has taught me nothing else, I've learned that life is too short to waste time placing blame. Yes, mistakes were made, but I can't spend my life holding that against you. I meant it when I said I forgave you. I really am at peace with it now."

"You're a good woman. Not many people could do what you're doing for my family and me. I thank you from the bottom of my heart."

"I'm just operating in my calling. Nursing is in my blood. My mom used to joke that I even tried to help the doctors out during my delivery."

He laughed a little. "I remember. How is Mama Ruby, by the way?"

"She's good. It's kind of you to ask."

"She was my mother-in-law, Angel. I'll always care about her . . . and you." Duke, looking at her the way he used to, made Angel feel things that she wasn't supposed to feel. He was much easier to deal with when she had convinced herself that she hated him. Now, she didn't know what to feel.

Duke seemed nervous. "Angel, I want to talk about the baby. Our baby, the one who died."

Angel felt a wave of sorrow all over again. "I guess Theresa told you about that, huh?"

"She did, but why didn't you?"

"I tried to. In fact, I was planning to surprise you with the positive pregnancy test for Christmas. But then—"

Duke closed his eyes. "Then I told you that Reese had just had my baby, and I walked out on you and our unborn child."

Angel nodded. "If the baby had lived, I would've told you eventually. At the time, though, I was just so hurt and confused. Once I miscarried, there really didn't seem to be a point in saying anything."

"Angel, if I had known that you were pregnant too . . ."

"Would you have stuck around?"

He looked down. "I don't know what I would've done." He raised his eyes to look at her. "Then again, if I'd taken just one look at you, knowing that you were carrying our child, I don't think I could have ever walked away."

"Duke, can I ask you something? It's been weighing on me all this time, and I don't think I can truly have closure until I know the answer."

"You can ask me anything you want."

Angel exhaled. "What happened between us? I know that it's a moot point now, but it's always been an unanswered question in my mind. I thought we were happy. To this day, I still don't know what went wrong."

He ushered her to the sofa, and they both sat down. "We *were* happy, Angel, but after a while, I started feeling trapped. Here I was, twenty-four years old, barely out of college, with a wife to support while she finished nursing school, bills to pay, a crappy apartment, and a job that I hated. My friends were still hanging out, having fun, being young. Then you started talking about having a baby, and it felt like I was living my parents' life." He lowered his head. "I couldn't handle the pressure, so I took the easy way out."

"Is that when you hooked up with Theresa?"

He nodded. "At first, being with her was just sort of an escape for me, you know, a way to forget about all of the stress waiting for me at home. That is, until she got pregnant. Her family was wealthy, though, and she pretty much told me that if I married her, I could go to grad school like I wanted and we could live here with her parents and not worry about money, plus have round-the-clock help with the baby. At the time, it seemed like the answer to my prayers. I see now how unbelievably selfish it was."

"Why didn't you tell me how you felt? I would've done more, even if I had to drop out of school and go to work. I certainly wouldn't have been trying to have a baby."

"I wouldn't have wanted you to leave college during your senior year to appease me, and I was too much of a coward to tell you I didn't think we were ready for a child."

"With all these misgivings, why did you ask me to marry you at all?"

He swept her hair back and gazed into her eyes. "Because I was crazy about you. I loved you. I just wasn't ready for marriage."

"That didn't stop you from marrying Theresa."

"I was on the fence about that too. But once Miley was born, everything changed. I had a child now, and I knew that I had a responsibility to her and her mother. Don't ever doubt that I loved you with everything in me that had the capacity to love. I was just stupid. There's no other word for it."

"You seem to have wised up now."

"It was a long time coming. Thankfully, God looks out for babies and fools."

"Which one were you?"

"At twenty-four, I probably was a baby. For leaving you, I probably was a fool."

Angel felt her blood rushing to her face, and she had to remind herself to breathe. With Duke's dreamy eyes staring back at her and him looking scrumptious in his tailored suit, Angel suddenly had a lot more compassion for Sullivan. "Well, it all worked out," she summed up. "You got your family; I got my degrees and my career. . . ."

"What about love? Do you have that, Angel?"

"Sure. I love my job. I love my friends, my church, my spin classes. . . ."

Duke tilted up her chin. "I mean romance. Do you have a man in your life?"

She trivialized his question with a laugh. "Who has time for a love life?"

"You should make time for it. Life is too short to spend it alone, and you're too good of a woman not to have the love of a good man."

Angel blushed. "I'll keep that in mind." She stood up to leave.

"Be safe, and thank you for everything you're doing for my wife and my family." He pulled her into a hug. Angel didn't know whether to back away or stay there forever.

"Daddy, look what I drew!" shrieked Morgan, running into the room, waving a sheet of paper.

Duke let go of Angel and kneeled down to face his little girl. "Let me see it."

Morgan pointed everyone out to him, "That's you, that's Mommy, that's Miley, that's me, and that's Miss Angel."

"You're quite the artist," said Angel, looking over Duke's shoulder at the drawing. "That's a beautiful picture. I feel so special that you included me in it."

"We have to find a frame for it and show it to Mommy," said Duke.

Despite whatever Angel felt during the moment of weakness in Duke's embrace, the picture reminded her very quickly about who he loved and where his priorities were.

"Well, good night, Duke," bid Angel.

"Good-bye, Angel. Get home safe."

Angel left, chiding herself for even going there with her emotions. Duke was married and, like it or not, she had to respect that. Nevertheless, she could still feel Duke's arms around her the whole way home.

Chapter 28

"I've apologized to you for the last time."
—Lawson Kerry

Autumn rolled on, and before Lawson knew it, it was October. The Sunday dinner plans that she had made to spend around the table with Reginell, Garrett, and Namon came to an abrupt halt when she found Mark on her doorstep.

"What are you doing here?" she demanded to know. "How do you even know where I live?"

"Lawson, ever since you told me I was Namon's father two weeks ago, you have completely avoided me at work. You refuse to return my phone calls or my e-mails, and I'm sick of it. I'm not playing these games with you any longer." Mark pushed his way into the house. "I want to see my son."

"Are you crazy? You can't just barge in here like this!" she screeched.

"Where is he, Lawson? Where's Namon? I'm not leaving until I see him."

Lawson pointed to the front door. "You're leaving *now*, Mark. Don't think I won't call the police." She darted toward the phone and picked it up.

Mark snatched it from her grip. "You're going to call the police and tell them what?" he roared. "How you kept my son from me for fourteen years? How you robbed both of us of time we'll never get back? That you got him thinking that some other man is his daddy?" He thrust the phone at her. "Yeah, Lawson, you call and tell them that!"

Lawson set down the phone. "I've apologized to you for the last time, and don't you dare stand here and act like the victim in all of this!" She pointed to her chest. "*I* was the one raising our son by myself while you were living it up in Germany. *I* was the one helping him with his homework and sitting up with him all night when he was sick. How many football practices did you have to rush home from work to drive him to? How many times did you have to get down on your knees and pray that there would be enough money to pay the bills and still put food on the table? And I'm supposed to feel sorry for you? *Please!*"

Mark watched her in disbelief. "Unbelievable! You're making this whole thing about you, Lawson! You wouldn't have had to do all that by yourself if you'd told me that I had a son. You let him think that I had walked out on him, which is something I never would've done. Even after we met again at work, you still didn't say one word about us having a child together. If I hadn't found his picture, you would've let both of us go the rest of our lives without knowing the truth."

"All right, maybe I should've handled things differently," Lawson conceded, "but I had to do what I thought was best for my child."

"I'm his parent, too, Lawson. You don't get to make all the decisions."

"I have for the last fourteen years, so what makes you think I'm about to stop now?"

"If I can't stop you, I'm sure a judge can!"

"No judge is going to listen to some irresponsible, belligerent ex-jock who—"

"Whoa, what's going on in here?" asked Garrett, rushing into the room with Namon at his side. "We could hear yelling way in the back."

Lawson exhaled. "Garrett, this is Mark."

Garrett froze and glanced over at Namon. "Is he here to see—"

"Yes," answered Lawson.

Mark slowly walked over to Namon. He began to choke up upon laying eyes on his son for the first time. He could clearly see himself in his child, and had to suppress the urge to take him into his arms. "Namon, do you any have idea who I am?"

Namon moved to Lawson's side. "No. Why are you yelling at my mom?"

"We were just talking, baby," Lawson explained. "We had a difference of opinion and things got kind of loud. I'm sorry."

Mark reached out for Namon, but stopped himself from touching him. "How are you, son?"

"I'm fine. Mama, who is this, and what's he doing here?"

"He's a friend from work and wanted to know if we had an extra plate for dinner." Mark admonished her with his eyes for lying. She mumbled, "This isn't the time, Mark."

Mark forced a smile. "So, Namon, I hear you like to play football."

"I play a little bit," he answered.

"Are you kidding me?" asked Lawson, putting her arms around Namon. "He's the best player on his team."

"I'm not half bad at it myself," touted Mark. "If you ever want someone to throw the ball around with you, let me know."

"My dad works with me," said Namon.

It crushed Mark to hear Namon refer to Garrett that way. "I'm the head football coach at the high school. If you're thinking about trying out for the team next year—"

"I'll probably quit the team," said Namon. "I want to be in band, and you can't do both since the band plays at all the football games."

"Well, if you change your mind and decide to play, you come up to the school and work out with some of the players. I could even give you a few pointers."

Reginell emerged from the dining room. "I was wondering where everybody slipped off to." She spotted Mark. "Hi, I'm Reggie."

He shook her hand. "I'm Mark."

She gulped. "*Mark.* Mark?" Sensing the potential for disaster, Reginell offered to drive Namon to Kina's to play video games with Kenny.

Namon looked up at his mother. "Can I go?"

"Sure, sweetie. Just be home by nine." Namon gave Lawson a peck on the cheek and left with his aunt.

"All right, now does somebody want to tell me what's going on in here? What did we just walk in on?" asked Garrett.

Lawson threw up her hands in frustration. "He's insisting on seeing Namon!"

Mark stepped forward. "He's my son. I have every right to see him."

"So, you were just going to spring it on him in the middle of dinner? When had you planned to talk to us about it?" interrogated Garrett.

Mark bestowed a cool glance on Garrett. "I hadn't planned to talk to *you* about it at all. No disrespect, but this is between Lawson and me."

"If it involves Lawson, then it involves me too," Garrett fired back.

"My beef is not with you, man, but if you try to interfere with me having a relationship with my son, it will be," warned Mark.

Garrett's voice deepened. "I don't take too kindly to idle threats, player."

"Neither do I, nor do I give idle threats, *player*. Now, I already told you that this is between Lawson and me. I'm not dealing with you, period."

"You don't have a choice," said Garrett.

Mark abruptly pushed Garrett in his chest. "Yo, man, what's your problem? She ain't your wife yet."

"You've got one more time to put your hands on me," cautioned Garrett.

Mark surrendered his hands. "Or what?"

Lawson tried to calm Garrett. "Baby, he's just trying to upset you."

"Are you *upset*, Garrett?" taunted Mark. "You *upset* because I was the first one to hit that? Are you trippin' off her having my seed instead of yours?"

Blind with fury, Garrett lunged and swung wildly at Mark. "You better not ever let me hear you say anything else to disrespect my woman!" he roared.

Lawson held Garrett back as he moved to strike. "Forget him! He's not worth it!"

Mark threw up his fists, ready to retaliate. "What kind of punk lets his woman fight for him? Is that what you've been teaching my son?" Mark went after him again.

Lawson lodged in between the two of them, and shoved Mark with all the strength she could muster. "That's it, Mark! Get out right now! The next time I catch you lurking around here, I won't hesitate to slap you with a restraining order. You got that?"

"You will not keep him from me," panted Mark, catching his breath.

Lawson marched to the door and flung it open. "Get out! Go! Now, Mark!"

Mark took a few deep breaths. "I don't care what I have to do; I will be a part of my son's life whether you or your boyfriend here like it or not."

"You can get out, or I can throw you out," Garrett warned him.

Mark ignored Garrett and held up his finger. "One week, Lawson. I'm giving you one week to tell Namon I'm his father, or I'll do it for you," Mark vowed and slammed the door behind him.

Chapter 29

"E'Bell is my husband and my problem."
—*Kina Battle*

"Mark has completely lost his mind!" wailed Lawson through the phone the next day while Reginell perused the snack food section of the grocery store.

"I'm sure by the time you go back to work tomorrow, Mark will have calmed down," Reginell assured Lawson as she wavered between Oreos and Chips Ahoy cookies. "You should've listened when Kina and I told you to be honest with him and Namon."

"I know. I was trying to protect my son."

"No, you were trying to protect yourself, and now you've created a monster in Mark. I don't think you're going to be able to stop him from seeing Namon. You saw what he did yesterday."

"He's not going to get away with pulling a stunt like that," warned Lawson. "He just doesn't know who he's messing with."

Reginell finished her shopping and was still thinking about her sister and nephew when she heard voices erupting from the parking lot as she walked out to her car. Both voices sounded familiar, and she jogged in the direction of the sound. She soon spied E'Bell and Kina.

Before Reginell could confront them, she witnessed E'Bell hit Kina. Kina crumbled to her knees as blood trickled from her nose.

"*Kina!*" Reginell cried and rushed to her aid. "Are you all right?"

"I'll be in the car," mumbled E'Bell. He didn't so much as glance at Reginell.

Reginell dropped her shopping bags and helped Kina to her feet. "Kina, what in the world is going on here?"

Kina covered her nose, not wanting Reginell to see the damage. "I'm okay."

"No, you're not! Your husband just hit you!" Reginell pulled out her cell phone. "We need to call the police."

Kina snatched the phone. "Don't!" she insisted and blotted her nose with her shirt. "Reggie, E'Bell is my husband and my problem."

"*Problem* is the operative word here. How long has E'Bell been hitting you?"

Kina lied. "This is the first time he's ever done anything like this. I brought it on myself, really. I said something to him that I shouldn't have, and he got upset."

"E'Bell got more than upset, Kina; he got violent. Where's Kenny?"

"He's at Lawson's house with Namon."

"All right, we'll just swing by and get Kenny, and the two of you can come home with me. E'Bell doesn't know where I'm living now. Both of you will be safe there."

Kina shook her head. "I can't impose on you like that."

"It's no imposition. You're family, and I can't have that fool hitting on you whenever he gets a notion."

"Reggie, that's sweet of you, but I've got this under control. Soon as we get home, E'Bell will apologize, and we can act like this whole thing never happened."

"Are you serious?" Reginell asked incredulously. "He can't just hit you and act like nothing happened! And if he hit you once, he'll do it again, Kina."

Kina looked back at E'Bell. "You remember the other day,

how you were saying you want to run your own life without everybody butting in?"

"So, what about it?"

"Well, I want the same thing," declared Kina. "You need to trust me to handle this on my own."

"At least talk to Lawson. She's more than your cousin; she's your best friend."

Kina shook her head. "Lawson wouldn't understand."

"*Kina, come on!*" yelled E'Bell from the car.

"Look, Reggie, I've got to go, but you'll keep this between the two of us, right?"

Reggie touched Kina's nose, which was starting to swell. "I wish you could see your face," she said softly. "You can't let him do this to you."

"Just promise me you won't say anything. Please, Reggie!"

E'Bell blared the horn. Reginell waved her hand dismissively. "Fine. I won't say anything this time, but if he ever puts his hands on you again . . ."

"Thank you, cuz." Kina gave her a quick hug. "I gotta go."

Reginell shook her head as she watched Kina jump into her car with E'Bell. He glared out the window as they rolled by. Reginell was not one who spent much time praying for herself, but with tears in her heart, she stopped right there in the parking lot and prayed for her cousins. Her spirit urged her to call Lawson, but before she could dial all seven numbers, she put her cell phone away. Reginell had her secrets, and she supposed that Kina was entitled to a few of her own.

Chapter 30

"Cast the First Stone."
—Sullivan Webb

"She's what?" gasped Lawson. Angel choked on her tea and Kina's jaw dropped to the floor following Sullivan's revelation as they gathered around Lawson's table for Sunday dinner the next day. The men had excused themselves to catch the game.

"That's right," confirmed Sullivan. "Stripping! An unnamed source saw her taking it all off at some seedy strip club last night, and I mean taking off all of it!"

"Reggie, how could you?" asked Kina, disappointed.

"I don't know why you all are acting so shocked," stated Sullivan. "The only surprise to me was that she didn't start sooner."

"Reggie, don't you know you're held accountable when you lure people into sin?" Angel reminded her.

"You're talking as if the Lord hasn't punished me enough already," spat Reginell.

"The Lord isn't punishing you," argued Lawson. "You're doing this to yourself. And for what—a little money? Some attention? That little change you're making is not worth your soul and your self-respect, Reggie."

"The wealth you get from sin robs you of your life," quoted Kina.

"Reg, you're too beautiful and talented to waste your life this way," said Angel.

"I don't need any of you judging me," shot back Reginell.

"I didn't ask for your permission or your approval on how to govern my life. I'm proud of my body and of what I do, and I don't care what none of you have to say about it!"

"If you're so proud, Reggie, why are we just now hearing about it?" asked Sullivan. "Why haven't you told anybody who'll listen, like with your stupid demo?"

"I'm doing this for my career," insisted Reginell. "Do you know how many famous people come through the club? All it takes is me getting noticed one time and being featured in one video, and I'll be set. I don't know anybody in the music industry. How else am I supposed to have a shot at fame?"

"Reggie, how do you expect anyone to take you seriously as a singer if your claim to fame is the ability to drop it like it's hot on a stripper pole?" posed Sullivan.

Reginell glared at her. "I can't stand you; you know that? I just wish that somebody would come along and bash you upside the head with a brick and put an end to your miserable life."

"You're taking it off for pocket change, and you're calling my life miserable?" questioned Sullivan. "You're pathetic, Reggie, and now the whole world knows it."

"Says the tramp who's slutting around with Vaughn," hissed Reginell. "Call me what you want, Sully, but cheating is ten times worse than stripping!"

"Are you two really going to fight over who's the biggest whore?" asked Lawson. "Mama is probably rolling over in her grave right now."

"Come on," said Kina, taking Lawson and Reginell by their hands. "Let's pray."

Reginell snatched her hand away. "*Pray?* Pray for what? What has prayer gotten you besides a man whipping your behind? If that's what your praying can do for me, you can forget about it!" The ladies all froze with horror. All eyes turned to Kina.

"Kina, is that true?" asked Lawson. Kina hung her head.

"Kina, if E'Bell is hitting you or your son, I can get you some help," insisted Angel. "You and Kenny can move in with me. You don't have to stay there."

Sullivan began dialing on her cell phone. "I'm calling Charles. His brother is a lawyer. We can see about getting that punk locked up right now!"

Kina grabbed the phone. "Guys, don't listen to Reggie. My marriage is just fine. She just *thinks* she saw something, that's all."

"So, it wasn't you who E'Bell gave a bloody nose to in the parking lot?" pursued Reginell. "It wasn't you who begged me not to say anything about it?"

Kina became flustered. "He wasn't trying to hurt me."

"But he did hit you?" interrogated Sullivan in a tone of both concern and outrage.

"Just look at her face," said Reginell. "Look at how red her nose is."

"He was drunk, all right? He was drunk, and we were arguing," admitted Kina.

"Don't make excuses for him!" ordered Sullivan.

"I'm not. In fact, I don't . . . I don't owe any of you any explanation at all," she professed quickly. "What goes on in my house is my business."

"Not if he's hurting you or my godson," spoke up Angel. "What he's doing is against the law, which makes it all of our business."

Kina rose. "He's never laid a finger on Kenny. I won't let him."

"So, you just let him use you as his punching bag instead," filled in Sullivan.

"My God, what's happening to us?" Lawson wondered aloud. "Sullivan is sexing up some grease monkey. Reggie is letting strangers disrespect her in ways I can't even imagine.

And you, Kina, you're getting slapped around by your no-good husband, and instead of being outraged by it, you're defending him! What's wrong with you people?"

"Let she who is without sin cast the first stone!" dared Sullivan. "Are you going to stand here and berate us when you have your own mess going on with Mark?" Lawson didn't say anything. "Yeah, that's what I thought."

Angel turned to Kina. "Kina, we can help protect you. You don't have to go through this alone. I'm a nurse, and I've seen and heard it all. Believe me— you don't want to know how much worse this can get."

"Kina, think about your son," implored Lawson. "Have you even considered what this is doing to him?"

"Kenny is fine, and so are E'Bell and me," said Kina. "There isn't anything in the Bible that says I have to put my friends or cousins ahead of my husband. I know you mean well, and I love all of you for it, but there's nothing for you to worry about."

"Kina, what kind of friends would we be if we didn't get involved?" asked Angel.

"The kind Mrs. Carswell warned me about. She said that the devil would try to use people closest to me to destroy my marriage, and I see she was right."

"What?" exclaimed Sullivan. "Who is the idiot who told you that mess?"

"Mrs. Carswell is a spiritual woman of God. Obviously, you wouldn't know anything about that," snarled Kina.

"This back and forth bickering isn't getting us anywhere," said Angel. "All of your lives seem to be spinning totally out of control. Where is God in all of this? Which one of you has sought Him in the midst of all this drama? Sullivan, you're the wife of a pastor. Your husband needs you to be his helpmeet, to be praying for him and supporting him and his ministry daily. Do you know what kind of demons he has to face every day? He needs his wife to have his back, not laying on hers with some mechanic young enough to be his son. I don't even know how you can stand to look at yourself in the mirror."

"It's quite easy when you look this good," replied Sullivan. "Then again, you don't seem to having any trouble looking into yours either, despite the fact that you're scheming on another woman's husband."

"I'm not scheming on Duke!" cried Angel.

"Not yet," weighed in Sullivan. "But we all know you want to."

Lawson turned to Reginell. "And don't think you're off the hook, little sister! You've been lying to us for weeks about having some fabulous new job, knowing all the while that you're just one trick away from prostitution. Those men may be giving you their money, but they don't respect you. Most of them probably have wives and families. How would you feel if some whore was trying to tempt your husband? Is this all you think of yourself? Don't you have any self-respect left, or did you leave it all on the floor at the strip club last night?"

"I'm grown, Lawson," contended Reginell. "As much as you like to pretend you are, you're not my mother. I don't have to answer to you or anyone else."

"Does that include the Lord too?" asked Angel.

Reginell rolled her eyes and pulled out a cigarette. "It includes *you!*"

"Well, excuse me," said Angel, slighted. "Kina, I love you, but you're an adult; you're supposed to be able to take care of yourself. But Kenny? He's just a kid. You're hurting your son and doing it in the name of Jesus. Kina, that's sick!"

Lawson took over. "You have a man beating you, but you called *us* the enemy. I'm starting to think you're about as screwed up as he is!"

Sullivan jumped in. "Lawson, try not to fall off that high

horse you're riding on. What gives you the right to sit here like self-righteous Sally and condemn us when your own ledger ain't that clean? Where was all this sanctimony when you were keeping Namon from his dad and lying to Mark?" Lawson was forced into silence once again. "Yeah, you're quiet now, huh? Shoot, I'll admit I'm a heathen and a liar and an adulterer, but at least I'm not a hypocrite like you! I don't go around judging my friends and putting myself on a pedestal that I never belonged on in the first place."

"*Judge not lest ye shall be judged also*," recited Kina.

Lawson shook her head and breathed heavily. "I'm not trying to judge anybody. You guys are my family, and I love you. It hurts me to see you ruining your lives."

Kina touched Lawson's hand. "They're our lives to ruin, Lawson, not yours."

Sullivan cleared her throat. "Well, thank you, ladies, for a lovely dinner. Next time, please warn me ahead of time if condemnation is going to be served with the potato salad and cornbread." She flung her napkin on the table and marched off.

Kina pushed her plate away. "Sullivan's right. Now, if you don't mind, my husband is waiting for me. E'Bell has always said I spend too much time with y'all, and I'm starting to see his point." With that, she excused herself and left.

Reginell shook her head and quickly backed away from the table. "Uh-uh, I'm not about to be the only degenerate at the table for all of Lawson's spiritual venom to be directed at me. I'll see y'all later." Reginell made her exit as quickly as the others.

"Dang, girl, you sure know how to clear a table," observed Angel, looking around at all of the now empty seats.

"Aren't you going to leave too?" asked Lawson.

"Nope." Angel rose and sat down in Reginell's vacant seat next to Lawson. "We're going to sit here and do what we know to do."

"I don't think I even have the strength to pray right now, Angel."

"Then I'll pray. You just touch and agree." She grabbed Lawson's hand and closed her eyes.

"God, we come to you in the name of Jesus, giving you the honor that you so richly deserve. You are our strength in times of weakness, our comfort in times of strife, and our fortress in times of trouble. Lord, I come asking forgiveness for not only my sins, but the sins of those around me who love you but who have lost their way. My friends are all confused right now, Lord, but we know that that is not of you, because you came to bring about peace, and it is the devil who is the author of confusion. Help them to heed your instruction and discern your voice from that of the enemy's. Help them to turn from their ways and come back to you. Amen."

"Amen," echoed Lawson. She opened her eyes. "I needed that. Thank you."

"Lawson, we all need help sometimes, even you with your stubborn self!"

"What am I going to do about my sister? Only God knows what else she's into now. And Kina? I mean, I always felt like E'Bell wasn't good enough for her. How am I supposed to sit here and do nothing while he terrorizes her and Kenny?"

"You're doing all you can do. It's up to them. They've got to want to change their situations. All we can do is pray and be here for them."

"That's my little sister, Angel."

"Your sister is a grown woman with a mind and a will of her own."

"My friends and my sister don't even want to be in the same room as me."

"They'll come around. Don't beat yourself up over it. It's hard for people to hear the truth sometimes. Besides, have you ever known us to stay mad for more than a day?"

"Yeah, who knows what kind of trouble that crew can get into within twenty-four hours?"

Chapter 31

"Marry a man I don't love or risk losing my son."
—Lawson Kerry

Mark barged into Lawson's classroom two days before her weeklong deadline to tell Namon the truth. He pulled Lawson off to the side, interrupting her lunch with Lydia. "I need to talk to you. You already know what this is about."

"Don't manhandle me," she replied, pulling away from him. "And I'm not going to discuss *that* here."

"Is everything all right?" asked Lydia, concerned.

"No." He took a deep breath. "I apologize for coming in here and interrupting you guys like this, but I need to speak to Miss Kerry alone."

"No, you don't have to go anywhere," said Lawson and crossed her arms in front of her. "I'm sure whatever Coach Vinson has to say to me, he can say in front of you."

Mark fumed. "I need to talk to you alone, Lawson, but if you want our business all over the school, then fine with me."

Lydia rose, but seemed reluctant to move. "Is everything all right?"

"No," Lawson confessed, but the thought of her baby daddy drama being fodder for the teachers' lounge was a bit too much to swallow. "However, it's something only the two of us can work out."

Lydia took the hint. "I'll be right across the hall if you need me." She collected what was left of her lunch and ducked out of the room. Mark closed the door behind her.

"Now, what was so urgent that you had to come storming in here like a maniac?" inquired Lawson. "Poor Lydia looked like she was scared half to death."

Mark sat down on top of one of the students' desks. "I want you to know that I've come to a decision."

Lawson gave him a sideways glance. "Oh, you have?"

"Yes." He paused. "I want Namon to come live with me."

Lawson looked at him in total disbelief. "Have you lost the little piece of mind you had left? After the way you acted the other day, you'd be lucky if I let Namon come over for a *visit*. You can forget about him living with you."

"I already told you that I'm willing to take this all the way to court if you keep denying me from getting to know my son."

"Do what you have to do, Mark. You and your court threats don't scare me. My money can retain a lawyer just as quick as yours can."

"You can stand here and talk all tough, but we both know you don't want to go toe to toe with me in a courtroom. You will lose, Lawson. I can almost guarantee that."

"It's a chance I'm willing to take."

Mark hopped off of the desk. "Going to court will be grueling and expensive and will take a lot of time from us that we can be spending with Namon. If we're honest, I don't think either of us wants that; therefore, I've come up with another solution."

She rolled her eyes and muttered, "I can't wait to hear this."

"I already told you that I'm a strong believer in doing the right thing when it comes to my child, so . . ." Mark took a deep breath. "I think we need to provide Namon with the kind of stability and family that he needs right now."

"He already has that."

"No, he has a *variation* of that, but not the real thing. We need to take ourselves out of the equation and do what's best for our son." Mark sighed and calmly stated, "I think you and I should get married."

"*What?*"

"I want to be with my son; you're not going to let him live with me without you. Getting married makes the most sense. It just seems like the most logical solution."

"Mark, we can barely stand to be in the same room together as it is. Why would you even consider something like that?"

"We got along just fine before all this came out about Namon. There were actually times when I felt chemistry between us. Marriage may not be the most conventional solution in this situation, but it's the only one that can guarantee that everyone gets what they want. Being raised by both of his parents is the best scenario for our son."

"While developing this master plan, did you forget that I'm marrying Garrett?"

"He's a good guy, but he's not Namon's father, no matter how hard he tries to be."

"He's the only father Namon has ever known, and he's the man I love."

"You said yourself that you all have been together for ten years, and you ain't made it down the aisle yet. That should tell you something."

"What it *doesn't* tell me is that I need to marry you."

"Lawson, I'm not going to beg you. It's either this or I fight you for custody."

"Mark, Namon doesn't even know you, and what he does know, he doesn't like. Why don't you stop thinking about yourself for five seconds and consider his feelings?"

Mark shook his head. "Fourteen years—*fourteen years* out of his life that I'll never have again. In four years, he'll be going off to college. If I'm going to build any kind of relationship with him, all I have is now. And like it or not, the key to that happening is being married to you."

"I don't know how being trapped in a loveless marriage could possibly be what's best for Namon or for anyone else."

"It doesn't have to be loveless if we don't want it to be," said Mark.

"Mark, I'll always love Garrett. I'll never love you."

"Never say never."

Lawson rolled her eyes.

"Hey, I'm no more in love with you than you are with me, but in time, our feelings could change, and we could end up having a great marriage. More importantly, Namon would have a real family."

"He already does."

"No, he's being raised by a single parent and her boyfriend. That's not the stable environment I want my son to have."

"Please explain to me how living with a single father who also has a child with another woman is better."

"It's not. I don't want our son torn between two families, having two sets of step-parents, two homes, and two different lives. He doesn't need that. But he does need both of his parents raising him in a Christian household as man and wife. Just think about it, Lawson. When you do, you're going to see that I'm right. In your heart, you know that being raised by the two of us is better for Namon than being raised by you and Garrett."

"Garrett has been nothing but good to Namon."

"But he's not his father," repeated Mark. "I am. We can give him the family that he's never going to have with Garrett. It's either that or drag this thing out in court."

"So, those are my choices, huh? Marry a man I don't love or risk losing my son."

"The choice is yours, sweetheart," Mark said and stood eye to eye with her. "I won't settle for anything else."

Chapter 32

"God will make him stop, baby, one way or the other."
—*Kina Battle*

Kina sashayed into the apartment and planted a wet kiss on E'Bell's cheek.

He looked up from the television. "What's with you?" he asked.

"I bought you something." She handed him a workbook.

"What's this for?"

"It's a study guide for college entrance exams."

E'Bell frowned. "Why are you giving this to me?"

"I've been thinking about it. Baby, just because you didn't go to college right after high school doesn't mean that you can't go now."

"I already told you that I'm too old to play college ball."

"I'm talking about getting your degree, not touchdowns. You're interested in starting your own business, right?" He nodded. "A degree can help you get there."

He snarled, "And just who is going to pay for all this college? You know I don't make enough money to be wasting like that."

"You might qualify for a scholarship, or you could get a student loan."

"Ain't nobody gon' give me no loan, and you know that."

"It's a guaranteed student loan. Anybody who applies can get one."

"And just who is gon' pay it back?"

"That's a bridge to cross after you graduate. Besides, with your degree, you can get a better paying job and make enough to pay back the loan." She sat down next to him and opened the book. "Just look at some of the questions. They're not even that hard."

E'Bell pushed the book aside. "Kina, I ain't been in school in fifteen years. I don't remember all this stuff."

"Just try. See what comes back to you." Kina set the book in his lap. "Okay, read number one."

E'Bell stared at the page, squinting his eyes. "Man, I can't read that little bitty writing. It's making my head hurt."

"I'll read it. The first one is an analogy. *Jettison* is to *accept*, as what is to what?"

"Huh?"

"Jettison. It's a verb."

"Like a person, place, or thing?"

"No, that's a noun." She pointed to the multiple-choice options. "Which one do you think is the best answer?"

He pushed the book away again. "I told you I can't read all this small writing."

"It's not that small, E'Bell."

"So, now you gon' tell me what I can see with my own eyes?" he charged.

"No, I wasn't trying to do that, but if you can't read it—"

"I can read!" he cut in. "You think I'm stupid or something?"

She touched him. "Baby, I wasn't insinuating that you can't read or that you're stupid. I just meant that you might need glasses."

"I don't need you to tell me what I need." E'Bell flung the book across the room. "And I don't need this book either. Since you think I'm so dumb, why don't you just take your fat behind somewhere else to live?"

"E'Bell, you're not dumb—"

"I must've been to marry you."

"All I'm trying to do is help you. Why are you getting so upset?"

Kina put her arm around him, but he jerked away. "Did I ask for your help, Kina? I work at a school, and seeing one every day is more than enough for me."

"But think of what it'll do for Kenny to see both of his parents in school, still pursuing their education."

"School just ain't for everybody, and we are the kind of people who ain't got no business being in somebody's school. Now, I don't want to hear no more of this foolishness. The house ain't clean, and there ain't nothing here to eat. If you got to be around here fretting over something, fret over that, and leave me alone."

Kina stood with her head held high. "Then I'll just have to go on to school without you."

E'Bell bolted up. "What? You gon' defy me like that?"

"When it comes to this, yes, I am."

Without warning, he slapped her, and she fell down on the sofa. He pulled her up by her hair. "Don't you ever talk to me like that again, you hear me?"

"Yes," she sobbed. "E'Bell, please stop! You're hurting me!"

"I told you one time that there ain't gon' be no school!" He shoved her to the ground. "I ain't telling you that no more!"

Kina wept, curled in the fetal position on the floor. E'Bell stepped over her body and grabbed his keys. "Either you get these silly ideas about school out of your head or I'll beat them out of you!" E'Bell slammed the door shut on his way out.

Kenny tore into the living room, crying as hard as his mother. He covered her with his own body. "Mama, why did he do that to you? You said he would never hit you!"

"Go back into your room, baby. You don't need to see me like this."

Kenny wiped his mother's tears with his sleeve. "Let's just go, Mama. Let's just go someplace where he can't hurt you anymore."

Kina sat up. "My place is here, Kenny, with you and your father."

"But why?"

"Because I love him. I just want him to stop hurting me."

"Who's gonna make him stop?" wondered Kenny.

"God will make him stop, baby, one way or the other." Kina sat up and hugged her son. "He will. Just trust Him."

Chapter 33

"If a man slaps me, it's a part of the foreplay."
—*Sullivan Webb*

Sullivan looked over her shoulder from her seat on the front pew. She hadn't spoken to Lawson, Angel, or Kina since the disastrous dinner a week prior. Even if they weren't speaking to her, she still wanted to know that they were there.

"I want to thank the choir for that beautiful selection," boomed Charles's voice from the pulpit. "And like they said, just a little talk with Jesus makes it right!" The congregation shouted in agreement. Charles cleared his throat. "You know, I usually don't bring politics to the pulpit, but as most of you know, I'm running for county commissioner. The general election is next Tuesday, and I'm facing the run-off on December first against my opponent, Willie Tucker. With the election being so close, I felt compelled to come up here and tell you all what's been on my heart. Is that all right?" The "amens" and applause told him it was.

"Over the past few weeks, there's been a lot of talk around here about political agendas and campaign supporters, but there's one person who's always supported me and always had my back with absolutely no hidden agendas. She's my anchor, my rock. Honestly, without her, I don't think I would have made it this far. I want to take the opportunity right now to invite her to come up here and stand by my side as my partner in this election, as well as the rest of my life. I

love you, Sullivan. Now, bring your pretty self on up here!"
A thunderous applause erupted from the crowd. Sullivan
timidly made her way next to Charles.

"I know that I haven't given you all of the attention and
accolades you deserve, but I thank you. You've been so patient and loyal, and you've proven that I can trust you with the
thing closest to me—my heart. You've never let me down, and
you've always been honest with me, even when you thought
what you had to say might hurt or disappoint me. It's my great
honor to have you as First Lady of this church and the only
lady in my life. I just wanted to say in front of the world how
much you mean to me."

The guilt that Sullivan had so cleverly avoided for the dura-
tion of her affair with Vaughn submerged her with full force,
drowning her in lies and betrayal. She was none of those
words that Charles had used so eloquently to describe his
idea of her. She was a liar and a cheater. She was selfish, and
she didn't deserve his praise any more than she deserved to
be standing there next to him. The shame she felt was almost
crippling.

"Baby, is there anything you want to say?" He passed Sullivan the microphone.

She looked down at the smiling, eager faces, not knowing
what words would come tumbling from her lips. She cleared
her throat. "I don't know if I'm worthy of all those things you
said, but thank you." She handed the microphone back to
him.

"Aw, come on, baby, you can do better than that. We all
know you ain't shy!" The congregation laughed.

Sullivan shook her head. "No, this is your stage, Charles."

"It's our stage. Any victory I have is just as much your
victory as it is mine. None of this would be happening if you
weren't in my life."

The shame now morphed into tears that trickled down her
cheeks.

"What? What's wrong, Sully?"

She wiped her tears. "I love you, and I'm just so proud of you, that's all."

He folded her into his arms and kissed her. "I love you too, baby. Always."

"You're an even better actress than I thought," teased Lawson as she approached Sullivan following the service.

"Oh, you're speaking to me now?" she asked sarcastically.

Lawson smiled. "Who else is going to give you a kick in the pants when you need it if I don't?"

Relieved, Sullivan heartily embraced her friend. "I missed you, girl!"

"I missed your ol' crazy tail too." Lawson grabbed Sullivan's purse. "Come on. Dinner's at my house today, and don't worry about clearing it with Charles. It's already taken care of. He said for you to come and have a good time. He's tired of seeing you mope around the house pretending to be mad at us."

Anyone watching the foursome laughing and talking around Lawson's table would have never guessed that they'd spent the last seven days not speaking. After a round of apologies and a slice of Lawson's banana cream pie, all was well in the sister circle.

"So, Reggie really moved out?" asked Angel, noting her obvious absence.

"Yep, she's in the back grabbing the last of her things as we speak."

"Have you seen her new place?"

"Not yet. Things aren't quite back to normal between us," admitted Lawson.

"Well, you did call her a whore," recalled Sullivan.

"I called you one, too, but you got over it," Lawson pointed out. "I'm really worried about her. If she's stripping, there's no telling what else she's into."

"Don't be discouraged. Remember the Prodigal Son. He had his time of riotous living, but he eventually came to his senses and went back home. Reggie will do the same. She's just rebelling right now."

"I just wish she'd rebel with her clothes on!"

"You looked real pretty up on the pulpit today, Sully. I like your hair all long and wavy like that," praised Kina.

She ran her fingers through her hair. "You do? I ordered this hair from Brazil. Doubtless, those hens on the mother board will just see it as something else to criticize."

"You didn't hear anyone criticizing you today, did you?" asked Angel. "Give people a chance, Sullivan. Not everyone is out to get you."

"I thought Pastor gave a wonderful speech." Lawson swallowed a mouthful of salad. "You should've felt like crap, Sully."

"I did. Still do. I'm thinking about coming clean, just telling Charles everything."

Angel looked up. "Why would you do that? Is Vaughn blackmailing you?"

"No, I'm emotionally blackmailing myself. The guilt is killing me. You heard him going on about me in front of all those people. I felt like such a hypocrite."

"What happened to all that big talk you were doing about being able to handle the situation?" jeered Lawson.

"I thought I could! Who knew Charles would start acting like a real husband?"

"Seeing as how I have a little experience in this area, I think you should tell him," Angel suggested, "but only if it's for the right reasons. Telling him to absolve yourself of your guilt is wrong and selfish. Plus, I'm not wholly convinced that you're going to stop sleeping with Vaughn."

"I will . . ." asserted Sullivan, "soon."

"What happened to all the good guilt and remorse you had five seconds ago?" asked Lawson.

"It was there until I thought about him kissing me . . . and nibbling on my ear . . . and that hurricane tongue . . ."

"Eww—T.M.I!" cried Angel. "I think I just threw up in my mouth a little bit."

Sullivan patted Angel on the back. "I'm sorry. I forgot you haven't had sex this millennium."

"Sully, how many times must we tell you how wrong this is?" chided Kina. "You heard your husband today. Anybody can see how much he loves you. This'll crush him."

"Why even risk him finding out and getting hurt?" asked Kina. "Just leave Vaughn alone."

Lawson poured the tea. "Aren't you taking an even greater risk staying married to Mike Tyson?"

"E'Bell hasn't laid a hand on me since that day in the parking lot," Kina fibbed.

"That doesn't mean he won't again. I don't trust him, and neither should you—not until he gets help," added Angel.

"He's never hitting me again. He promised."

"So, Sully promised to be faithful, and we see how well that's worked out!" said Lawson.

Sullivan shook her head. "Don't even think about comparing me to that ogre E'Bell. If a man slaps me, it's a part of the foreplay, and it's never on my face."

Angel closed her eyes and balled her fists for emphasis. "Again, Sully, *T.M.I!*"

"None of us want to see you or Kenny hurt, Kina. I pray for you and your safety every single night. My prayers won't amount to a hill of beans, though, if you don't remove yourself from this dangerous situation," Lawson warned her. "As a teacher, it's my obligation to report it if he's hitting Kenny."

"There is no dangerous situation! E'Bell and I are fine. We're doing better now than ever. Things are going so well that not only is he okay with me going back to school, he's even decided to join me. Lawson, you'd be doing us a huge favor if you'd lend E'Bell some old textbooks. He needs them to brush up before he takes his entrance exams." Kina was surprised and impressed with how adeptly she could lie.

Lawson was shocked. "Really?"

"You all were wrong about E'Bell. He really does love me and Kenny. He just lost his cool that day, but we're putting it behind us. I wish you would too."

"I will give him the benefit of the doubt for your sake," said Angel. "I still think he needs help. You both do."

Kina quickly changed the subject. "So, what's going on with you and Mark, Lawson? You haven't said much about him lately."

Lawson pushed her food around her plate. "What's there to say other than that Mark has lost his mind?"

Angel sliced her chicken. "Uh-oh. What did he do now?"

"Oh, this one's a doozy!" Lawson wiped her hands. "He asked me to marry him! He claims that he wants to give Namon a family."

"And give you a reason to kill him!" added Sullivan. "What is he thinking?"

"He's thinking about his son," filled in Kina. "I can't really say I blame him."

Angel turned to Lawson. "You're not considering his proposal, are you?"

"No . . . not really," Lawson replied slowly.

"*Not really?*" echoed Sullivan.

"He brought up some good points," granted Lawson. "I mean, he is Namon's father, and he deserves to be a part of his life."

"What about Garrett?" asked Angel.

"I haven't really told him about the proposal yet," Lawson confessed. "You know he's already anxious about us getting married. If I tell him this, it'll confirm his belief that I've been holding out for someone better. I'm probably going to turn down Mark's proposal anyway, so why upset Garrett unnecessarily?"

"Because you're using words like *probably* to say whether or not you're going to accept another man's proposal!" replied Sullivan.

"Ladies, you know that I have every intention of being Garrett's wife; however, if letting Mark think that I'm considering his proposal will keep him off my back and out of my son's life for the time being, I'll tell him whatever it is that he wants to hear."

Angel dug her fork into the pasta salad. "That's a mighty big risk you're taking, Lawson, and a very dangerous game to play."

"There's no game. I'm just letting Mark think what he wants to think."

"But you're deceiving Garrett while you're at it," said Kina. "He's going to feel like you betrayed him when he finds out."

Lawson raised her glass. "Then here's to men not finding out!"

"Amen!" agreed Sullivan. They clanked their glasses together.

Angel raised hers. "And here's to God having mercy when they do!"

Chapter 34

"Instead of us sharing him, we may have both just lost him."
—*Lawson Kerry*

As Lawson, Sullivan, Angel, and Kina chatted in the living room over dinner, Reginell snatched her clothes from the closet and replayed her sister's censuring in her head. "Who does she think she is, talking to me like that?" grunted Reginell as she flung the last of her belongings into a box. "She thinks she's better than somebody, but you've got skeletons, too, Lawson!" she said, raising her voice loud enough for Lawson to hear.

Lawson knocked on the door then opened it. "We're headed to the park to watch Namon and Garrett play football. Lock up when you leave." She closed the door without further conversation.

Reginell heard the front door open, and the ladies' laughter as they filed out. "Good riddance!" she called after them. The fact that they didn't invite her to tag along perturbed Reginell even more.

As Reginell secured her boxes with tape, the doorbell rang. She opened it and found Mark standing before her.

"Hi. It's Reggie, right?" he asked.

"Yes. How are you doing, Mark?"

"I'd be doing a lot better if I could see my son. Is Lawson home?"

"No, she left. Namon's with her. Did she know you were coming?"

"I told her that I was giving her a week to tell Namon the truth. She knows that her time is up." Mark shook his head. "I was really hoping to see Namon today. It's been driving me crazy knowing that I've got a kid ten miles from my house who doesn't even know I'm alive."

Reginell empathized with him. "I can imagine. Just so you know, Mark, I'm on your side in this. I told Lawson she is wrong for keeping you from your son."

"I appreciate that." Mark smiled. "It's good to know that at least one family member agrees with me."

"I'm on your side. So is my cousin, Kina. It's cold out here. Why don't you come in for a minute?" She let him into the house.

"Thank you." Mark seemed genuinely humbled by Reginell's support. "Please keep talking to Lawson on my behalf. Although, after our conversation the other day, I think she may be coming around."

Reginell sat down. "Really? What happened?"

"I asked her to marry me. I think it's what's best for our son. I think she's considering it."

Reginell thought about what she'd overheard Lawson saying during dinner and rolled her eyes. "I wouldn't get my hopes up if I were you."

"Why not?"

"Because she's playing you. Lawson is not the good girl she tries to come off as. She can be very mean-spirited and hurtful. She plans to string you along with this marriage thing as long as she can. She has no intention of breaking up with Garrett or marrying you. Lawson just wants to keep you quiet so you won't blow her cover to Namon. She was talking and laughing about it with her friends ten minutes ago."

Mark stroked his face, taking in the disclosure. "So, Lawson thinks she can make a fool out of me, huh?"

"Yes," replied Reginell, "unless you plan to show her differently. Don't let her get away with this, Mark."

Mark pressed his lips together and stood up. "Thank you for being honest."

"It was the right thing to do. Lawson can't get away with hurting people."

"Do you happen to know where she is now?"

"She's at the park. Namon, too."

Mark stalked off, and Reginell smiled to herself. "Now we'll see who has the last word, Lawson."

"*Go long!*" cheered Lawson as Namon sprinted across the field with Garrett tailing him. "*Whoo-hoo!*"

Sullivan laughed. "Ol' Garrett is showing his age out there."

"You leave my baby alone!" teased Lawson.

"You talking to me?" asked a male voice behind her.

Lawson turned out, stunned to see Mark. "What are you doing here?"

"I should be asking you that. Just what *do* you think you're doing, Lawson?"

Lawson shook her head. "Mark, you should leave. This isn't a good time."

Mark stood firm. "Your time is up. I want to see my son, and I want to see him now."

Sullivan came to Lawson's aid. "Is this clown giving you a hard time?" She turned to Mark. "If you're here to cause trouble for Lawson and Namon, you've got to go through me first!"

"How did you even know we were here?" fired Lawson. "Are you stalking me?"

Mark shook his head. "I have better things to do with my time than that. Now, you can bring Namon to me, or I can just go out on the field and get him."

Lawson anchored her hands to her hips. "I won't be bossed around, Mark."

"And I won't be strung along, Lawson! Now, I've done everything you asked me to do. I kept my distance; I gave you a chance to break the news in your own way, but you refuse to hold up your end. Now it's time to do it my way."

Angel scampered off of the bleachers and over to Mark, Lawson, and Sullivan. "Don't look now, but Garrett and Namon are coming over," she mumbled, watching them cut across the field.

Lawson panicked. "Mark, please don't say anything to him," she pleaded. "I promise you, we'll sit down and do this the right way, but not today, not like this."

Mark shook his head. "I'm through playing by your rules, Lawson. Namon is going to find out right now who his real father is."

"Will you stop being such a jerk?" fired Sullivan. "Think of Namon! You're so selfish. The objective is to do what's best for him, not what's best for you."

"That's what I'm trying to do," answered Mark. "Lawson, have you thought any more about my proposal?"

Lawson sighed. "Yes, of course."

Lawson cut her eyes to Sullivan, who knew full well that she was lying.

"Getting married might not be such a bad idea, but you can't expect me to just run off and leave Garrett in the wind. He deserves better than that."

"He deserves to know the truth," said Mark.

Garrett approached Mark with Namon at his side. "Are you harassing Lawson *again*?"

"This isn't harassment," he reported. "You know why I'm here. You both do."

Garrett exhaled. "This isn't the time or the place."

Mark fumed. "You know, I'm tired of all you people trying

to dictate to me when and where I see my son. That stops right now!" He moved toward Namon.

Lawson reached out for him. "*Mark, no!*"

"Namon," began Mark, placing his hands on Namon's shoulders. "Do you remember me?"

Namon shirked away from him. "Yeah, you were the one yelling at my mom."

Mark nodded. "Well, we were arguing about you."

He frowned. "Why?"

Mark glanced over at Lawson before going on. "Because I wanted to see you, I wanted to spend time with you. You see, Namon . . . I'm your dad. You're my son."

Namon's expression changed. He shook his head and sidled close to Lawson. "You ain't my daddy!" he spat. "Mama, why is he saying that?"

"Because he is, baby," confirmed Lawson, squeezing Namon's hand as her tear ducts began to rupture. "Mark is your biological father." Garrett wrapped his arms around her.

Mark extended his arms. "Namon, I'm your father. I've been waiting all this time to tell you that, to hold my son."

Namon shunned him. "Garrett's my daddy. I don't even know you."

"We can get to know each other, starting today," offered Mark.

Namon snarled and asked, "If you're my daddy, where have you been all this time? Why are you coming around now? Why didn't you just stay gone?"

"Son, I didn't know. I hadn't seen your mother since we were kids. If I'd known about you, I would have been in your life from day one." Mark turned to Lawson. "Lawson, tell him."

Lawson stepped forward. "He's right, Namon. He never knew I was pregnant with you. He didn't even know you existed until a few weeks ago."

"I tried to tell you when I came over," explained Mark. "Your mother didn't feel like it was the right time, though."

Namon looked at Lawson. "So, you lied to me, Mama?" He dropped her hand.

Sullivan stepped in. "She was trying to protect you, honey. She didn't want to just spring this on you."

"So, all of y'all knew and nobody told me?" asked Namon. "You knew too, Garrett, and you didn't tell me?" A flash of sadness broke in his eyes.

"This is why I wanted to prepare him," Lawson uttered to Mark. She faced her son. "Sweetie, I know what a shock this must be to you, but it doesn't change anything. I'm still your mom. Garrett still loves you just the same. Mark just wants a chance to get to know you too. Maybe it wouldn't be so bad if you got to know him."

Mark kneeled down beside him. "Your mom and I have been talking about a way to make that happen and to make things easier on you." He hesitated. "We've been talking about getting married, so we can raise you together as a family."

Garrett broke away from Lawson. "*What?* Baby, what is he talking about?"

Angel and Kina dropped their heads.

"Mark, it's not your place to say anything!" admonished Lawson.

"It's obvious that you weren't going to," retorted Garrett. "Is all this true?"

"Garrett, I can explain," stammered Lawson, "but not right now. Our focus needs to be on Namon. There's nothing between me and Mark that you need to worry about."

Mark joined Lawson at her side. "I asked her to marry me, and she's thinking it over. It's what's best for our son."

Garrett glared at Lawson. "When were you going to mention this to me?"

Angel mediated. "Can we just keep our attention on Namon? This is about him. You can sort out all this other stuff later."

"She's right," agreed Mark. "This is about our family—Lawson, me, and Namon."

Garrett sidestepped Lawson. "Obviously, this is a *family* matter, and I'm not part of that equation. Excuse me."

"Garrett, don't leave like this," entreated Lawson. "You *are* my family! You're the only father Namon's ever known."

Garrett turned around. "Have you really been discussing marriage with this guy?"

"We've done more than *discussed* it," bragged Mark. "We've picked out the dress, even practiced the first dance."

Lawson was flustered. "It wasn't like that, Mark, and you know it! Garrett, don't listen to him. Let's just go home. You, me, and Namon can go home and figure this out together. We're solid. Don't let Mark make you question that."

"If that was true, Lawson, you would've been straight with me about what's going on. You've been talking marriage with him and ain't said one word to me about it! What does this say about our relationship? What does that tell me about you?"

Garrett went to Namon. "You know I love you, and I'll always be here whenever you need me, but you've got your real father now."

"I want to go with you," Namon told him. "I want *you* to be my dad. I don't want him!"

Garrett hugged him. "You just need to get to know him, that's all." He released Namon. "I'll see you around."

Garrett turned to walk away. Lawson gripped his sleeve. "Garrett, don't go!" He broke her hold on him and kept walking.

"Shh, just let him cool off," advised Sullivan, draping her arm about Lawson. "He feels betrayed right now, but he'll be back."

Mark approached his son. "Namon, if it's all right with you and your mom, I'd love to take you somewhere to eat and we can start getting to know one another."

"No, it's not all right with me!" screamed Lawson. "Why don't you get out of here? Go home, Mark. You've done enough damage for one day!"

"You can't keep him away from me! I'm his father!" yelled Mark.

Namon shot back, "No, you're not, and you never will be." He ran to catch up with Garrett.

"Namon!" called Lawson. He ignored her.

"I'll go after him," said Mark.

Lawson held him back. "No, that's the *last* thing he needs. I'll go."

"No, Lawson, you stay here and get this straightened out with Mark. I'll check on Namon and Garrett," offered Angel. She raced to catch up with the two of them.

Lawson pounded Mark in the chest and shoved him. "What were you thinking?"

"How could you be so stupid, Mark?" asked Sullivan. "Do you think he's going to want anything to do with you now?"

Mark defended his actions. "All I wanted was a chance to know my son."

"Then what was the point of blabbing to Garrett about the proposal? You lied to him. You knew that I didn't pick that dress to wear for you. That was plain cruel."

Mark pointed to himself. "*I'm cruel?* Weren't you just laughing it up with your friends about how big of a sucker you think I am and how you were going to string me along until you got what you wanted?"

Lawson was livid. "What have you been doing, Mark, eavesdropping? Lurking around my house so you could listen to my conversations?"

"No, a reliable source told me."

"What source?" Lawson shook her head and exhaled. "It was Reggie, wasn't it? Of course it was. She's the only other person who could've told you that. My sister really played you. She used you, Mark, to get back at me, and you walked right into it."

"That's the same thing she says about you."

"If you had been patient, none of this would be happening right now."

"*Patient?* It's been fourteen years! If you had been more concerned about your son than your boyfriend's ego, it wouldn't have come down to this!"

"Don't you dare mention Garrett! And if I lose him over this stunt you just pulled, I swear to God—"

"Both of you just chill out," issued Kina. "The most important thing is making sure that Namon's okay. The two of you going at it like this isn't going to help anybody."

"She's right," agreed Sullivan. "You're in it together now. You're stuck with each other, so you might as well find a way to make it work."

Angel returned. "Garrett is taking Namon back home. He said he'll wait there with him until you come back."

Lawson hugged her. "Thank you, Angel. How did Namon seem to you?"

"He's confused, but he's a tough kid. He'll be okay," Angel replied.

"And Garrett?"

Angel sighed. "I don't know . . . I don't know if he can get past this," she admitted.

Lawson glared at Mark. "Are you happy now? Is this what you wanted?"

"All I wanted was for my son to know who I was."

"Well, you got what you wanted, didn't you, Mark? Now, instead of us sharing him, we may have both just lost him."

Chapter 35

"You couldn't come to this conclusion before we had sex?"
—*Sullivan Webb*

Sullivan fell back on the bed. "You sure know how to put a smile on a girl's face."

Vaughn reached into his nightstand and pulled out a pack of cigarettes. "You want one?" he asked as he and Sullivan lay sprawled across his bed while Charles beat the campaign trail.

"I haven't smoked since I was about eighteen."

He passed her a cigarette and lit it. "Here's to being eighteen again."

"So, tell me, Vaughn, why don't you have a girlfriend?" she asked him, exhaling the smoke.

"I have a few friends who I kick it with every now and then."

"Are they friends or lovers?"

"Both, I guess," he replied casually. "We have sex sometimes, but we're still friends."

She blinked. "Just like that—you sleep with all your female friends?"

"Not all of them, but for the ones who are down, we all know what we want, we get it, and that's that."

"What about love and commitment?"

"What about it?"

"What's making love without that?"

"We're not talking about making love; we're talking about sex."

"How can you be intimate with someone and not feel anything for the person?"

"I'm pretty much a loner. I don't have time to get caught up in relationship drama. I'd rather just get in the studio and do my own thing. I don't need a lot of people around me to do what I do. In fact, people get in the way of my creativity."

She sat up. "What about what just happened between us? Am I just sex too?"

"You have a man, and you make love to him. We have sex. That's all you should want it to be."

"Is that all *you* want it to be?"

He blew out a ring of smoke and closed his eyes. "You think too much and ask too many questions."

"Are you afraid of the answer?"

"Nope."

"Then why are you avoiding the question?"

"I'm not avoiding the question; I'm avoiding the consequences of answering it."

"Why?"

He seemed annoyed. "Because it's a messed-up question. There is no right answer. If I say I'm just sleeping with you, you'll get offended and start acting all hurt. If I say I want more, it puts you in a difficult position with your marriage."

"The fact that you care so much about how I might react says a lot."

"Don't read too much into that. I care more about how your reaction will affect me than how it affects you. I don't want to say or do anything that might trigger a stalker or a violent reaction from you, that's all."

"Whatever, Vaughn." She ground up the cigarette and turned over in bed.

Vaughn glanced over at her. "Hey, don't get too comfortable over there."

"I told you that Charles wouldn't be home tonight."

"I don't let women sleep over at my place. It sends the wrong message." Vaughn rose and slid into his boxer shorts. "It's time for you to bounce."

"We're still in afterglow here."

"Afterglow is for couples. You and I just have sex."

Someone knocked on the door. "Are you expecting company?" grilled Sullivan. "Is that why you're in such a hurry for me to leave?"

Vaughn grumbled something inaudible and opened the door to an over-zealous campaign aide who thrust a flier in Vaughn's face.

"A vote for Willie Tucker is a vote for equality," he sang, peering into the studio apartment, giving him a clear view of everything inside, including Sullivan.

Vaughn balled it up and tossed it over the railing. "Nah, man, I ain't interested."

"Perhaps if you have a few minutes, I can change your mind, and together we can make sure that William Tucker gets re-elected for another term."

"Did you hear what I said?" asked Vaughn in a cool but threatening tone.

The aide nodded, taking the hint. "Thank you for your time. Have a nice day, sir." Vaughn slammed the door shut.

"I guess he won't be counting on your vote," joked Sullivan.

"That li'l dude's been coming around here every day, nonstop," griped Vaughn.

"I must say, Charles is doing better than I thought he would. He's got Slick Willie running scared."

"Got to be for them to be coming to this neighborhood." Vaughn turned to face her. "You ought to go on and get out of here. They might come back around, and they don't need to see you laying up in my bed."

Sullivan buttoned her blouse. "Yeah, you never know who Tucker has got on payroll snooping around here."

Vaughn grabbed a beer out of his refrigerator. "I think maybe we ought to just chill out for a while."

"What?" exclaimed Sullivan. "Why?"

"It's been cool, but I don't think we need to do this anymore. Do *us*, I mean. It's getting hot, and I told you I don't do drama."

"You couldn't come to this conclusion *before* we had sex?"

"Why are you trippin'? You got what you came for. It ain't like this was some romance type of thing."

"Then what was it?"

He shrugged. "You had an itch, and I scratched it."

"So, I violated my vows, risked my marriage, and broke enough commandments to earn me a cozy little corner in hell because you thought I had an *itch*?" posed Sullivan as she wriggled into the rest of her clothes.

"It is what it is." Vaughn clicked on the television with the remote and crawled back into bed.

"How can you lie there and act like what we had was nothing?" she demanded.

"What are you talking about?" Vaughn seemed genuinely perplexed. "We looked at a few paintings, we shared a couple of laughs, and we had sex. That's all it was. What more was there supposed to be?"

"Feelings!" she blurted out.

"Sullivan, let's be real. You're not going to leave your million-dollar mansion to come be with me, and I don't intend to give up my lifestyle to please you."

"That's not the point!" she contended. "I thought we had something special."

"I'll put it to you like this." Vaughn took a pull from his cigarette. "In my business, some cars are loaners; some are keepers. I always saw you more like a loaner."

"A *what?*" That's when the reality hit Sullivan like a ton of bricks. For the first time since she spotted Vaughn in the garage, she saw him for who he truly was. More importantly, she saw herself for what she had been. She and Vaughn weren't kindred spirits; they weren't even friends. She finally understood what it was like to be used.

"I am such a fool," surmised Sullivan. "All this time, I thought you were some force that had come into my life to restore all of the excitement that I was missing with Charles. But you're none of those things. You're an immature, self-indulgent kid who knows nothing about life outside of this dingy apartment or that rusty garage."

Vaughn adjusted the volume on the television. "Lock the door on your way out."

Sullivan couldn't believe that she'd been played . . . by a twenty-three-year-old . . . a twenty-three-year-old mechanic . . . whose whole apartment could fit into her bathroom with room to spare. More specifically, she had allowed the devil to enter into her life and take control over her mind, body, and spirit.

It was the longest drive home she had ever traveled.

Chapter 36

"The truth can change your whole world in an instant."
—Kina Battle

"Here are the books you wanted," said Lawson, unloading various textbooks into Kina's arms. "Just try to keep up with them. I need them back. The school doesn't know that I borrowed them yet."

Kina returned the books to Lawson. "I don't need them anymore. E'Bell doesn't want to go back to school, so he doesn't need to take the entrance exam."

"Why not?"

Kina shrugged and let Lawson into the house. "He says he's too old to try."

"That's nonsense! We're practically the same age, and I just finished school myself. Heck, half the people in class with me were over thirty."

"Lawson, you know E'Bell. He's got all that pride and doesn't like to look stupid in front of anyone. Between you and me, I think he's ashamed."

"What is he ashamed of?"

"Needing glasses. I tried to study with him the other night, and he couldn't read the print. It made him frustrated, and he didn't want to try anymore."

"I've never known E'Bell to have vision problems."

"Me either. I think it's just when he reads. He does everything else just fine."

"If he's that self-conscious about wearing glasses, he can just get contacts. There's no need to forgo his education over something as minor as that."

"It's not just that, Lawson. It's something about school *period*."

Thoughts began to churn in Lawson's mind. "What kind of student was E'Bell when we were in school?"

"Average, I guess. He clowned around in class and slept a lot. He never wanted to do any of his work, and I usually ended up having to do it for him. He hated going to class, especially English. All he wanted to do was go to lunch, P.E., and football practice. I guess you get a lot of kids like that."

"Does he ever read around the house? Magazines, the newspaper, the Internet?"

"E'Bell reading?" Kina laughed. "You can't pay that man to pick up a book."

"He doesn't even read the sports pages as much as he loves football?"

"He gets all his scores and highlights from TV, so he doesn't have to."

Lawson took mental notes. "What about helping Kenny with his homework or reading to him? Does he do that?"

"He leaves all that to me. I told you—he hates anything having to do with school. It's probably because he has to work in one."

"I guess he doesn't read the Bible much either, huh?"

"I try to encourage him to; he says he'll wait for the movie."

Lawson took a deep breath. "Kina, have you ever considered . . ." She exhaled and shook her head. "There's no easy way to say this, but E'Bell is exhibiting all of the signs. Sweetie, it sounds like E'Bell can't read."

"That's impossible. I mean, we all went to school together; we saw him graduate. I know that he was never an honors student, but he did enough to get by."

"E'Bell was a jock, and a lot of teachers feel pressured to pass the athletes. I see it every day at work."

"Lawson, no one can go to school twelve years and not know how to read. I just don't see it. Besides, I live with the man. I think I would know if he couldn't read."

"He might be functionally literate, reading at maybe a second or third grade level. Between teachers who are burnt out or don't care and pressure from the coaches, it's very easy for someone like E'Bell to skate through high school without knowing how to read."

Kina shook her head. "I just don't believe that."

"Think about it, Kina. You admitted that he never reads to Kenny or picks up a newspaper. Have you ever seen him reading anything around the house?"

"I'm the bookworm in the family. He'd rather watch TV or play video games."

"The more I think about it, the more it makes sense. It would certainly explain why he never went to college."

"He did that for me, to help me raise our son."

"He could've gone to school locally and still been a father to his son and a husband to you. Look at the kinds of jobs he's had since graduating. There was his job as a fry-cook, his pizza-delivery gig, and now his job cleaning up at the high school—all low-level positions that require minimal education and no reading. He's never been promoted or been given any responsibility that will require him to read or to write."

"Lawson, you know you can't get a good job without going to college these days," rationalized Kina.

"There are still lots of jobs he can get without a degree, but the decent ones will demand that he read or write at some point, so he shies away from those."

"I hear what you're saying, but I know my husband, and I know he can read. He just doesn't like to."

"Kina, do you know how many classes and programs there

are out there to help him become literate? Most are free and accommodating to his work schedule. There's help out there for him, and he doesn't have to be ashamed. Neither do you."

Kina collapsed onto the sofa. "Lawson, you don't understand. Everything I've put up with and gone through has been because I thought E'Bell gave up his life's dream for me and Kenny. If it turns he never had a shot at that dream in the first place . . ."

"I don't want to upset you, Kina. Don't jump to any conclusions without getting all the information. Talk to E'Bell. Talk to some of his old teachers. Do whatever you have to in order to get to the truth."

"Okay, so I find out the truth. Then what?" Kina lifted her eyes toward Lawson, desperate for answers. "Do I confront E'Bell with it? Do I leave, or get him the help he needs? How can I forgive him if he's been lying to me for all these years? Do I even have a right to be mad at him for not knowing how to read?"

"Kina, I can't tell you what to do other than to pray for the strength to face whatever comes next. I know that if it were me, I'd want to know the truth. Learn from my mistakes with Mark. The truth always comes to light whether we like it or not."

"It's scary, you know? The truth can change your whole world in an instant."

"I know, but you have to ask yourself what's scarier: finding out the truth or living a lie."

Chapter 37

"What's done is done. Just don't do it again."
–*Lawson Kerry*

"I didn't think you'd have the nerve to show your face around here after that stunt you pulled," directed Sullivan to Reginell as she and the other ladies collected donations for the church's holiday toy drive.

Reginell smacked her lips. "Hey, if you don't want these—"

"We *do* want them, okay?" assured Angel, taking the two shopping bags of toys from Reginell's hands. "We thank you, and so do the children of Chatham County."

"We just want to know which one of your faces is gracing us with your presence today, considering that you have so many," added Sullivan.

Reginell rolled her eyes. "I'm out!"

"No, you're not," said Kina, dragging her by the arm. "We need to talk about this."

"We all know what you did," muttered Sullivan.

Lawson glared at Sullivan. "What she means is Mark showed up unexpectedly at the park last week, and we thought you might have some insight as to how that happened. You were gone when I got home that day, and you haven't exactly made yourself available for answers since then."

"No mystery there. I told him," boasted Reginell.

Sullivan boxed up some toys. "Why would you send him after Namon and Lawson like that? Didn't you know he was gonna blab everything?"

Reginell crossed her arms. "Yes, that was the point."

Lawson's mouth gaped open. "Reggie, why would you want to hurt me like that? I'm your sister."

"What's the difference between me hurting you and you hurting me? Did you forget how mean you were and all the names you called me the other day?"

"I wasn't trying to be mean," Lawson clarified. "I was trying to knock some sense into that thick head of yours. What you did was out of pure malice. Not only did you hurt me, but you hurt Namon and Garrett too."

Reginell felt a twinge of guilt. "So, Namon knows?"

"Yes, and he was devastated," broke in Sullivan. "Now Garrett doesn't want anything to do with her because Mark made it seem like the two of them had something going on."

Reginell gasped. "Garrett dumped you? Lawson, I'm so sorry. I didn't think he—"

"You didn't think *period*," threw in Angel.

"Guys, can you keep it down?" whispered Kina as more people came in to drop off gifts.

"Well, how's Namon now?" asked Reginell.

Lawson shook her head. "He's quiet, confused. I mean, here's a man that Namon has no connection to claiming to be his father, and the man that he knows as his dad has moved on."

"Lawson, I can't tell you how sorry I am. I just wanted you to know how it felt to have your own blood turn on you. I had no idea it would lead to this."

Lawson shrugged. "Well, what's done is done. Just don't do it again."

"At least let me talk to Garrett," offered Reginell. "Let me help get the two of you back together."

"I'm afraid that boat may have sailed," concluded Lawson.

"You can't give up, sis. Garrett loves you, and you love him. He's a great guy. Believe me, there aren't too many of those around. You have to fight for him."

Lawson patted Reginell's hand. "We'll see. Either way, I don't want you getting involved. It's not your fault I wasn't completely honest with Garrett. It was mine. If the Lord wants us to be together, I have to trust that it'll happen."

Kina cut wrapping paper along the edge of a board game. "So, Reggie, when are you going to let us check out your new digs? It's never too soon to have your first visitor."

"You can come by anytime you want, although technically you won't be my first visitor."

"Just who was that honor bestowed upon?" teased Angel.

Reginell smiled. "Just this guy who's been hanging around."

"Hanging around the strip club?" asked Angel.

"No, hanging around me. He's sweet, but he's not really my type."

"Are you sure?" grilled Lawson. "That twinkle in your eye says differently."

Kina creased the paper. "What's his name?"

"Jody Blash. He's a barber. He owns a couple of shops in town."

"Oh, he's an entrepreneur," mused Sullivan. "I see you've learned a thing or two from me after all."

Angel cleared her throat. "Does he know about the, um, *dancing?*"

"Call it what it is, Angel," exclaimed Lawson. "Does he know you're *stripping?*"

"Yes, he does," said Reginell in a huff. "And unlike you people, he also realizes that it's just a means to an end, not a long-term career move."

Lawson exhaled. "I'm still not happy about you working there. I've gotten into my car more than once to go over to that strip club and drag you out of there kicking and screaming if I had to."

"I hope you don't humiliate me that way, Lawson. Don't

forget that I'm old enough to make my own decisions, and this is what I've decided to do for now."

"I know you say he's fine now, but how comfortable is Jody going to be with you stripping if the two of you get serious?" posed Angel.

"He's not judgmental like that," replied Reginell.

"Can we refrain from all the pole talk while we're working for the Lord?" asked Kina.

"While we're on the subject of things we shouldn't do," jeered Sullivan, "what's up with you and Mr. King?"

Angel raised an eyebrow. "There's nothing up with me and Duke. I'm his wife's nurse. That's as far as it goes."

Sullivan snickered. "Nobody said you couldn't be a nurse to Theresa while playing doctor with Duke."

Angel adhered a bow to a gift-wrapped box. "Obviously, I have more respect for marriage than you do."

"Marriage-smarriage!" cried Sullivan. "You had him first. You broke him in. It's only fair that you get to ride him—pun intended."

"Next subject please," Angel deadpanned.

"Have any of you checked out that new restaurant that just opened on River Street?" asked Lawson.

Angel poured Reginell's gifts out onto the floor for wrapping. "No, but I heard they have an excellent salad bar. We should check them out for lunch, Kina."

"Okay, but let's not go Monday. I have to go up to the high school during my break."

Sullivan grimaced. "Are you still bringing E'Bell his lunch every day like clockwork? Kina, you're better than any trained puppy I've ever seen in my life!"

Kina appeared shocked. "Don't you do that for Charles?"

Sullivan gave her a sideways glance. "Kina, don't make me cuss you out in the middle of this vestibule."

"Well, anyway, I'm not really going to see E'Bell. I wanted to visit one of my old teachers."

Angel smirked. "Take a picture for Lawson so she can see what she's going to look like in a couple of years."

Lawson sidled up to Kina and spoke low enough so that no one else could hear. "I think you're doing the right thing."

Kina nodded. "I decided that the only thing worse than knowing is not knowing."

"Well, you know I'll be here for you if the news isn't good. Together, maybe we can get E'Bell the help he needs."

Kina smiled, but her smile hid the fear of her wondering if she would have the help *she* needed once she confronted E'Bell with the truth.

Chapter 38

"You'd be amazed at what you can do when you let go and let God."
—*Angel King*

Theresa was sitting up in the bed with a beautiful array of yellow roses sprouting out from the vase on the nightstand next her.

"How are you feeling?" asked Angel.

"I'm okay— just happy to be able to see another day."

"I think we're all happy for that." She began taking Theresa's vital signs. "Those are beautiful," she noted, nodding toward the roses. "Where did you find roses this time of year? It's Poinsettia season."

"Duke got them for me this morning. You'll have to ask him where."

"That was sweet of him." She released Theresa's arm after taking her blood pressure.

"Duke bought them because I asked him to. They're not for me; they're for you."

Angel checked Theresa's pulse. "For me? Why?"

"Angel, you've been a lifesaver for me and my family. Sometimes I really do believe you are my guardian angel."

"Don't exalt me to sainthood yet. My wings are as crooked as everybody else's."

Theresa shook her head. "I don't think so. Most women couldn't have done what you've done for me, not even the ones who profess to be Christians."

"It's been a struggle, but you'd be amazed at what you can do when you let go and let God."

"I thank Him for you every day. I really do. I don't know what we would've done without you, especially the girls. I've seen the way you are with them. They love you so much. They're going to need your strength after I'm gone."

She squeezed Theresa's hand. "You know I'll always be there for them."

Theresa raised her eyes. "Duke is going to need you too."

Angel thought about her feelings for him and tried her best to mask her uneasiness. "Duke will be fine."

"Angel, you know him as well as I do. The whole macho thing is all an act. I know he thinks he's being strong for me, but I worry about him. I know he's not as tough as he pretends to be."

"I'll look after him too. I promise."

"Do you still love him?"

Angel looked away.

"It's all right. You can tell me if you do."

Angel sighed and sat down next to her. "I guess a part of me always will."

Theresa smiled. "It's okay to love him, you know."

Angel shook her head. "No, it's not. He's your husband."

"He was yours too."

"Okay, this is a little awkward for me, so why don't I go and let you rest." Angel rose. "I'll come back and check on you in a bit."

"No, I want you to stay. Please, sit back down."

Angel sat down in a chair beside the bed.

"Do you know why I asked Duke to get those roses specifically? Because they're yellow, and yellow roses represent friendship. Despite our colorful history, I'd like to think that we're friends now."

"Of course we are."

"Then as a friend, I would like for you to do something for me."

"Anything. Just name it."

"I want you to look after my girls when I'm gone. I don't mean a phone call every few weeks and a gift at Christmas. I want you to be a part of their lives."

"Theresa, I told you I would."

"No, I mean . . . I want you to adopt them. I want you and Duke to raise them together."

Angel blinked her eyes, stunned into silence for a moment. "You want me to what?"

"I want you and Duke to raise the girls together, to be a family. Angel, my family is the most precious thing in the world to me. You're the only one I trust enough to ask to do this. I know that you'll love them and take care of them the way I would. I know that you'd be an excellent role model for my daughters, and I know that you can make Duke happy."

Angel shook her head. "No one can make Duke as happy as you do. Any ties he had to me ended a long time ago, and I know I could never replace you in your daughters' hearts. I don't even want to try."

"It's not about replacing me. It's about making sure that Duke and the girls don't miss out on life because I'm not here. You've always wanted a family, Angel. You told me so yourself. This can be the family you never had."

"Theresa, I can't just come in and claim your family as my own. It's not right."

"You'd be honoring my memory. It would give me so much peace to know that my guardian angel was watching over the ones I love the most, and I want to be able to die in peace. Besides, you would be the perfect woman to help Duke manage his grief and to build a life with."

Angel thought about it. "It just wouldn't feel right to me. Duke is your husband, and that's the only way I see him now."

"I know, but there will come a time when he'll come out of his grief and accept that his obligation to me has been fulfilled. One day, his heart will open enough that he'll be ready to love again. I want you to be there when it happens."

"I can't do that."

"Why not? The Bible says that if a woman separates from her husband, she should either remain single or return to him."

"I don't mean from a biblical perspective. This is from a personal one."

"What do you mean?"

Angel held Theresa's hand. "I know that we have gotten past all this now, but the fact remains that Duke left me. He betrayed me, and he broke our vows. Regardless of what I may feel about him, I don't think I could ever trust Duke with my heart again."

"He's not the same man he was eight years ago."

"Then I don't know who he is, and I definitely can't commit my life to a stranger," said Angel. "I meant it when I said I'll always be there for those girls, and I will try to help Duke through his grief. Anything more than that is not in the cards for us. No offense, but I just don't trust him."

"Are you sure it's Duke you don't trust? Maybe it's yourself and the feelings you want to pretend don't exist anymore. Don't be afraid to love again, Angel. Life's too short for that."

Angel plucked one of the roses. "I'm not afraid to love," she said. "I'm afraid to love the one man who has hurt me the most."

Chapter 39

"Why didn't you tell me that getting dumped sucks?"
—Sullivan Webb

"Well, don't we look tired and spent?" said Lawson, looking up and seeing Sullivan drag through the door later the next day. "I take it that Vaughn has the same haggard look on his face too."

"Vaughn who?" murmured Sullivan as she dropped her purse at her feet. "That oil rag can kiss my well-sculpted derrière!"

"Looks like somebody got dropped off at the Heartbreak Hotel," teased Angel.

Sullivan fell in between Lawson and Angel on the couch. She turned to Angel. "Why didn't you tell me that getting dumped sucks?"

Angel rose. "Any sympathy I might've had for you just upped and boarded a plane to Timbuktu."

"What happened?" asked Lawson.

Sullivan rested her head on Lawson's shoulder. "He treated me like I was dirt. Less than dirt. Like last season's shoes."

Lawson looked down at her feet. "Well, considering that my shoes are circa 2003, I need you to put this in terms I can relate to."

Sullivan fumed. "He kicked me to the curb! *Me*—Sullivan Raquel Webb! Do you know what he referred to me as? A freakin' used car!"

A snicker escaped Lawson's lips. "I'm sorry, girl, but a used car?"

"Sully, it's not like you're in love with the guy," consoled Angel. "Or are you?"

"Love is a little strong," admitted Sullivan. "But it was a very passionate *like*. I actually thought we were soul mates."

"Really? Honestly, I thought it was just about the sex," disclosed Lawson.

"I had real feelings for him . . . at least I thought I did," said Sullivan. "Maybe I was just caught up in the excitement of it all."

Angel nodded. "Sin is like that. It always takes you further than you want to go and leaves you there, lost and broken, for far longer than you ever wanted to stay. No matter how much the devil tempts you, God always leaves a way for you to get out of it."

"Well, God had a little help from Mr. Lovett with getting me out of that one."

"Sully, it's for the best. You should be thanking God that no one got hurt, namely Charles."

Sullivan pointed at herself. "*I* was hurt!"

"No, your ego took a beating, and that's not the same thing," reasoned Angel.

Sullivan stretched her legs out on the sofa. "I still can't believe I allowed myself to get sucked in like that."

"Don't be so hard on yourself. Even when we mess up, God still loves us, flaws and all. We still love you too."

"I suppose," resolved Sullivan sadly. "You got anything to drink around here?"

"Choose your poison," replied Lawson. "We've got milk, Kool-Aid, juice, bottled water. Take your pick."

"If you don't have anything that requires an ID, I'll pass." Sullivan's eyes wandered over to Angel, who was staring out of a window. "What are you doing over there, Angie?"

Angel peeked through the wooden blinds. "Just thinking."

Lawson leaned forward. "About what, or shall I say *who?*"

"I was thinking about my life and how I thought it would turn out," revealed Angel. "It's kind of ironic really. Theresa stole my family; now I may be getting hers."

Sullivan looked up. "So, you've decided to go after Duke after all. I don't blame you, honey. Finders keepers . . ."

Angel shook her head. "It's not like that. Theresa wants to me look after her family when she dies."

"Of course you'll stay in touch them," said Lawson. "I'm sure they'll appreciate you stopping by for birthdays, graduations, and holidays, things like that."

"I don't think she meant it that way," Angel explained. "She said she wants her kids to come live with me. Duke too."

"She said that?" asked Sullivan. "Reese actually said she wants you to marry her husband and raise her kids?"

Angel nodded.

"I know that I can be a little self-absorbed, but even I wouldn't stoop to that! How selfish can you get?"

"How is that being selfish, Sully?" questioned Angel.

"Ol' Reese just wants to ease her conscience before she meets her Maker. It's selfish of her to put that kind of pressure on you."

"Sully, the woman's dying. Have some sympathy," said Lawson.

"Reese destroyed Angel's family, so now she wants to atone for it by giving her another one?" posed Sullivan. "That's sick! It's sick and it's creepy."

"I think she sees it like a gift," said Angel.

"If she wants you to have a gift, she can *buy* you one, not recycle her used family. Saddling you with her brood sounds more like a curse than a gift anyway."

"Sully, Angel loves those girls." Lawson turned to Angel. "And if you're honest with yourself, you'll admit that you love Duke too. Is this something you're giving serious thought to?"

"I don't know. It's not really up to me. Nobody has asked
Duke what he wants. He may not want me involved with
them once Theresa dies."

Sullivan pressed, "But what do *you* want, Angel?"

"You know that I've always wanted kids, and God knows
that I love those girls with all my heart."

"And Duke?" asked Lawson.

Angel exhaled. "Duke was the love of my life . . . eight years
ago. I'm not the same woman he married back then. Plus, I
don't want to be his rebound chick, and I'm not trying to take
Theresa's place with him."

"She certainly had no qualms about taking your place!"
argued Sullivan.

"This isn't about revenge," replied Angel. "I've already
made my peace with what happened."

Lawson joined her. "Well, it looks like you've got some
praying to do."

"Yeah, I know, and I have been. Not just for me. I pray for
Theresa all the time."

"I never thought I'd ever hear you say that," admitted
Sullivan.

"I never thought I'd be *doing* that," replied Angel. "She's
really not a bad person. It sounds crazy, but I actually think
I'm a better person because of Theresa King."

Lawson smiled. "I admire you, Angel. Sullivan, you could
learn something."

Sullivan frowned. "Me?"

"Yes, you!" Lawson's cell phone rang. "Hey, Kina, what's
up?" She moved out of their range of hearing.

"I don't trust this fake Mother Theresa, and I don't think
you should either," whispered Sullivan.

"Sully, you can't blame the woman for wanting to get her
house in order."

"Just don't forget that she was the one who got *your* house
out of order."

Lawson scurried back into the living room and shrieked, "Pull up the city's Web site! Hurry up!"

"What's going on?" asked Sullivan as Angel booted up the computer.

"We're logging on now," said Lawson into the phone. "I'll call you back."

Lawson and Angel crowded around the monitor. Angel's eyes widened and her mouth dropped open when she found the Web site in question. "Oh my God! Sully, you need to take a look at this."

"What?" Sullivan peeled herself off of the couch. "Is Willie slinging mud again?"

"He ain't just slinging it!" exclaimed Lawson, staring at the monitor. "He's got pictures to back it up!"

Sullivan squinted her eyes and studied the screen, "*What the–?*"

She couldn't breathe. It felt like her heart caved in when she saw pictures of her and Vaughn posted online under the heading: SEX SCANDAL SPUN INTO WEBB'S CAMPAIGN. The photographs ranged from snapshots of the two of them hold-ing hands to their kissing in front of his apartment. "Who would do this?"

"*A Tangled Webb*," read Angel from one of the captions. "How apropos."

"It doesn't say who's responsible for these pictures, but it doesn't take a genius to figure out that it was someone from Willie's campaign," surmised Lawson.

Sullivan's mind flashed back to the smarmy campaign aide who had been slithering around Vaughn's complex. Her cell phone vibrated in her purse and she raced to answer it. "Hello?" Sullivan shouted, "No comment!" then hung up the phone.

"Was that a reporter?" asked Angel.

Sullivan nodded. "Apparently, the newshounds have pic-ked up the story."

Lawson winced. "Do you think Charles knows?"

"I don't know." Sullivan threw back her head. "What am I going to say to him?"

"The bloggers are going crazy with this story," informed Angel, reading the online posts. "They're calling for Charles to drop out of the race or divorce Sully. One guy is demanding you make a public apology to the church and the people of Savannah."

"Just turn it off," commanded Lawson. "Sullivan, don't worry about what they have to say. As long as God and Charles forgive you, that's good enough."

Sullivan buried her face in her hands. "There's nothing I can say or do that will make anything other than a political nightmare for my husband."

"Forget about the campaign," urged Angel. "What about your marriage?"

Sullivan's phone rang again. "I don't want to talk to another reporter."

"Give it to me," ordered Lawson. "Hello . . . This is clearly a vicious smear campaign on behalf of Commissioner Tucker in order to avoid the issues and distract the voters. Mrs. Webb has no further comment." She hung up the phone.

"You handled that like a pro," complimented Angel.

"You'd be amazed at what you learn if you put in enough hours watching political scandals on *CNN*." Lawson put her arm around Sullivan. "You need to figure out what you're going to tell Charles. I'm sure he's caught wind of it by now."

"What *can* I tell him?" Sullivan fell to the floor. "What is there for me to say to him when the truth's right there for the whole world to see?"

"Tell him that the pictures were photo-shopped," suggested Lawson.

"If I do that, Charles is going to try to move heaven and earth to clear my name. If he tries to sue—and I know he will—

it's going to come out that these pictures are authentic." The tears began flooding from her eyes. "How could I have let this happen?"

"Sully, we all tried to tell you that you were playing a very dangerous game," Angel reminded her. "Now you have to deal with the consequences."

"Do you think that Charles is going to leave me?"

"I don't know, Sully, but I do know that Charles loves you. He's a good, patient man. Chances are that his love is strong enough to forgive you regardless of what happens with his campaign. You know how these news cycles run. This whole thing'll blow over in a couple of weeks," predicted Angel.

"I don't have a couple of weeks," wailed Sullivan. "The election is in five days."

Lawson shook her head. "Forget the election! Angel, what man do you think is going to want to stay married to a woman who's been banging another man the whole time she's been sleeping with him? There are some things that the male ego is not structured to handle, and this is one of 'em, especially when it's plastered all over the Internet. This could very well cost Charles not only the county commissioner's seat, but also his business contacts, his standing in the church, and in the community."

"I expected a little more sympathy, Lawson," whined Sullivan.

Lawson reeled back. "Why? Sullivan, you screwed up big time! As usual, you just didn't think. All you were worried about was your libido, and Charles is going to be one who ends up paying for it. He doesn't deserve that."

"I can't think with this much pressure on me! I need a drink," sobbed Sullivan.

"No," argued Lawson, "what you need is to face up to your responsibility in this. You have to find a way to make this right, save your marriage, and Charles's campaign."

Sullivan's phone rang again. "Should I answer it?"

"It's probably another reporter," said Angel. "You're too upset to talk to them. Just let it go to voice mail."

"I'll handle it," insisted Lawson, answering the phone. "Hello?" She swallowed hard and passed the phone to Sullivan.

Sullivan refused to take it. "What are you doing? You know I don't want to speak to the press."

"It's not a reporter, Sully," said Lawson gravely. "It's Charles."

Chapter 40

"Your wife is dying and more than ever, you need to be dealing with reality."
—*Angel King*

Angel heard muffled sounds coming from inside the Kings' pool house. She cracked open the door and found Duke inside on the loveseat. She joked, "I thought this was *my* hideout."

Duke sat up. "I'm just taking a load off. What's your excuse?"

Angel sat down in the recliner across from him. "I needed a minute to clear my head. Do you remember my friend Sullivan?"

He nodded. "She was your roommate in college, right?"

"Yes. She did something so incredibly stupid." Angel shook her head at the thought of Sullivan's antics. "Don't worry. You'll hear all about it on the news tonight. Anyway, I needed a minute to mentally distance myself from her drama before I went into the main house. How's Theresa?"

Duke dropped his head and, without warning, succumbed to his grief and tears. "She's dying, Angel. My wife is dying and there's nothing I can do to fix it and nothing I can do about it. I don't get it, you know? Why her? Why now? She's so young and vibrant and beautiful. Why did this have to happen? How do I get my little girls through the pain of losing their mother?"

Angel rushed to his side. "God is still in control, Duke. I know it doesn't feel like it right now, but He is. And you *are* doing something about it. You're making sure she's comfortable and that she has everything she needs. You're taking great care of the girls, so that's one less thing she has to worry about."

"The girls?" He looked up at her through his watery eyes. "What am I supposed to tell them? They think I'm some kind of superhero, that Daddy can do anything. How do I explain to them that their superhero can't save their mother? How do I break their hearts and tell them that they're never going to see her again, not on this side of heaven? How do I make them understand what I barely understand myself?"

"You tell them the truth, Duke. They need to know that Mommy's sick, but she's going to a place where she'll never have to be sick, in pain, or hurt again."

"I tried that, and you know what Morgan told me? She said that she wanted to die too, so she could be with her mother. It broke my heart."

"She's four. She doesn't have a real concept of death or know what she's saying. I'll talk to her and try to help her understand."

Duke seemed to take some comfort in that. "If anybody can get her to understand, it's you. Morgan is crazy about you, you know?"

Angel smiled. "The feeling's mutual. You have two beautiful, special little girls. I can see why you and Theresa are so proud of them."

"As much as I love my daughters, I can't help but think about the child we lost," he admitted. "I'll never forgive myself for playing a part in your miscarriage."

"Duke, this is not the time for you to be dwelling on that. Right now, your focus needs to be on Theresa and the girls and getting through this as a family."

"None of us would even be going through this if I'd just stayed married to you."

"That might be true, but you wouldn't have Morgan and Miley either if you'd stayed married to me. I know you wouldn't give them up for the world."

Duke shook his head. "Things would've been so different if I hadn't been so stupid. Remember all the dreams we had about the kind of life we wanted and how we'd raise our kids?"

She laughed a little. "We were going to have twins—a girl and a boy— and live in a cottage on the beach and collect sea shells and build sand castles with our babies."

"You would've been a great mother," he said.

Angel felt uncomfortable and moved away. "Maybe we shouldn't be doing this."

"Doing what?"

"Playing 'What If.' Your wife is dying, and more than ever, you need to be dealing with reality."

"I have more reality than I can take right now. I just want to sit here and forget about it for a minute."

She sat down and rubbed his back. "You're tired, aren't you? I spend so much time worrying about Theresa and the girls that I forget that you need a break too."

"You're a good woman, Angel. I don't think I deserved you. I know I don't deserve your help and your kindness now."

"I try not to worry about who deserves what and when. Theresa doesn't deserve what's happening to her; neither does your family. I'm no better than you all are."

He sighed. "Reese is the one who holds our family together. As the head of the household, I know I'm supposed to be this big tough guy, but I can be strong because I know she's got my back. She's fearless, and she loves her family more than anything."

"Even in her fragile state, she's trying to make provisions for you to make the transition easier."

Duke nodded. "Well, I know that she arranged her funeral some time ago. She's already written down the mortuary home she wants to use, the dress she wants to be buried in, and even the songs she wants played at her funeral. She didn't want her parents and me to have to worry about any of that."

"That's not all she didn't want you to worry about. She asked me to take care of you and the girls. She even went so far as to say she wanted us to re-marry and raise the kids together. That's how much she loves her family."

"Angel, I know that my wife had the best intentions, but you've got your own life to live. You have your business, your family and friends. I don't expect you to keep looking after the girls and me."

"Looking after you guys is something I want to do. Besides, I promised Theresa that I would. You guys mean everything to her, and she wants me around to make sure that you all are okay. That's her dying wish."

"Angel, nobody expects you to give up your life for us. She shouldn't have put you in this position."

"She only did it because she knows that I love those girls just like they came from my own body." Angel paused. "And she knows that I love you."

Duke faced her. "She knows that I loved you, too, in my own way. As incredulous as it sounds, I love both of you. The love is different, but it's love nevertheless."

"In her mind, she is the one who tore us apart, so she wants to be the one who brings us back together."

Duke smiled. "That's Reese for you. She always tries to make everyone else happy. She knows what an incredible woman you are, Angel. You're amazing. I don't know why I couldn't see it before." He hugged her, and she let herself wallow in his solace. It was nice to be in his arms again.

As they were pulling away, there was a moment when their eyes met. She felt the way she used to whenever he looked at her, and she could sense that he felt it too. Duke touched her face and slowly drew Angel into a kiss.

The guilt set in as soon as she realized she was kissing him back. She dragged her lips away from his and whispered, "We can't do this."

He pressed his forehead against hers. "I need you, Angel."

"You don't want to do this. You're hurt and you're confused." She rose. "I can't let you do something that you're going to regret."

"There's still something here between us."

"Of course there is. We were in love, and we were married. But you have a new wife and a family now. They need to be your only focus."

He stood before her. "Am I supposed to just ignore how I feel?"

Angel shook her head and crossed her arms. "You're doing it again, Duke! It's just like when we were married. You feel trapped and you feel the pressure mounting, so you look for an escape. First it was with Theresa, now me."

"That's not what I'm doing."

"That's *exactly* what you're doing. You can't run away this time. You have to face this. Your wife is dying; you've got to accept that. Within the next few weeks, those beautiful girls are going to lose their mother. You're going to be a single father, and those kids are going to be totally dependent on you. You've got to accept that too."

"You're right." He nodded. "I need to grow up and take responsibility whether I like it or not. Forgive me for over-stepping the boundaries like that. I know that you're not the kind of woman who would help a man break his vows."

She touched his shoulder. "I know it may feel like it right now, but you're not alone, Duke. You've got family and frie-nds." Angel cupped his face. "You also have me, but don't try to turn this into something it's not. That won't help either of us."

"I know," he conceded. "It just hurts so bad, Angel. It's hard to come to terms with the fact that she's leaving me."

"She's not leaving you," said Angel. "She's going home."

They heard Morgan and Miley right outside of the door, calling his name.

"Duty calls," Duke said and stood up.

"You want me to take them to the park for a while to give you some time to get your head together?"

"No. If I'm going to get used to facing my responsibility, I may as well start now."

Angel put her hand on his shoulder. "I'm glad to hear you say that."

He opened the door for the girls and let them in. "What have you two munchkins been up to?"

"We were looking for you, Daddy," answered Miley. "Are you hiding from us?"

"I was," he said, then looked at Angel. "But I'm not hiding from you anymore. From now on, you never have to worry about where I am."

"What if you get sick like Mama?" asked Morgan.

"Then Miss Angel will take care of us, stupid!" Miley looked up at Angel. "Won't you, Miss Angel?"

Angel nodded. "Yes, I'll be around whenever you need me."

"See, I told you," assured Miley. "Miss Angel's going to be our new mama, aren't you?"

Angel stooped down to her level. "Sweetie, you already have a mama who loves you very much. She loves both of you girls, and nothing brings her more joy than being a mother to you."

"But when she goes to heaven, you're going to be our new mama 'cause she told us," revealed Morgan.

Duke stepped in. "Girls, you can't just ask somebody to do that."

"Yes, you can," insisted Morgan. "Don't you want to be our new mommy, Miss Angel?"

For someone who usually had all the answers, Angel didn't have a clue about what to say.

Chapter 41

"You started taking me for granted the minute we got married."
—*Sullivan Webb*

"Hello, Charles," whispered Sullivan when she found him in the study, staring at the computer, after he summoned her home with a terse, "Come home. I need to talk to you," before hanging up the phone. There was no point in telling him that it wasn't what it looked like, so Sullivan did the only thing more selfish than cheating on him: she shifted the blame to him.

She put down her purse. "In all fairness, you were the one who set all of this in motion. If you had taken my car to the mechanic like I'd asked you to, I never would've met him and this never would've happened."

Charles stared at Sullivan in anger and disbelief. "You know, I bet that honestly makes sense in your warped, twisted mind. I had actually convinced myself that you would come home and tell me that it was all lies and that the pictures had been doctored somehow." He laughed bitterly to himself. "The joke's on me, right?" Charles smashed one of their framed wedding pictures against the wall.

Sullivan shrieked. "Charles, let me explain . . ."

"How could you, Sullivan? You're my *wife*, for God's sake!"

"I never wanted to hurt you. Please tell me you believe that," she whimpered. "Please say you forgive me."

"I trusted you. I gave you my heart and all I had in me to give. There was *nothing* I wouldn't have done for you." He put his hand over his heart. "You know, I knew that perhaps you didn't love me as much as I loved you, and I accepted that. But for you to turn around and do this . . ." He pushed over the desk, sending the computer monitor and keyboard crashing to the floor. "My God, Sullivan, do you have no conscience? Does Christ live anywhere in you?" No longer able to stand the sight of her, Charles headed upstairs to their bedroom.

Sullivan followed him up the steps. "I never meant for any of this to happen," she sobbed.

"You never meant for what to happen, Sully? When you laid down and took off your clothes for this man, you never meant to sleep with him—is that what you're saying?" All she could do was shake her head. "No, you meant for that part to happen, right? And don't give me this crap about not meaning to hurt me because you knew that sleeping with another man would devastate me. The only thing you didn't mean to happen was me finding out." He tore open the closet door and grabbed a duffel bag.

"Nobody was supposed to get hurt, especially not you," she cried. "It was just a fling; it was nothing, Charles."

"You had an affair. You slept with another man. How could you disrespect our vows like that? We went before God," he continued, stuffing clothes into the bag. "We promised to be faithful and honest with each other no matter what."

Sullivan tried to grab him, but Charles pulled away from her. "We have to talk about this, baby. Let's just pray, or yell at each other, or make love, or anything other than you looking at me with such contempt in your eyes."

"I can't look at you any other way right now." He moved about the room, tossing in items.

"Moving out won't solve anything. I still love you, and I

know that you still love me. You know it too. Don't you even want to hear what I have to say?"

"Not really." Charles stopped packing momentarily, granting Sullivan a smidgen of hope. "I do love you, Sullivan, and believe it or not, I forgive you, because not only are you my wife, but you're also my sister in Christ. But forgiving you doesn't mean I have to hang around while you make an even bigger fool out of me."

Sullivan took a deep breath. "I made a horrible, selfish mistake; I admit that, but you've made mistakes too."

Charles zipped his bag and tossed it over his shoulder. "The only mistake I made was trusting you." He walked past her.

"Go on, leave," Sullivan called after him. "That's the one thing you've been good at lately." He stopped in the doorway. "You've been so wrapped up with this campaign until it's like I'm not even here. You've been too busy to notice what was going on under your own roof. When was the last time you even asked me how my day went or took an interest in what I wanted?"

"You know how important this race is to me. You said that you understood."

"I do understand, but I'm human. I get lonely, and I need more than these stupid campaign posters and speeches to make me feel wanted."

Charles faced her. "And you don't think I've been lonely? This race has been my whole life, and most days, the only thing that keeps me going is knowing I'm going to come home to you. I thought that you had my back, my helpmeet. I thought you'd be there when no one else but God would."

"I've been here with you and for you through the ups and downs, disappointments and bad days, but you started taking me for granted the minute we got married. You're just as much to blame for this as I am."

"You know what? I accept that, Sully. I know that there are thousands of things I've done wrong, but I never cheated on you. I never even thought about it."

"Just stay, Charles," pleaded Sullivan. "We need to talk until we work this out."

Charles nodded. "We can do that . . . if it only happened once."

Sullivan blinked. "What?"

"I can forgive you, Sullivan, and we can work on putting this behind us if it was a one-time moment of weakness that you gave in to."

She swallowed hard. "Charles, I—"

He reached for her hand. "Just look me in the eyes and tell me that it was just this once, that you haven't been making a fool out of me time and time again."

"I can tell you that it'll never happen again," vowed Sullivan.

"But you can't tell me that it hasn't happened before, can you?" She shook her head, her eyes burning with tears. Charles dropped her hand. "I'll be back to get the rest of my things in the morning. It'll be better for both of us if you weren't here."

Sullivan blew into a tissue. "You're not wasting any time, are you?"

"I've done enough of that already." They were silent for a moment. "Look, I haven't made any announcements to the press or anything about us breaking up. I'm trying to hold it off as long as I can because I think that it'll just draw unnecessary attention to my personal life instead of the issues. I'm hoping that you and your boyfriend will respect that and use some discretion, at least for now."

"Vaughn is not my boyfriend. He isn't anything to me. It's over now."

"It's funny," said Charles. "Before today, the rest of the world thought that we were the perfect couple, but I think we both know that hasn't been true for a long time. I didn't want to see it, but you and your lover have made it very clear. Obviously, he knew that things weren't right long before I did."

"Charles, don't talk about Vaughn like he was the great love of my life. He's barely out of high school. He's just a kid."

"But it's true, right? All of those nights that you were lying there in that bedroom with me, you were secretly pining away for him."

"It wasn't like that."

"I still can't get the image of the two of you together out of my head. There you were, on the computer screen, kissing and touching him, when I have to beg for the least bit of affection from you."

"It's different with you. We have a relationship based on respect and partnership. Despite what you saw on that Web site, I love you, Charles. I always will."

"What, like a brother? Does he love you, Sully? I did. I wanted a future with you. I had already picked out the names for our kids, and I stood up in front of everyone in the church and professed my everlasting love for you. I saw myself sitting on the porch in a rocking chair next to you, watching our grandkids run around the yard. Just last week, I was joking with some of the deacons about having to trade in your BMW for minivans and getting a dog and taking trips."

"We can still have all of that," she assured him.

"I wanted it with you." He dropped his head. "But you want it with him, don't you? Didn't you know how much I loved you? I would have given you everything. You could have just told me that you didn't love me anymore. You didn't have to jump in bed with another man."

"I wanted to tell you about him; I just couldn't."

"You couldn't tell me, but had no problem sleeping with him behind my back."

"Charles, please tell me what I can do to fix this. If you

want me to make a statement to the press, I will. If you want me to go before the church and apologize, I'll do that, too. Just tell me what to do."

"All I know to tell you to do is ask the Lord for His forgiveness."

"What about us? You said I have your forgiveness, so I don't see why we can't work this out. A lot of couples have to face infidelity. We've had several in the church who have dealt with it, but emerged stronger in their marriage and their walk with God. Think of what it would do for the congregation if we could show them that couples can survive a hit like this and still stay together. What could be a more powerful testimony?"

"All that sounds real good, Sullivan, but this ain't about my campaign or putting on a show for the church. I don't care about those things right now. It's about us, and me opening my eyes to the kind of woman I married."

Sullivan fumed. "Newsflash, Charles: your wife ain't perfect," she said sarcastically. "She's not the innocent little First Lady who sits on the front pew with her white gloves and hat. She's a woman who's passionate and sexual and creative."

"Don't you think I know that, Sullivan? And I knew that with our age difference could come some complications. I was prepared for that. What I wasn't prepared for was a wife who could lie to my face and run around with another man behind my back and have the whole world witness my humiliation. Now I have everything I need," he said as he picked up his suitcase, "and thanks to you, a few things I didn't."

Chapter 42

"I made myself believe that I deserved it."
—*Kina Battle*

Kina knocked on the door of her former English teacher's classroom. Everything looked almost as it did the last time she was there. "Mrs. Evans, you got a minute?"

"Hey, Kina Anne, come on in." Mrs. Evans walked over to the door and gave Kina a hug. "I was shocked when the office buzzed down here and said you were looking for me. You just missed E'Bell. He was headed toward the gym."

"Actually, I was kind of hoping that the two of us could talk alone."

"Sure. Have a seat. Your old desk is still right there in the front."

Kina squeezed into the desk. "I don't remember it being this hard to get into when I was seventeen."

"I could get into my desk a lot easier then too," quipped Mrs. Evans. "So, what can I do for you?"

Kina folded her hands together. "Well, I wanted to talk you about E'Bell."

Mrs. Evans sat down. "I have to confess, Kina, I don't really say too much to him these days, pretty much just hello and good-bye. From what I can see, he seems like a pretty good worker, if that's what you're wondering."

"No, not quite. I want to know about when he was a student in your class. I know it's been a while, but anything you can remember would be a big help."

"Okay, exactly what do you want to know?"

"What kind of student was he?"

Mrs. Evans thought back. "E'Bell was an okay student, I guess. He was never disrespectful or anything, probably because he spent most days asleep in my class. I don't think he worked as hard as he could, but in those days, things were different. There wasn't all the accountability that students and teachers have placed on them now. E'Bell was the star football player, one of the best in the state. It was sort of understood that you didn't fail our best athletes."

"Did he seem to struggle at all with the assignments?"

"He didn't put forth enough effort to struggle. He would do enough to get by, or rather, get his girlfriend to do it for him."

Kina smiled bashfully. "Guilty as charged. What about when he did work on his own?"

Mrs. Evans nodded slowly as she remembered. "He got frustrated a lot, but rather than try, he'd just give up and put his head down. I remember him never wanting to read aloud in class, afraid that the students would laugh at him, I suppose. He just . . . I don't know, didn't really like being in school. To tell you the truth, I think he would've dropped out if it weren't for football."

"Did you ever hear him read?" asked Kina.

"No. It often concerned me that I never saw E'Bell read anything. Even the kids who didn't like to read the books I assigned to them would still read their little romance novels or sports magazines. That wasn't the case with E'Bell."

"Why did it bother you so much?"

"I was afraid that he might be illiterate. I tried to have him tested, but his mother and his coaches fought me on it and won."

Kina looked at her with skepticism. "Can a person really go to school for that long and not know how to read?"

"It's easier than you think. Kids fall through the cracks all the time, I'm sad to say. Now we have all of these state-mandated tests that the students have to take, so it's harder for kids to make it all the way to graduation without being able to read. In most cases, though, those are the kids that end up dropping out."

"They would still have to read at some point, right?"

"People can be functionally literate. A person might read well enough to fill out a job application or something like that, but if you're an adult reading at a third or fourth grade level, you're still considered to be illiterate."

Kina closed her eyes and murmured, "So, Lawson was right about him."

"Kina, are you worried that E'Bell can't read?"

Kina nodded her head. "It's crazy, huh?"

"Not at all. It would actually make a lot of sense."

"Why do you say that?"

"Because of his test scores."

"What about them?"

Mrs. Evans filed away some papers. "Well, you already know the story with Duke and USC and those other colleges that were looking at him."

"I thought those schools accepted him."

"They did, pending his test scores. Once the scores came back, they all rescinded their offers." She noticed the pained expression on Kina's face. "Didn't you know about that?"

Kina shook her head. "All I knew is that he was offered scholarships, but he changed his mind about going when I told him I was pregnant with Kenny."

Mrs. Evans turned away, mortified.

"What else is going on here?"

"Kina, it's really not my place to get into it. I honestly thought you knew."

"Knew what?"

Mrs. Evans held up her hand. "You need to talk to E'Bell. I've said too much as it is."

"Mrs. Evans, please. You don't understand. For the past eleven years, I've blamed myself for E'Bell not going on to college like he wanted to. I've always felt like if he didn't sacrifice everything for me and the baby, he wouldn't be in the situation he's in now. I need to know the truth."

"I understand all that, but it's E'Bell's business. I don't want to get involved."

"Mrs. Evans . . . he hits me," admitted Kina aloud for the first time. "He beats me and he blames me for him not being able to go to college. I've stayed with him and taken his abuse all this time because I believed him. If there is some other reason that E'Bell didn't go to school, I need to know that."

"Oh, Kina, you poor child." She pulled Kina into her arms and held her. "We have to get you some help. We've got to involve the police. E'Bell can't get away with this, and you can't risk your life staying married to a man who abuses you."

She pulled away from her former teacher. "I don't want to call the police right now. I just need to know the truth."

"He's not supposed to be hitting you for any reason. No one deserves to be treated that way."

"I know, but I felt so guilty that I made myself believe that I deserved it."

Mrs. Evans took a deep breath. "Kina, it wasn't your fault that E'Bell didn't get into college. His test scores kept him out, not you."

"What do you mean?"

"E'Bell never really finished high school. He doesn't have a diploma."

"Yes, he does," argued Kina. "I was there. I saw him graduate."

Mrs. Evans shook her head. "I'm not supposed to be telling you this, but he never passed his graduation tests."

"What?"

"His scores were extremely low, like in the third percentile for the high school exit exam. They were just as low on the college admissions tests. With scores like that and no diploma, no school would even look at him, not even some of the local colleges. It had nothing to do with you being pregnant."

"That can't be right," said Kina, confused. "I saw him graduate. I saw him walk across that stage and get a diploma. I saw all the letters from the colleges and the scholarships they wanted to give him. This doesn't make any sense."

"Yes, he walked across the stage the same as you did, but what he got was a certificate of attendance, not a diploma. He received a paper that said that he'd been to school for twelve years, that's it."

"But he said it was because of me," wailed Kina, trying to piece it all together. "He said that he was trying to do the right thing by marrying me and raising our baby together. He told me that he had sacrificed his whole future for Kenny and me."

"That may be what he told you, probably was what he told himself, too, but E'Bell's football career was over long before you had that baby. Marrying you just gave him an excuse for not going off to school, his way of saving face."

"He probably never even loved me." Kina felt numb. Her entire marriage was a lie. She had been beaten for nothing, degraded for nothing, ashamed for nothing. It was the price for believing in her husband.

"Kina, I can talk to our principal if you want. He needs to know what E'Bell's been doing to you. We have campus police right here at the school. I can go with you if you want to file charges."

Kina scooted out of the desk. "That won't be necessary, Mrs. Evans. E'Bell needs this job; I'm not going to file charges." She did, however, have every intention of filing for a divorce.

***

Kenny sat on his bed, clutching two pillows over his ears so he wouldn't hear his parents arguing. The pillows muffled their words, but he could still hear them yelling. He knew he had to do something before his father got angry enough to hit his mother again. He threw the pillows down and ran to his parents' bedroom.

"All this time!" screamed Kina. "All this time I let you blame me for everything that happened. You let me think it was my fault that you didn't have your big football career, that it was my fault that you couldn't go to college, that it was my fault that we had to live this way. All along you knew that it was all because of you, because you couldn't read."

"Shut up before I come over there and shut you up," threatened E'Bell.

"Here you are, the big shot football player," she said mockingly, "so tough that you have to beat on your wife in order to feel like a man."

E'Bell walked up on her. "Who do you think you're talking to?"

Kina dug her finger into his chest. "I'm talking to this ignorant, cowardly, pitiful excuse for a man named E'Bell Ricardo Battle! I let you take my hope and my self-esteem, but you won't take another day of my life and happiness away." Then she announced, "I'm leaving."

A menacing scowl washed over E'Bell's face. "You gon' do what?"

"I'm taking my child, and we are getting as far away from you as we can."

His eyes turned cold. "Kina, I'll kill you. You know that?"

"You don't scare me anymore, E'Bell. You can say and do whatever you want, but nothing's going to stop me from leaving. If you've got to kill me, then fine. Either way, I'll be free from you."

E'Bell grabbed her by the arm and twisted it. "You think you better than me now, huh? You getting your little degree, so you think you better than somebody?"

Kina looked him dead in his eyes. "You're doggone right!" She snatched her arm away from him. "It's over, E'Bell," she declared with finality.

E'Bell roared, "You ain't going nowhere. You hear me?" he pushed Kina hard against the wall. She hit her head against one of the sconces, sending an excruciating pain through her entire body. Too groggy to stand, she slumped to the floor.

E'Bell kicked her in the stomach. "Talk bad now! Get up!"

Kina tried to stand and defend herself, but he smacked her back down. "You think you gon' leave somebody? If you leave here, it'll be in a hearse! Today will be the last day you ever take that tone with me!"

E'Bell punched Kina in the head. Her vision went blurry, but in her haze, Kenny appeared like an apparition, brandishing something in his hand. She couldn't make out what it was. She did, however, make out E'Bell raising his fist in the air as he prepared to strike her.

"Stop it!" cried Kenny. "Leave her alone!"

Kina braced herself for the blow to her head that never came. Instead, she heard a loud crackling noise followed by blood spattering the living room wall. The last thing she heard was the thud of E'Bell's gun hitting the ground as it slipped from Kenny's hand. The last thing she saw before the room went dark was E'Bell's body dropping to the floor.

Chapter 43

"No more stalling, no more games."
—Lawson Kerry

Lawson opened the door and greeted Garrett with a smile. "Thanks for coming."

"Well, you said Namon needed me, so I'm here."

She let him in and closed the door. "Namon does need you. So do I."

"Lawson," Garrett sighed, "we've been here before. The fact is you were stalling about us getting married long before Mark even came in the picture. I have to accept that we're not meant to be. Maybe you are better off marrying Namon's dad."

She shook her head. "Mark is not the one for me. You are."

Garrett took off his jacket. "And how do you know that?"

"Mark can't look at me the way you do and know what I'm feeling, what I'm thinking. We know what every sigh, every touch, every kiss means to the other one. I could never have that with Mark. I don't even want to."

"Then why would you let him think he had a chance with you?"

"I just needed more time, and it was the only way I could stall him. But that's over now. Namon knows the truth, so no more stalling and no more games. I want to marry you, Garrett, if you'll still have me. More than anything, I want to be your wife."

Before Garrett could reply, the doorbell rang. Lawson opened the door and let Mark in.

"What's he doing here?" asked Garrett as the two exchanged harsh glares.

Lawson escorted Mark to where Garrett stood. "He's here
because I asked him to come. Like it or not, we're all stuck
with each other. We all love and want what's best for Namon,
and what's best for him is all three of us, one dysfunctional
blended family."

"For that to work, your boyfriend here is going to have to
respect the fact that I'm Namon's real father," pointed out
Mark.

"And, Mark, you're going to have to respect the fact that
Garrett has been a fantastic father to Namon. I'm not cutting
him out of my son's life to appease you."

"How is Namon supposed to accept me as his father if this
joker's always hanging around?"

"I don't know, but we'll figure it out. There's no better
time to start than now." She called Namon out of his room.

"What's going on?" asked Namon, entering the room.

Lawson brought him over to Mark. "Your father would like
to spend some time with you today."

"Do I have to?" whined Namon.

"Yes, you do. You can spare him a few minutes of your
time. Go on, grab your coat."

She addressed Mark. "There's a football in the backyard. I
guess that's as good a place to start as any." Namon snatched
up his jacket and grudgingly headed out of the back door with
Mark behind him.

Garrett waited until they closed the door behind them to
speak. "I have to be honest with you, Lawson. I don't know
if I can do this. I was cool when Mark wasn't around, and I
could pretend that I was Namon's father, but I can't do that
anymore."

Lawson grabbed him by the collar and looked squarely into his eyes. "Do you love me?'"

"Lawson—"

"Do . . . you . . . love . . . me?" she enunciated slowly.

He exhaled. "You know I do."

"Do you believe that I'm the woman God created for you?"

"I did. . . . I do."

"Do you still want to marry me and spend the rest of our lives together?"

Garrett exhaled and nodded.

"Then hold on to that,"—she pulled him into an embrace—"and hold on to me."

Namon and Mark tossed the football back and forth in silence until Mark raised a question.

"So, you like football, huh?" he asked Namon.

"Yeah, I've gotten pretty good at it."

Mark threw the ball to him. "What position do you play?"

Namon stated, "QB," and tossed it back.

"Like father, like son," said Mark and chuckled.

"My mom said you used to play over in Germany."

Mark nodded. "I did. I went over there right after college. The GFL is the German version of our NFL."

"Who'd you play for?"

"I played for the Berlin Eagles for a couple of years and played arena football after that. Then I hurt my knee and that kind of ended the football thing for me. Coaching is cool, though. I actually like it more than playing."

"Did you make a lot of money when you were playing football?"

"I made a li'l' something . . . and blew *a lot* of something!"

"You think I could play for the NFL?"

"Maybe. I thought I could, but you see where I ended up. I

thank God that I had my degree to fall back on." He walked over to Namon and put a hand on his shoulder. "Son, there's nothing wrong with wanting to play in the league, but you should definitely have a Plan B. Always have a back-up. Stay in school and get your education. That's the one thing that no one can ever take from you."

"That what my mama always tells me."

"Your mother is a very smart woman. You should listen to her."

"Why didn't you guys ever get married?"

"That's a tricky one," answered Mark. "We were really young when we met, not much older than you are now. We didn't know anything about love and marriage back then. I did ask her to marry me when I found out about you, though."

"What did she say?"

"She said that she loves someone else."

"She's talking about Garrett. He's her boyfriend, but they're supposed to be getting married soon."

"Yeah, she told me. How does he treat you?"

"Who, my dad?" asked Namon without thinking. "I mean, I know you're my real dad."

"No, Garrett's been the one who's been your real dad all this time, not me. Hopefully, in time, we can change all that."

"He's been really good to me and my mom."

"I can tell. Hey, did your mom tell you that you have a little sister?"

"No."

Mark pulled out his wallet and flashed a picture of his daughter. "Her name is Mariah. She's six. She lives in North Carolina with her mother."

"She's pretty. It's weird that I have a sister who I haven't even met yet."

"Well, she'll be down here this summer. I'd love for you to come over and spend some time with her, get to know her."

He nodded his head. "It might be cool to have a little sister to boss around."

"It might be cool to have two dads, too," added Mark. "What do you think about that?"

Namon turned the football around in his hands. "It might be all right. We can try, I guess."

"Look, Namon, I know that I missed the first fourteen years of your life, and I know that we didn't get off on the right start." Mark stooped down. "But if you give me a chance, I promise to be the best father to you that I can be."

"Well, you two seem to be getting along," said Lawson with a smile as she and Garrett joined Namon and Mark in the backyard.

Namon grinned. "I've got a little sister."

"Yeah, I know," replied Lawson. "It looks like you've got an extra dad as well."

Mark turned to Garrett. "So, I guess you'll be sticking around."

He nodded. "As long as this beautiful lady will have me." Garrett kissed Lawson on the forehead.

Mark dug his foot in the ground. "Hey, man, I want to apologize for how I came at you earlier. I was trippin' because I was jealous of your relationship with Lawson and my son, but that's no reason to overstep like that. I'm sorry."

Garrett extended his hand. "There are no hard feelings. Lawson and Namon are wonderful people. I can't even say I blame you."

Mark shook his hand. "And rest assured that you're the only man Lawson wants. I pulled out all my best stuff, but she never took the bait. All she kept talking about was how much she loved you."

Lawson smiled. "Thank you, Mark. It means a lot that you would say that." Lawson's phone rang. "Hello . . . What? Wait, slow down . . . Oh, no . . . I'll be right there!" She hung up the phone.

"What's wrong?" asked Garrett.

"We've got to go," she informed him. "That was Kina's neighbor. E'Bell's been shot. We have to go to the hospital."

"What about Kenny?" asked Namon, worried about his cousin. "Is he okay?"

"Sweetie, I don't know. I just know that the ambulance is over there, and they're on the way to the hospital."

Garrett pulled out his car keys and tossed them to Namon. "Why don't you go and unlock the doors for us." Namon dashed out of sight. "Now, tell me what you were afraid to say in front of Namon, because I can see it in your eyes."

Lawson shook her head. "All I know is that E'Bell was shot, and Kina's been badly beaten. Right now, I don't know if it looks good for either one of them."

Chapter 44

**"I'm not thinking about next year. Live for the moment
. . ."**
—Angel King

"You're awake." Angel set the tray down on the coffee table
next to the living room sofa, where Theresa lay. "How are
you?"

"I'm fine," she said, her voice tired and wispy. She yawned.
"What time is it?"

"It's a quarter past four."

"Where are the girls?"

"Upstairs with Duke. They were giving him their Christmas lists when I last looked in on them. The holidays are just
around the corner. Can you believe it?"

"Christmas?" Theresa coughed. "Seems like such a long
way off. If I'm this tired and weak now, there's no telling what
I'll be like a month from now. I don't know if I'll have the
strength to put up a tree or go shopping for the girls."

"You have plenty of time to worry about getting the house
ready for Christmas. Don't worry about that. Everybody is
focused on taking care of you; nobody's even thought about
a Christmas tree. I haven't put one up at my house in years."
Angel stopped short of telling her the reason was because
Duke left her at Christmastime.

"The girls deserve to have Christmas," said Theresa.
"I want them to have a tree and to celebrate Christmas like

we always do. I can't let this illness get in the way of that, especially with Miley's birthday coming up on Christmas Eve."

"Miley and Morgan just want to see their mom feeling better. That's all they really want for Christmas this year."

"I used to make them gingersnap cookies," recalled Theresa. "We'd eat some and use the rest for tree ornaments. Promise me—" She gasped for breath. "Promise me you'll make gingersnap cookies with them this year."

"I will," vowed Angel.

Theresa closed her eyes, waiting for the spasm of pain to pass. "Angel, let's not wait."

"Wait on what?"

"The tree, the cookies, none of it. Call the girls and Duke down right now. I want to smell those cookies baking and hearing my daughters laughing and see that big beautiful tree all lit up."

"You want to put up the tree? Don't you think it's a little soon for that? The girls haven't even eaten all their Halloween candy." Angel patted her hand. "I know you're worried, but we have time. I promise."

Theresa shook her head. "All we're promised is right now. Please, Angel, help me to have one more Christmas with my family."

Angel reassured her with a smile. "Okay, I'll go get the girls and Duke."

Theresa sat back and smiled as the house was soon buzzing with activity. Duke dragged the Christmas tree and ornaments from the attic, and the aroma of nutmeg and cinnamon from Angel's cookies filtered into the living room from the kitchen.

Theresa sighed and lay back on the sofa. "Now it feels like Christmas."

"Mommy, look." Morgan brought a picture of herself that

had been turned into a tree ornament. "This was me when I was a baby. See, *Morgan's First Christmas*."

"I remember that. Now my baby's all grown up." Theresa kissed her daughter's brow. "We should take another picture to hang on the tree. Duke, where's the camera?"

He dug the camera out of the armoire and called Angel into the room. Duke and the girls gathered around Theresa on the sofa while Angel snapped the picture.

"Be sure to hang it on the tree," said Theresa. "I want the girls to always remember today."

Angel nodded. "They will. I'll make sure of it. And as soon as these cookies are done, I'll print out the picture, and we'll hang it on the tree."

"Next year," whispered Theresa, "they can take another picture with you."

Angel squeezed Theresa's hand. "I'm not thinking about next year. Live for the moment, remember?"

Theresa watched from the sofa as Angel, Miley, and Morgan decorated the tree with bells, bows, and gingersnap cookies. Duke sat attentively at his wife's side.

Morgan pulled him by the arm. "Daddy, Angel is about to light the tree. Come on!"

Miley held her mother's hand. "You can come too, Mommy."

"Sweetie, Mommy needs to take a little nap first. I would love a kiss, though." Both girls rushed into their mother's arms. She hugged them, pouring all the love she had for them into that embrace. The gesture took the last bit of strength she had. "Now, you go on and help Angel. Mommy loves you so much."

"We love you too, Mommy!" they said in unison as they skipped into the foyer where the tree stood in front of a bay window.

Angel approached them. "I wanted you to see the last ornament before we put it on the tree." She handed Theresa the family picture they'd taken thirty minutes earlier.

"I don't look half bad," joked Theresa.

"You look beautiful," said Angel. "Peaceful and happy."

"I am happy." Theresa's eyes seemed to sink into dark pockets around their sockets. "It's a happy, happy day." She passed the picture back to Angel.

"I'm going to find a hook for this, and I'm going to take lots of pictures of the girls with the tree lit. And we'll set the pictures all around you, so your family will always be smiling and close by."

Theresa nodded a little. "I'd like that very much, Angel. I'm so glad we've had this time to get to know one another."

"I am too," Angel admitted. "In fact, I feel blessed to be able to call you my friend."

"You're my friend and my sister in God's kingdom," replied Theresa. "I couldn't have asked for a better nurse, friend, and confidante over the last few weeks."

"It's been my pleasure." Angel reached down and gave Theresa a hug. "Now, I'm going to light that tree over there before those munchkins eat all the ornaments!"

Theresa gave Angel a slight wave and settled her head snugly into the pillow.

Duke brushed her hair back. "You all right, baby? You look a little pale."

"I'm just tired. All I want to do is lie here and count my blessings and think about how happy I am right now."

"You sure I can't get you anything?"

"I'm fine. You go on back up front with Angel and the girls."

He kissed her hand. "You know how much I love you, right?"

She nodded. "Thank you for loving me and making the past nine years worth living."

Duke scooted next to her on the sofa. "I don't want to leave you here by yourself while we're out there."

"No, it's okay. It makes me feel good to see you all happy and carrying on like old times. It lets me know that no matter what happens, everything is going to be all right."

He brushed his lips softly across hers. "I'll be right out here. I'll be back to check on you in a few minutes."

"Go on. I'm fine," she whispered. "The girls are waiting." He walked to the door and turned to smile at her one last time. Theresa looked on and smiled as they trimmed the tree. Their laughter was music to her ears. She was finally at peace. Then she closed her eyes and quietly slipped away.

Chapter 45

"This may be the last chance I have to say good-bye."
—*Kina Battle*

Riding in the ambulance, Kina sat numb as the paramedics fought to save E'Bell's life. Everything had happened so fast: one minute she was trying to escape for her and her son's life; the next, E'Bell was hemorrhaging from a bullet wound, inflicted by their son, that had pierced from his back to his chest. E'Bell had gained consciousness, but Kina knew that his condition was grim. He'd lost a lot of blood, and she overheard one of the medics say that his heart rate was dropping. No one was sure if he'd even make it to the hospital alive.

Once they'd reached the hospital, Kina made a brief call to Lawson to let her know what was going on. She watched helplessly as the surgeons rushed E'Bell down a hospital corridor. She declined one doctor's offer to examine the gash on the side of her head from the sconce; she only wanted them to focus on E'Bell. His surgeon only stopped long enough to inform her that they wouldn't be able to tell her anything definitive for several hours, and she should pray.

Pacing the waiting room floors, Kina found herself torn between being E'Bell's wife and E'Bell's victim, but the stakes were a lot higher now. He was her husband and the man she'd loved since she was fifteen years old, and he lay just a few feet away from her, close to dying. If he died, she'd have to raise their son alone, and her son would have to live for the rest of his life with the guilt of killing his father. If E'Bell lived, she would have to decide whether to leave him or stay. Her conscience wouldn't let her leave to fend for himself a man who had barely escaped death, but she knew that if she stayed, there was every possibility that E'Bell's violent rages would escalate. She would have avoided one bad situation only to end up in a worse one. Would resigning herself to spending her life with a man who it turns out she barely knew at all force her to forgo someone who could be the love of her life, a man who could give her and Kenny the family that she'd always longed to have?

Her search for answers led her to pray at the hospital's chapel. It was the one place on earth where she expected to find answers.

Kina lit a candle once she entered the modest chapel and kneeled down at the altar and prepared her heart to speak to God.

She looked up and saw Lawson smiling down on her. "I knew I'd find you here."

Kina rose and smiled. "Thank you for coming. Did you pick up Kenny from the neighbors?"

"Yeah, he's right outside. Garrett and Namon are with him."

"How is he?"

"Quiet. I tried to get him to open up, but I think he's still in shock."

"I can't imagine what he must be going through right now."

"Kenny will be fine. He's strong and resilient. We'll all help him get through this." Kina nodded. "How is E'Bell? Better yet,"—Lawson examined the gash on Kina's head from her fall—"how are you?"

Kina touched her head. "This is nothing. I'll heal, but

E'Bell . . . the doctors are in with him now." She shook
her head, trying to hold back tears. "It doesn't look good,
Lawson."

Lawson put her arms around her cousin. "God is still in
control. Nothing is going to happen that He can't give you
the strength to handle, okay?"

Kina wiped her eyes. "Did you tell the others?"

"Yeah, Sullivan is on her way. I couldn't get in touch with
Reggie, but I left a message telling her to come. Angel is at
Duke's. I think Theresa has taken a turn for the worse, so I
told her to stay there with the girls and Duke."

"That's probably best. There's not much she can do here
anyway. I need to see my son. Please take me to him."

Lawson led Kina to where Kenny, Namon, and Garrett
were waiting. Kenny rushed into his mother's arms, sobbing.
"It's my fault!" he wailed. "I did this to Daddy! You told me
not to mess with Daddy's gun, and I didn't listen."

Kina rubbed his head. "Nobody is blaming you, Kenny.
You probably saved my life. You're a hero."

"But Daddy's gonna be real mad now! What if he tries to
hurt you again?"

Kina shook her head. "We don't have to worry about that
anymore, I promise." She hugged her son tightly.

Garrett tapped Kina on the shoulder. "The doctors need
to have a word with you. Kenny can stay here with us if you
want."

Kina nodded and released Kenny. "Thank you, Garrett."

A nurse approached Kina. "Ma'am, if you don't mind following me, I can take you in to speak with your husband's
doctor."

"You don't have to go in there alone," said Lawson. "I'm
right here with you."

Holding on to Lawson's hand, Kina took a deep breath and
followed the nurse, praying that she had the strength to face
whatever news was waiting for her.

The doctor's prognosis was bleak at best. After surviving the harrowing surgery, E'Bell was moved to the intensive care unit and listed in critical condition. The doctors held out little hope for a full recovery. They had managed to dislodge the bullet, but not before tremendous damage had been done to E'Bell's organs. That, coupled with the fact that he'd lost so much blood, worried his physician. Too much internal damage had been done, and E'Bell, still unconscious, seemed to have lost his will to live.

"I need to see him," Kina told the doctor after hearing the prognosis. "I just want him to know we're here. This may be the last chance I have to say good-bye."

The doctor consented to the visit, and he and Lawson left to join the rest of the family.

As Kina crept into the room, the first thing she heard was the ominous beeping from the machines assuring that E'Bell's heart was still beating. Seeing him bandaged and hooked up to machines brought tears to her eyes.

Kina made her way over to his bed and pulled up a chair beside him. She felt his hands. They were cold and didn't flinch at her touch. His eyes were closed, and he was perfectly still. If the monitors hadn't assured her otherwise, she might have thought he was dead.

"I'm so sorry this happened to you," she whispered and wound her fingers around his hand. "The doctors are doing all they can, but it's really up to you now . . . and God." She looked eagerly into his face, hoping to see some eye movement, even a flutter. He lay motionless.

"I was so scared for you when they wheeled you in here. I thought we'd lost you. If that had happened, I don't know . . ." Her voice trailed off. "Can you squeeze my hand? Just let me know if you can hear me," she entreated. Nothing happened. "Maybe it's better this way. At least now you have to listen to me before putting your two cents in." She laughed a little.

"You know what I was thinking about earlier? The night of our senior prom and how happy we were that day. I remember thinking, 'He's the one, Kina.' And it wasn't just because I was pregnant with Kenny. I was in love with you from the day we first met."

She sighed and laid her head down on his stomach. "What happened to us, E'Bell? Maybe if I'd found out the truth sooner, or if we'd gotten help for both of us, things would be different. Perhaps you'd be somewhere happy instead of tied to some machine for something our son did because of what you did to me." She began to cry. "I want you to know that I forgive you. I have to, as much for you as for me. I'm sorry that we weren't what the other one needed and that we didn't turn our marriage over to God like we should have.

"I want you to know that I tried to be a good wife to you. I don't doubt that you wanted to be a good husband for me; you just didn't know how to." Kina wiped her tears and regained her composure.

"The easiest thing in the world for me to do right now would be to say that you brought this on yourself and that you deserve to die for what you did to me, but I'm not going to do that. Instead, I'm going to pray for God to keep you under His protection and release any ill will I have for you in my heart. It's also my prayer that you can forgive Kenny and forgive yourself."

She sat up. "I just want you to get better, E'Bell. Even if I never see you again, I want you to get well, be strong, finish school, and live to see our son become a man. If I could take back a lot of what went wrong in our marriage, I would. But I want you to know that I don't regret the good times that we did share and bringing our precious baby into the world together. I just wanted you to know that."

The door cracked open and a nurse poked her head in the door. "Ma'am, I need to check on our patient. It'll only take a minute."

"Well, I guess that's my cue," Kina said, rising. "You take care, E'Bell, and I'll be back to see you as soon as I can." She leaned down and kissed him on the forehead. "God still loves you no matter what you've done."

Kina sent for Kenny when the doctor alluded that E'Bell may not make it through the night. When Kenny entered and saw his father hooked to tubes and breathing machines, he was frightened and just quietly stared at him.

"What's wrong with him, Mama? Why isn't he moving?" he asked.

"Your dad is very sick, and he needs to know that we are here for him and that we want him to get better."

"Didn't the doctors get the bullet out?"

"Yeah, champ, and they're doing all they can to help him, but it might not be enough."

"But he's not going to die, right?"

Kina exhaled and looked her son in the eyes. "I don't want to lie to you, Kenny. He might die; that's still a possibility. But I want you to know how much he loves you. He always will."

"But he's my dad. He's not supposed to die!" he protested through his watery eyes.

"Believe me, Kenny. Everybody is trying to do whatever it takes to save your father. Maybe if you talked to him, and he heard your voice, he'd fight harder to come back to us."

Kenny kneeled down beside his father and begged him not to die. Kina ached for her son. She could hardly watch him suffering that way. She kneeled down next to Kenny and lightly touched E'Bell's arm.

"E'Bell, I know that you can't see it right now, but you have a lot to live for. Kenny needs his father, and you still have a lot of living to do. This isn't your time to die. I need for you to fight. I need you to hold on."

Kenny cried on his mother's chest, and Kina tried her best to comfort him. After a while, Kenny dozed off to sleep, and he and Kina kept vigil at E'Bell's bedside. Despite everything he' done, Kina still cared about E'Bell and didn't want to see him succumb to his injuries. She wanted him to live a long, full life, even if it was going to be without her.

"I know that there is a lot of good in you, E'Bell," she whispered. "You've always had so much love to give. Somewhere down the line, it just got misguided. I want you to know that I don't hate you and that I forgive you."

Suddenly, E'Bell's eyes began to flutter.

"Kenny, look! I think he's waking up!" said Kina, rousing him to attention. E'Bell partially opened his eyes and turned his head to look at them.

"You came back!" exclaimed Kenny.

Kina cupped his face in her hands. "I'll be right back. I want to tell the doctor you've regained consciousness."

E'Bell grunted, trying to speak. His eyes motioned her to sit down. His chest heaved up and down with seeming difficulty. Again, he tried to force himself to speak. "Sorry . . . Ki . . . sorry . . . hurt . . . you."

"I forgive you. Don't worry about that now. Concentrate on getting better. I need to get your doctor."

E'Bell shook his head then shifted his eyes to Kenny. "Not mad, son . . ." He gazed at Kenny for a moment. "Try'na . . . protect . . . your mama."

Kenny wrapped his arms around his father. "I love you, Daddy."

E'Bell smiled briefly before taking what was to be his last breath. The heart monitor flatlined. He was gone.

Chapter 46

"He was a very complicated man who had a lot of demons inside of him."
—*Kina Battle*

"Ma'am, I'm Detective Keith Ross, and I need to ask you and your son a few questions," grumbled a detective waiting for Kina the moment she and Kenny emerged from E'Bell's room once he was pronounced dead.

Kina frowned. "Questions about what?"

The officer pulled out a notebook and a pen. "A man is dead, and we need to get to the bottom of why."

Lawson stepped in front of Kina and Kenny as if to shield them. "Kina and Kenny are the victims here." Lawson pulled Kina's hair back to reveal the cut on the side of her head. "My cousin was just trying to protect his mother."

"Don't say anything else, Lawson," ordered Sullivan. "You either, Ki. Not until we have an attorney present."

Kina panicked. "Is my son under arrest, officer?"

"We just need to clear up a few things," replied the detective. "According to the statements we got from your neighbor and the 9-1-1 operator, your son is the one who actually pulled the trigger. Is that correct?"

Kina clung to her son. "He wasn't trying to kill him. He saw his father beating on me and tried to save me."

"The kid's father just died. Give him a break!" screeched Lawson.

Detective Ross was unfazed as he addressed Kina again. "Do you mind bringing your son down to the station?"

Sullivan whipped out her cell phone. "She will do no such thing! I'm calling my lawyer."

The detective continued his line of questioning as Sullivan stepped off to speak with her lawyer. "Mrs. Battle, were you aware that there was an unregistered gun in the house?"

"That was E'Bell's gun," blurted out Kina. "I asked him to get rid of it a thousand times."

The detective scribbled something in his notebook. "Did your husband have a license to carry it?"

Kina shook her head. "I don't know, but I doubt it."

Kenny seized Kina's arm. "Mama, what's going on?"

"Honey, the police just want you to talk to them about what happened to Daddy," answered Kina.

Kenny gulped. "Am I in trouble?"

Kina offered him a reassuring smile. "No, baby, God is going to see to it that everything will be all right. We just have to trust Him, okay?"

Sullivan returned. "My lawyer is meeting us down at the station. He said not to say anything else to the police until he gets there."

"Do we have to go this minute?" questioned Kina. "Sir, my husband just died. Can't this wait until tomorrow or next week?"

"It's better to go ahead and get it over with while the details are fresh in everybody's mind."

Kina relented, fearing that the nightmare she thought was finally over had only just begun.

Kenny yawned as Kina unlocked the door to their apartment. She could tell that her son was just as drained physically as he was emotionally. After a grueling interrogation at the police station, it was determined that Kenny acted in self-defense. Because of his age and the extenuating circumstances, no further action would be taken against him.

"It's been some day, hasn't it?" asked Kina as she led Kenny to the sofa.

Kenny laid his head on his mother's lap. "I feel tired, but I can't go to sleep."

"I think we're both feeling that way, champ. A lot has happened today. It's going to take a while for it all to sink in. I want you to try to get some sleep, though. Tomorrow might be a busy day too."

"Why?"

"Well, we have a lot of family and friends who love us and cared about your father. They'll probably want to drop by to offer their condolences."

"What's condolences?"

"It's when people feel bad for your loss, and they want to share that pain with you and help you grieve. It's their way of comforting the family."

"Are they gonna be mad at me for shooting Daddy?"

"No one is upset with you for that, Kenny. People will understand why you did it. Even your dad understood. Didn't he tell you he wasn't mad before he died?"

Kenny nodded. "What did they do with Daddy's body at the hospital?"

"They have this place where they keep all the deceased people. It's called a morgue."

"Isn't he gonna be cold in there and lonely?"

"No, that's just his body. His soul—the part of him that made him alive and that makes all of us special—is gone. Without the soul, the body has no feeling. It's like a shell, just dead skin."

"Is Daddy's soul going to hell?"

"No. Why would you think that?"

"'Cause he was a bad person. He hit you, and he was mean. People like that don't get to go to heaven."

"Your dad wasn't a bad person. He was a very complicated man who had a lot of demons inside of him."

"What do you mean?"

"Sometimes people can get so ashamed or so hurt about something that they harden their hearts. Then they can't hear God when He's trying to talk to them. They don't hear Him telling them right from wrong."

"Why was Daddy so mad all the time?"

"Your father couldn't read, so that limited a lot of his options. He couldn't go to college or get the kind of job he wanted, and it made him angry and frustrated. He could've gotten some help, but he never told anyone the truth about his problem with reading. That's why it's so important to let people know when something is wrong or if you're hurting. They can't help you if they don't know."

"Do you let people know when things are wrong? Did you tell Lawson and Reggie how mean Daddy was to you?"

Kina was convicted by her own words. "No, I didn't," she admitted. "And because I didn't say anything, the situation just got worse. Now, it's affected all of us in ways I could've never imagined."

"But you said when you're scared or sad, all you have to do is pray."

"That's true. God didn't give us a spirit of fear. Even though you pray, God expects us to do some of the work too. I prayed for your dad, but I should've gotten some help too, and made sure that we were both some place safe."

"Are we safe now?"

"Yeah, baby." She held her son close to her body. "Thank God, we're safe now."

Chapter 47

"I think I've finally figured out what I want in life and what's really important."
—*Sullivan Webb*

"How are you holding up?" asked Lawson, bringing Kina a cup of hot cocoa as she, Angel, and Sullivan sat around her apartment following E'Bell's graveside funeral.

Kina curled her legs underneath her and wrapped her hands around the mug. "I'm okay, I guess. I expected today to be difficult. Kenny took it a lot harder than I thought he would."

Angel empathized. "I know. I think it really hit him that his father is gone when they lowered his casket into the ground. My heart ached for him. Are you putting him in counseling like we discussed?"

"He has his first session tomorrow afternoon," replied Kina. "I was thinking it wouldn't be such a bad idea if I went for counseling myself."

"It's a great idea," said Lawson. "You've been through a lot, Kina. It's time to start the healing, and talking about it with a professional can help you do that."

Kina nodded. "How's Duke's family, Angel? They must be about as big of a mess as I am right now," lamented Kina.

"Well, we all knew Theresa was sick, so her death wasn't really a shock to anyone. The girls have a lot of questions, and Duke and I are doing our best to reassure them that everything will work out for the best. Her funeral is tomorrow. That'll be the real test."

Sullivan shook her head. "Two funerals in one week. As jacked up as my life is right now, I don't envy you having to go through that."

"You know, I work with dying patients every day; death is a part of my job. But when it hits home like it has this week, I feel totally helpless and unprepared for it. My heart goes out to them and to you and Kenny, Kina."

"Thank you, Angel. And thanks for being so cool about letting me have some time off. I just needed some time to get my affairs in order and get my mind right."

"No problem. Take as much time as you need. Sully's been pitching in and taking up the slack."

Kina blinked back. "Sully, you actually set foot somewhere other than a mall?"

"Or in a smoldering pile of you know what?" joked Lawson.

"Thanks to stepping into that pile of you know what, I have a lot of extra time on my hands," answered Sullivan. "Who knows? I might be able to score a few brownie points from God and Charles by volunteering my services."

"It's nice to see you serving others as opposed to *servicing* others," teased Lawson. "You know I'm just playing with you. We're all happy to see you thinking about someone other than yourself these days."

"How are things between you and Charles?" asked Kina.

"He left me," reported Sullivan. "Charles is gone, and I don't think he's coming back. I tried to call to let him know that I was thinking of him today and that he could count on my vote. He wouldn't even come to the phone."

"It's only been a few days," Angel pointed out. "He just needs some time. The election will be over one way or another tomorrow; then he can settle down some and focus on your marriage."

"Now, this might sound a little insensitive, but I hope you weren't too distraught to cast your vote this afternoon," said

Lawson, sitting down after re-filling her cup. "I think Charles is going to need every vote he can get."

Sullivan huffed. "You can say it, Lawson. He needs every vote that my little tryst with Vaughn doesn't cost him."

Lawson sipped her drink and muttered, "Well, you said it; I didn't."

"It's Charles's election night. I should be there with him," insisted Sullivan.

Angel held Sullivan down. "You should stay put! I drove by the church on the way over, and it was crawling with people and camera crews setting up shop. Save yourself the hassle and the embarrassment."

"But I'm Charles's wife!"

"You're also the woman who got caught creeping with Vaughn, and now the whole world knows it. If you go over there, you'll only cause a scene. The pastor has enough on his plate without you adding to the drama," warned Lawson.

"Vaughn and I aren't even together anymore. Besides, I think the press needs to hear my side of the story instead of feeding off Willie Tucker's diet of sleaze and scandal."

Angel turned on Sullivan's television. "Don't make this about you, Sully. If you go down to that church, it *will* be all about you. This is Charles's night. Let him have it."

Lawson pointed to the screen. "Hey, they're about to do an election update. Turn that up!"

Angel turned up the television in time to hear the reporter announce that Charles had just called his opponent to concede the election after the numbers showed him trailing by forty percentage points once the last precinct entered its results.

"Poor Charles," said Angel. "He must be devastated."

Sullivan bolted up. "I'm going over there. Charles needs me."

Lawson tried to stop her. "You going over there is the *last* thing he needs. If it'll make you feel better, I'll call and let him know you're thinking about him."

Sullivan slipped into her coat. "No, this is something I have to do. I've got to face the firing squad sooner or later, right? Might as well get it over with."

Sullivan stood in front of the church doors, daring herself to go in. She knew that Charles and his supporters had gathered there to watch the campaign results trickle in, and she knew that she would be blamed for his crushing defeat. Despite that, she felt like she needed to be with Charles and offer him a word of comfort, even though she risked getting cussed out in the name of Jesus in the process.

For the first time, she felt alone. She didn't have her girls to back her up or her expensive clothes to hide behind, just a worn blue wrap dress she'd purchased three years prior. There was no drink to calm her nerves, and she had no prepared venom to hurl at her naysayers.

"It's just you and me today, Lord," said Sullivan. "If they dish it, let me be strong enough to take it."

Sullivan walked into the sanctuary with her head held high, though not quite as high as usual. Rather than inconspicuously taking a seat in the back, she strutted to the third pew and sat down, nodding "hello" to the onlookers who watched her with wide eyes and opened mouths.

Sullivan heard a woman behind her mumble, "I know she didn't just walk up in here like she's the virtuous woman we all know she's not."

"Is that Pastor Webb's so-called wife?" asked the female seated next to her. "I hardly recognized her without a tongue down her throat."

"I guess Satan does exist!" exclaimed a choir member as she brushed past Sullivan. "She's the devil, and she's wearing her blue dress to prove it."

"Look at her," spat one of the deaconesses. "She ain't got no shame."

A couple in front of Sullivan turned around to personally snub her with their condescending looks. "How can she show her face here after what she did to a good man like Pastor Webb?" asked the wife as they faced the pulpit again. "Pastor ought to stone her like they did cheatin' women back in the day."

Sullivan didn't mind being hated for the right reasons, which for her were always tied to envy and jealousy. But to be hated because they thought she was scum brought Sullivan to a low that she'd never experienced. She figured there was no point in letting them sharpen their tongues on her, so Sullivan grabbed her purse and stood to leave.

Charles spotted his wife as she made her way down the aisle toward the door. "Wait!" he shouted and rushed to the pulpit. "I want to say something. I want everyone to hear it, especially you, Sullivan."

Sullivan stopped and groaned inwardly but took a seat on the pew closest to her. As if her semi-private humiliation weren't enough, Charles had now gotten on the microphone to ensure that the damage done was total. Even though she didn't want to hear what he had to say, she knew he needed to say it for his own peace of mind, so she sat and braced herself for being made a public spectacle all over again.

Charles cleared his throat and began speaking. "First of all, I want to thank everyone who supported me. The countless hours you put in campaigning for me, knocking on doors, posting signs in your yards, and driving people to the polls is appreciated more than you could ever know. I thank you from the bottom of my heart." The people applauded.

Charles looked directly at Sullivan. "Now, I know that there are going to be many theories and rumors about why I lost this race, but I've learned that God has a way of working things out according to His will. If this position isn't what He wants for me at this time, I thank Him for removing me from a situation that might've led me away from His will and His plan for my life.

"I won't go into the details of the shady tactics that my opponent tried to use against me, but everyone here knows that the most brazen one was an attack on my wife. Regardless of what she may or may not have done, Sullivan Webb is still my wife, and I love her. She has my utmost respect and always will."

His words incited an uproar from those seated in the audience. One campaign aid jumped out of her seat and shouted, "You've got to *earn* respect, and that stuck-up heifer don't deserve your respect, Pastor, and nobody else's! She has brought shame to you and shame on this church! I know you're too good a Christian to say it, but don't worry. I'll say it for you!" Her tirade was met with "amens" and approving nods from the others.

Sullivan pursed her lips together and silently reminded herself that the Bible said to bless those that curse you. She dug her nails into the pew's cushion to keep from slapping anyone.

Charles quieted the congregation. "I realize that my wife may not fit your preconceived notions of what a First Lady ought to be. She might not look the way you think she ought to. She probably doesn't dress the way you think a First Lady should. Her walk and her talk are a little different. She's got *swagger*, as the kids say. She's beautiful; she's got style.

"But there is so much more to this woman that I'm so proud to call my wife. She's got a heart big enough to fill this whole room. She genuinely cares about people, and you would be hard-pressed to find a more loyal and more giving friend."

Charles disconnected the microphone and carried it as he moved into the audience, traipsing up and down the aisle. "I'll be the first one to say that Sister Webb has her faults, just like the rest of us. The enemy tempts and attacks her the same way he does everyone else in this room. In fact, the only difference between anything she's done and what most of you have done is that she got caught. That shouldn't make her *less* human in your eyes; it should make her *more* human. Don't judge her or judge our marriage, and don't ever forget that your own marriages are just one mistake away from being in the same position as ours.

"You know, I could take this trial and let it make me bitter and angry and question the very existence of our loving and merciful God. Instead, my praise and my faith have only gotten stronger. Now, the next time a member comes to me who's dealing with betrayal or adultery in a marriage, I can say, 'I know how you feel,' and mean it. More importantly, I can say, 'God can lead you out of it. I know because He did it for me and here's how.'

"Some of you have demanded that Sullivan come before the church and confess her sins and beg for the church's forgiveness. A few of you have even called to tell me I ought to shame her in front of the entire congregation, but I'm not going to do that.

"Yes, my wife has sinned; she's fallen short, just like the rest of us. But the fact remains that sin is sin. You may not have done what she did, but if you've ever lied on somebody, you've sinned. If you participated in gossip and slandered my wife's name, you've sinned. If you had an abortion or cussed somebody out or lusted after someone else's husband or wife, you've sinned. If you woke up in somebody else's bed this morning, or skipped out of church to sleep in, or used the Lord's name in vain, you've sinned. My sins are no greater or better than yours. And yours are no better or worse than my wife's.

"You want me to stand up here and parade her sins, but what if it was you? Would you want to stand here in judgment and condemnation for everything you've ever done wrong in your life? We've all messed up, but the important thing is that she has acknowledged her sins and repented. She is forgiven by her God and her husband, so it's really nothing for anyone else to say about it."

Charles stopped in front of Sullivan's pew and extended his hand. "Sweetheart, come here." Sullivan cautiously tip-toed over to him and placed her hand in his.

"You are my wife," stated Charles, "and you are the First Lady of this church. Hold your head high, and know that you are the righteousness of God, no matter what anybody in here has to say.

"My saying this might drive some people away from the church or cause them to turn on me, but I can't worry about that. I'm not looking for a church made up of perfect people. This is a rest haven for the weak and weary who come seeking the Lord and His protection and forgiveness. No one in here has a heaven or hell to put you in, and that includes me. I can't waste my time focusing on the crisis, but rather, how God is going to lead us out of it."

"Do you mind if I say something?" whispered Sullivan.

Charles passed her the microphone. "Say whatever is on your heart."

Sullivan gripped the microphone and looked out into the congregation. "First off, I want to thank my husband for the kind words and his forgiving nature. I know that despite your best efforts, some of you—probably most of you—will still think I have no place at your side or at this church. If my actions have crippled anyone's walk, I'm sorry. Whether or not you believe that, I truly am, but this isn't about me.

"The fact that my husband can stand here and stick up for me when he has every reason not to shows what an extra-ordinary man he is, and if you've ever questioned whether or not he is a man of God, I think he's answered that question." Several people applauded. "I messed up. I know I did, and I accept whatever repercussions may come of it. Even though

God is forgiving, nature and society are not so forgiving. I will have to reap the harvest I've sown, but please don't take my sins out on my husband. He's a good man and an anointed pastor. Don't turn on him for loving me. He's only doing what God told each of us to do, which is walk in love. That's all I wanted to say." She gave the microphone back to Charles.

A few people clapped; others grumbled amongst themselves. Charles held onto Sullivan's hand as he spoke again. "Now, you've heard from me, and you've heard from my wife. You are free to stick around as long as you want to dissect the 'hows' and 'whys' of it all. There's plenty of food in the back. Feel free to help yourselves and take some of it home if you'd like. Again, I thank you all for coming. I thank you for your support, and I love each and every one of you in here. God bless and good night." With that, he whisked Sullivan to his office and locked the door behind them.

"Charles, you really didn't have to do that," said Sullivan, who was appreciative but didn't feel worthy of his public support.

"Yes, I did. That wasn't just about you, Sullivan. I'm tired of the church keeping down the very people we're here to lift up. Do you think you're the only spouse in there who's cheated? A lot of people who needed to be convicted were, and a lot of people who needed to be were set free."

"Well, I was if they weren't. I thank you for that."

"Don't thank me; thank the Lord. I'm only trying to follow in His footsteps. I can't really claim to have faith and be forgiven if I can't withstand the pressure when I'm being tested."

Sullivan nodded. "You're right—no test, no testimony. I hope you'll remember that when the press is ripping me into shreds in tomorrow's paper, saying that I cost you the election."

"Things like that don't happen without God cosigning on

it. I don't blame you. It just wasn't the thing for me to do, not now anyway."

"You ran a good campaign," she replied. "You have nothing to be ashamed of."

"Yes, I do. I let winning blind me. Power can be an alluring drug. I wanted it so badly, you know? So much so that I didn't realize everything that I was sacrificing in the process."

Sullivan put her arm around his shoulder. "You lost the election—big deal. You still have your job, your friends, and who says you can't run again in a few years and win?"

"I lost a lot more than the election, Sully. I lost you too."

She exhaled. "Well, if it's any consolation, I lost me for a while there too. I get it, you know."

"You do?"

She nodded. "Last night, I took a hard look at myself. I kept replaying our wedding over and over again in my head. Usually, when I do that, I think about my dress or how good it felt to have all my friends and family around, but last night was different. I thought about our vows and what we pledged to do for one another. I failed you, and I failed God. I felt so ashamed of my actions. I truly know what it means to be sorry for what I've done."

Charles laughed a little. "Wow, look at us. It's been a wild ride, hasn't it?"

"Yep." She rested her head on his chest. "It hasn't been a total loss, though. I think I've finally figured out what I want in life and what's really important."

"What's that?"

Sullivan raised her head. "You. I'd give anything to have the chance to start over and get it right this time."

"Can I make a confession? I've been thinking the same thing."

"Do you really mean that, Charles? Even after everything I put you through?"

"It wasn't all your fault, Sully. Anytime there's a screw-up this big, more than one person is usually the culprit. I blame myself too. I didn't take of care you or put you first like I should have. I practically handed you over to Vaughn."

Sullivan chuckled. "You know, if I never hear that name again, I could die a happy woman."

"Is that how you feel about me too?"

She shook her head. "I could never feel that way about you."

"Wow, it almost sounds like we're ready to give this marriage another shot." He dropped his head. "Almost."

Sullivan nodded, somber. "Yeah, I know. It's not that simple, is it?"

"You know, the first time I saw you, I thought, 'My God, she is the most beautiful woman I've ever seen in my life.' I just wanted to love you and wanted you to be mine. Nothing else mattered, and that's where the problem started."

"What do you mean?"

"Sully, the only major decision I've ever made in my life without praying about it first was marrying you. I just wanted you so badly that I didn't care what the Lord had to say. That was my biggest mistake."

"I'm guessing you don't think that God approved of this marriage."

"Whether He did or not is irrelevant now. We stood before him and made vows that we're responsible to uphold."

"So, you're saying it doesn't matter," inferred Sullivan. "Even if God didn't approve, we still have to try because we made that covenant to Him and each other."

"Yes, but that means that, as a couple, you'll have it that much harder. Sullivan, I counsel couples all the time, and the one thing I tell them over and over is that they have to be equally yoked. That goes far beyond just both being Christians. It's about sharing the same morals and beliefs and vision for the kind of family you want to raise and the life you want to lead. With us, though, I didn't take my own advice."

"You don't think we're equally yoked?"

He chuckled. "Do you? You're this beautiful, free-spirited soul who wants to spend her days shopping in Europe and her nights jetting off to some other exotic place to live out another wild adventure. I'm just a simple, church-loving man, who wants to sit on the porch with my kids and my wife."

"Nothing scares me more than spending my life doing that," admitted Sullivan.

He patted her hand. "I guess we just want different things out of life, that's all. These are the issues we should've tal-ked about and asked God to reveal to us *before* we got married. Marriage is a lifelong commitment, so it can't be an emotional decision like it was for us."

"So, where do we go from here?" wondered Sullivan. "This sounds so final, you know . . . the end of an era."

"It doesn't have to be the end, Sully. We vowed 'til death. This can be a new beginning if we're both willing to pray and make the changes that need to be made. If we're committed to each other and seeking God's will for our marriage, we'll be fine."

"What if we try but nothing changes?"

"Things will change if you ask God and wait on His timing. Whatever happens, though, I don't regret a single day of my life that I've spent living with you"—he lifted her chin—"or loving you."

"I was such an idiot. Why did it take you leaving me to realize what a good man you really are? I could kick myself— and Vaughn!"

"I want you to know that I'm not worried about the affair. I've forgiven you for that. You're human. I just hope you can forgive me for making you feel like that was your only way out."

"There's nothing to forgive. You didn't do anything wrong. Let's just try to do this thing one step and one day at a time," offered Sullivan. "Let's see where it goes and try to enjoy the ride."

"You know, I could really go for a strong cup of coffee. What about you?"

"Won't you be ashamed to be seen out in public with me?"

"How could I be ashamed to be seen with the most beautiful woman in the city?"

She smiled. "You always know exactly what to say. I would love to have a cup of coffee with you."

He extended his hand in a courtly affectation. She laughed and curtsied before sliding her hand into his. She didn't know what the future would hold, but for the moment, Charles was holding her hand. For the first time, that was good enough.

Epilogue

"Promise me it'll always be like this."
—*Lawson Kerry*

Six Months Later

"And you thought this day would never get here," said Lawson as she smiled up at her groom during their first dance as man and wife.

"Well, it took long enough, but I would've waited a lifetime to make you my wife."

Lawson laid her head on his chest while they swayed to the music. "Promise me it'll always be like this."

"If I promise you that, it means our life can never get any better." Garrett lifted her chin and kissed her. "This is only the beginning, Mrs. Bryant."

Lawson held onto her husband, allowing herself to be totally in the moment and consumed wholly by his love. "I feel so blessed right now."

Garrett gazed down at her. "Are those tears?"

"Don't worry—they're the happy kind. I'm still taking it all in."

"You want to sit down for a while? You've been on those pretty feet all day."

Lawson shook her head. "I'm fine. I'm going to dance and smile and eat all night. I've never been this happy, and I want to savor every second of it. I have the rest of my life to sit down, but not tonight." They danced a while longer before they were interrupted.

"Can I cut in?" Mark smiled bashfully. "I just need to talk to Lawson a minute before heading out."

Lawson nodded, signaling to Garrett that it was okay.

Garrett kissed her on the cheek. "I think I'll go ask your new mother-in-law if she'd like to take a whirl on the dance floor."

"Don't stay too long. Leave and cleave, remember?" teased Lawson before allowing Mark to enclose her in his arms. They stared at each other a second before succumbing to laughter.

"Well . . ." began Mark.

Lawson smiled. "Well . . ."

He gave her the once-over. "You know, I didn't think you could get any more beautiful than you were the day you bought this dress, but you've managed to outdo yourself."

"I had a lot of help," admitted Lawson. "That Sullivan is a one-woman glamour army."

Mark shook his head. "It doesn't have anything to do with the hair or the makeup or the dress. You're happy. In fact, you're glowing. You made the right choice marrying Garrett. I don't think I could've made you shine like this."

"You're part of the reason I'm so happy, you know. If things were still tense between us, I don't think I'd be feeling so good right now. I'm not even worried about Namon staying with you this week while Garrett and I are in Aruba on our honeymoon."

"I appreciate you having that kind of confidence in me. We're riding up to North Carolina tomorrow to bring his sister down for the summer. I can't wait for them to meet each other."

"Namon's excited about that too. It makes my heart smile to see the two of you forming a real relationship. To be honest, I never thought I'd see this day come."

"Well, it wouldn't have happened without you."

She pulled back. "Are you kidding me? I'm the one who kept the two of you apart."

"But you're also the one who brought us together, and for that, I'm grateful." He hugged her. "I love you, Lawson."

"Is that the kind of thing you tell another man's wife on their wedding day?" asked Lawson, teasing him.

He kissed her on the cheek. "That's the kind of thing you tell family every day."

Lawson smiled. "I love you too, Mark. Now, get out of here and stop hoggin' the bride!"

Garrett approached them as Mark was leaving. "We appreciate you coming out tonight and supporting us."

"Well, we're fam now, right? Just remember that I'm one of those witnesses who heard you vow to love her forever. I intend to do everything in my power to make sure you stay true to your word," warned Mark.

"Hey, that's what family's for." The two shared an awkward hug.

"All right, enough of this male bonding," teased Lawson, wedging between them. "How about some spouse bonding?"

Garrett swept his bride up in his arms and carried her off. Lawson shrieked with delight.

"Get a room, you two," ribbed Reginell as she and Jody strode by the amorous couple.

"I'm sure they already have that covered," replied Jody.

"Don't hate," called Lawson over Garrett's shoulder. "You kids could be next."

"*Whatever!*" Reginell replied and grabbed Jody's hand. "Come on, let's dance."

Jody wrapped his arms around Reginell's waist, pressed her body against his, and said, "It wouldn't be such a bad idea, you know?"

"What?"

"Me . . . you . . . a church . . . long white gown . . . some vows, some rings . . . 'til death do us part."

Reginell raised an eyebrow. "Let's just stick to dancing for the time being."

Jody took the hint and let it go. "It was just a thought."

"Yeah, a thought whose time has yet to come," said Reginell. She closed her eyes and swathed herself in his embrace. She laid her head on his chest. "Then again, 'til death do us part might not be so bad, and I *do* look good in white."

"Mark my words: they're gonna be next," predicted Kina, watching Reginell and Jody sway to the music.

Sullivan nodded. "They look great together," she admitted, then followed up with, "and you better not tell her I said that!"

"I'm just thankful that he was able to convince her to give up all that dirty dancing. Lawson said that Reggie's actually thinking about joining the choir. I think singing for the Lord will be good for her," said Kina.

"Kina, you have to try this cake," gushed Angel. "It's so moist and delicious."

"None for me, thank you." Kina patted her stomach. "I'm trying to watch my figure, you know."

"Mama, how come you're not dancing?" asked Kenny, licking cake frosting from his fingers.

She tickled his belly. "Because nobody's asked me yet."

Kenny held out his hand. "Well, I'm askin'."

Kina giggled and accepted the offer. "Wow, I must be special! The most handsome man in the room just asked me to dance." Kenny and his toothy grin escorted Kina out onto the dance floor.

"He seems to be doing well," noted Duke, watching Kina and Kenny dance.

Angel agreed. "Yeah, he's in counseling now. They both are. They're happier than I've ever seen them."

Duke leaned into her ear. "You know what would make *me* happy right now?"

Angel eyed him suspiciously. "I'm almost afraid to ask."

"If the most gorgeous woman in the room would dance with me."

"Do you think Garrett would mind?" joked Angel.

"Lawson's all right, but the most beautiful girl is right here. Just don't tell Lawson I said that." Angel laughed and joined Duke on the dance floor.

"Daddy, what about us?" cried Miley, chasing after them with her sister in their matching flower girl dresses.

Duke turned to Angel. "You think there's room for two more?"

Angel scooped up Morgan as Miley jumped into her father's arms. "The more, the merrier."

Charles stealthily crept up to Sullivan's side. "You remember when that was us?"

She smiled. "You were so handsome in your tux, so proud and loving." She sighed. "I felt like the most beautiful woman in the world that day."

"You were . . . still are." Sullivan blushed. "On our wedding day, I promised that I would always love you, didn't I?"

"You did, but I'm not holding you to that promise, especially not under the circumstances. I've been a pretty rotten wife to you."

"Don't be so hard on yourself. We both made mistakes in the marriage."

"Today marks eight months since the last time I've had a drink," touted Sullivan. "The Christian-based support group you put me in contact with has been really good for me."

Charles beamed. "Congratulations, Sullivan! I'm very proud of you."

She smiled. "I'm kind of proud of me too. Now that I'm back to painting full time now, and we're slowly but surely getting back on track, my life seems to be making sense again."

"We'll understand it better by and by," quoted Charles.

Sullivan glanced around at all of the dancing couples and

longed to join them. "How about a dance for old time's sake?" she asked Charles. He complied.

As if on cue, the ladies all looked at each other at the same time and broke into laughter. Their smiles were partly due to being happy to have survived the tumultuous year, but mostly because they were able to see each other through God's perspective. It was only then that they could see past all the flaws and imperfections. The road ahead wouldn't be easy, but with God and friends, it wouldn't be traveled alone, and was bound to be interesting.

Reading Discussion Questions

1. By the end of the story, which character evolves the most as a person? Who remains most stagnant?

2. Does the friendship between the women seem to hinder or support each woman's spiritual growth? Explain.

3. Considering his stature in the church and the community and the magnitude of Sullivan's betrayal, should Charles have taken her back? Why or why not?

4. Was Sullivan just spoiled and self-indulgent, or did she have a legitimate reason to be so unhappy with her life and in her marriage?

5. Should Sullivan, Angel, or Lawson have called the police on Kina's behalf once they found out that E'Bell was abusing her, or should they have let Kina handle the situation on her own? Why?

6. Would you have liked to see E'Bell live? If he had lived, do you think Kina would have been strong enough to walk away from him for good?

7. In the Angel/Theresa situation, would it have been harder for you to forgive, befriend, and take care of the woman your husband cheated with, or to watch your husband's ex-wife take the place you once held with him and your children?

Reader Discussion Questions

8. Should Angel have given Duke a second chance with her? Based on his past actions and integrity (or lack thereof), do you think he would cheat on her again?

9. Would you have liked to see Lawson end up with Mark as opposed to Garrett? Why or why not?

10. Was Lawson justified in keeping Namon away from his biological father? Why or why not?